STEVEN MOORE
I, VIGILANTE

BOOKS

Vinci Books

vinci-books.com

Published by Vinci Books Ltd in 2026

1

Copyright © Steven Moore 2021

The publisher and the author have made every effort to obtain permissions for any third party material used in this book and to comply with copyright law. Any queries in this respect should be brought to the attention of the publisher and any omissions will be corrected in future editions.
A CIP catalogue record for this book is available from the British Library.
Paperback ISBN: 9781036706906
The EU GPSR authorised representative is Logos Europe, 9 rue Nicolas Poussion, 17000 La Rochelle, France contact@logoseurope.eu

By Steven Moore

The Alexandria Ridley Vigilante Thriller Series

I, Vigilante

I, Guardian

I, Salvation

I, Destroyer

I, Redemption

The Hiram Kane International Action Adventure Series

The Condor Prophecy

The Tiger Temple

The Feathered Serpent

The Samurai Code

Of Curses and Kings

The Shadow of Kailash

The Oak Island Enigma

Killing Koreana

The Rising Kingdom

Prologue

His mind floated up from the darkness like a leviathan rising slowly from inky depths. As consciousness gradually returned, his initial thoughts were of pain. Nothing specific yet; just general but acute, all-encompassing, infernal pain. For those first agonising minutes, pain was his entire existence.

But those minutes seemed like hours, until other aspects of his consciousness began to re-form. The pain did not subside. It remained constant as it was joined by other thoughts and sensations. Next to appear was rage. Without the cognitive ability to place blame for the pain yet, his anger was merely directed outward, at anything and everything. Focusing that anger on someone or something would have to wait until later.

Next, sensory input began arriving from various parts of his body. The pain began to coalesce, to concentrate into specific areas. There, the head. Massive pain, as if having been clobbered with a cricket bat. Or a boot to the temple. His nose, probably broken. His jaw, unmovable. The sharp-

1

ness around his torso, which was now pulsing with every breath, could only mean broken ribs.

Then the smell assaulted his nose. Smoke, thick and heavy as it filled the air. Mixed with it, prominently, like the stench of sweat and perfume on a cheap whore, was the sharp but sweet aroma of charred meat. His empty stomach began to growl at the aroma. How long had it been since he'd eaten?

Wait, that's not roast mutton. Nor pork…

It was human flesh.

His gorge began to rise at the thought, though he managed to suppress it by refocusing his mind away from the sickening stench.

He forced his eyes to open. His swollen lids felt heavy. At first, he thought himself blinded, which would have been no surprise considering the pain enveloping his head. Gradually, the dim glow of naked incandescent bulbs, hanging haphazardly from wires running along a rough-hewn stone ceiling, resolved to illuminate the cavern around him.

What he saw jarred his memory. It was starting to come back to him now. Bodies lay strewn about. Most of the corpses were dressed in the digital-green camouflage uniforms of the People's Liberation Army. They were Chinese.

That's right… there was a fight…

He rolled over onto his stomach and pressed his hands to the cold, hard stone floor. It felt good against his palms. Fire and ice. Though the rest of his body screamed in protest, he pushed himself up off the ground, first to his knees, then to his feet. He wobbled, then stumbled, and stuck a hand out to find the stony wall of the cavern to steady himself.

A glint of metal caught his eye, there on the floor near

where he had lain. He carefully bent over to examine it. As he did so his head swirled. After a moment, the dizziness passed. He picked up the heavy object and stood back up.

A gun. It felt good in his hand. Familiar. Like an old friend. He knew at once it was his own. The nearest overhead bulb was a few feet away. He shuffled slowly towards it, stepping over one of the bodies that had fallen around him. Under the weak light of the bulb he lifted the gun to his face and saw that it was indeed familiar. The Daewoo K5. Though his vision was still blurry, he could just make out the small letters that had been etched into the handgun's frame, just behind the serial number. "DHK," he muttered.

That was him. Along with his own identity, the memories came flooding back. Do-Hyun Kim remembered it all now. Everything until he'd blacked out, that is. He looked around at the dark, oily rock that formed the interior surfaces of the cave, dimly lit by the overhead bulbs.

Kailash, he remembered. The cave system beneath the mountain. The base of operations for the Chinese human-trafficking outfit that he had been working within. Drugs and guns had been lucrative, but it had been the slave trade that had made him rich. The proceeds had brought him up from the slums on the outskirts of Seoul after his dishonourable discharge from the R.O.K. Army so many years before.

It was all gone now. This place had been destroyed. The team that operated the slave market here, decimated. The inventory, stolen. The secret facility here in the shadow of Kailash, infiltrated and violated. Not to mention the damage to himself; beaten, both physically and mentally.

By her. The bitch he had abducted from that group of do-gooders back in the town of Mood. Despite her age—a bit above that of his usual livestock—she was to be his prize offering at the next auction. A mixed-race beauty with spirit, and the fight of a lioness. Ready to be tamed by the highest bidder. But the fucker had somehow gotten free. Her meddlesome friends had found their way into the compound as well, and all hell had broken loose.

Kim looked around at the bodies discarded about him. There was a trail of them leading off in the direction of the narrow passageway that led to the main chamber. They had been shot by him, in his fit of rage, as that fucking bitch was being been dragged away by her comrades.

Yes, this was all her fault.

She had caused everything that had happened here. She would pay.

Ridley was her name, Kim thought as the memories continued to flood back in. *Alexandria Ridley...*

Had he shot her too? He couldn't remember. He hoped he had.

He didn't know how many he had shot, those unlucky bastards who had just happened to be there when rage had eclipsed his self-control. So, he pulled the magazine from the K5 and held it in front of his eyes. It was one of the extended 15-round magazines he had bought from an American arms dealer. There were three rounds left, 9-millimetre parabellum.

That will have to do for now, he mused as he slammed the magazine home and stuffed the gun back into his waistband.

The narrow passage was the only way through the main part of the complex. Kim began stumbling in that direction. He carefully picked his way around and over the dead Chinese guards, cursing them under his breath as he went.

The interior of the passage was a horror scene. Charred

bodies lay everywhere. The cloying smell of cooked human flesh hung heavily in the air. At one point the press of blackened corpses was so thick that he had to move some of them aside in order to clear a path. The bodies were still warm. Not from the life that had coursed through them, but from the fires that had consumed them, still smouldering in places. As Kim grabbed the arm of a charred woollen coat to drag its owner aside, the arm came loose, with half the flesh of the man's shoulder and side coming with it, sloughing off the bones like perfectly barbecued galbi ribs. Kim turned his head and retched, steadying himself against the soot-stained wall of the tunnel.

He finally emerged from the narrow passageway into the large central chamber. He had stepped over what looked like the burned remains of an immolated monk, small pieces of red robe still clinging to the few sections of skin that remained unburnt.

Several feet into the chamber, near the edge of the bottomless pit that was located at its centre, one of the Chinese guards sat on the floor, leaning against a stone. Kim made out a snail trail of blood and seared flesh where the man had dragged himself away from the flames. To his amazement, the guy was still breathing.

Kim nudged him with the toe of his boot. The man winced in pain, then his eyelids parted. When he saw Kim, the eyes opened wider.

"Mr. Kim?" the man asked haltingly in Mandarin, pain dragging out each syllable. Kim did not know him by name, but he looked down and saw the crossed rifles and single chevron of his rank insignia.

"What happened here, corporal?" Kim replied, in the man's own language.

The soldier struggled to sit up, in obvious agony as he

did so. Kim saw that there was a canteen attached to the man's utility belt. He unclipped it, unscrewed the cap and touched it to the man's lips.

The man greedily, yet gingerly, accepted several sips from the canteen, then nodded in appreciation. "The *gweilos*," he managed. "They were fleeing, but... we were gaining on them. Until..."

Kim waited impatiently, and finally prodded: "Until what?"

"The monks—both of them, but the young one first— set himself on fire, blocking the passage. Then the older one pushed him away and took his place." The corporal shook his head in disbelief.

"The women?" Kim asked.

The soldier waved his hand weakly. "All gone. All of them. Even the whore you brought in this morning." The corporal shuddered as he said it.

Ridley, Kim thought with contempt.

"How long ago?" He still had no idea how long he had been unconscious.

The corporal lifted his left arm to his face. The fingers of that hand had been mostly burned away. Only charred black nubs remained, oozing fluid from their ends. His PLA-issue watch seemed to be surprisingly intact. He rubbed the surface of it with the sleeve of his other arm and looked at the face. "Eight... almost nine hours," he said.

Shit, Kim thought. *A nine-hour head start!*

He looked down as he heard the man struggling to get to his feet.

"There's a base about twenty miles down the valley," the corporal said. "They will have a field hospital there." He extended his unburnt hand to Kim, for help to his feet.

Kim pulled the K5 from his waistband and placed the

barrel against the soldier's head, directly between two bulging eyes. "Sorry," he said, this time in his native Korean. "I don't have time for that, corporal."

The sound of the shot was deafening in the otherwise quiet cavern.

Chapter One

Alexandria Ridley watched as the bubbles rose swiftly through the light amber liquid, joining their fellows in a frothy head at the top of the glass. Condensation formed on the exterior of the vessel, beading into droplets, and occasionally sliding back down to the tabletop to form a watery ring around the base. She traced a condensation trail with her finger as she gazed through the droplets, through the glass, through the beer, and through the bubbles to the spectacular view past the edge of the rooftop patio, not really seeing any of it.

It had been a few days since their mad dash through the mountains, down from the lofty peaks and valleys of southwestern Tibet. It had been a hasty retreat from the wreckage they had left within the caverns below Mount Kailash's snowy peaks. She and Hiram Kane, her stalwart friend and sometime lover, was at her side and giving her the strength to do the right thing. They had fled along with a host of women and girls they had rescued out of bondage from beneath the shadows of the holy summit known as Mount Kailash.

Ridley's wounds were still fresh. Both the physical ones and the mental. Among them the gunshot wound in her shoulder, through which a bullet had gone, with luck cleanly, in one side, out the other and thankfully hit nothing vital. The long, vertical gash on her chest. The smaller, but still deep, cuts on her chin and temple had been well tended but were still tender. Those would heal, she knew. Any traces of scars that couldn't be easily covered or lasered away would endure as badges of honour, earned in the service of good against nearly insurmountable evil.

Yet, she had triumphed, in the end.

What would take longer to heal, she feared, would be her psyche. She had been abducted and taken into the tunnels against her will. When she had gained her freedom, rather than escape to safety she had charged deeper into the mountain, hell bent on stopping her captors and their entire operation. She had been determined to free her fellow captives. She hadn't had time for fear. Her reckless abandon had almost gotten her killed. It wasn't for the first time.

She shivered now, at the dark memory of it all.

Ridley flinched slightly as a hand came to rest on her shoulder.

"Are you going to drink that?" someone said from behind her. Then Kayla Stone's smiling face appeared as she moved around to the opposite side of the table, smoothly sliding into her seat. "Or are you going to study it for a little longer?"

Ridley smiled at her new friend. The two had endured that hell beneath Kailash together. On their long, hasty journey back to Mcleodganj from Tibet, Kayla had shown her true colours. Though she was among the youngest of the abductees, she had taken charge; looking after her fellow rescuees, encouraging them with motherly tenderness. She was tough, too. She had acted as a triage nurse, sewing up the worst of Ridley's wounds and tending to her and the others until they could get to professional medical attention back here in India.

"I was waiting for you," Ridley said, and then betrayed the little white lie by picking up the glass and taking a long, satisfying swallow of the ice-cold beer.

"Liar!" Kayla teased.

"I know how you Aussies are about your beer. I didn't want to pick the wrong one for you and incur your wrath." They shared a laugh.

Kayla called a waiter over and ordered a Kalyani Black Label. "I actually love the beer here, though I'm not a fan of that Kingfisher swill," she said, nodding towards Ridley's now half-empty glass.

Ridley rolled her eyes, but took another sip and, as she set the glass back down, said, "When in Rome... "

The McLlo Beer Bar was normally one of the busier spots in Mcleodganj. In the middle of the day, though, they had most of the rooftop beer garden to themselves, along with its spectacular view of verdant foothills stretching away to the snow-capped Himalayas in the distance. The two had met here for drinks several times in the days since returning from Mount Kailash. It had become a routine they both looked forward to.

Kayla leaned across the table and gingerly pulled the neckline of Ridley's shirt to the side, to inspect the worst of her wounds.

There were few people Ridley would allow into her personal space, but she had become somewhat used to the younger woman's gentle forwardness and assumption of familiarity.

"It's looking good," Kayla remarked, as she leaned back into her own seat. "Better already."

Ridley nodded, her gaze returning to her beer and the lacing of white foam that now decorated the near-empty glass.

"What about you?" Kayla prodded. Ridley looked up to see Kayla pointing at her head. "Up here?"

"You mean mentally? I'm fine. I'll be fine. I'm a rock."

Kayla nodded slowly as she stared at her. "Yeah? I'm not so sure. Nobody's a rock. That kind of shit back there takes its toll, no matter how tough you think you are." Her bright blue eyes were piercing. Almost electric. Ridley looked away.

"You already know me that well, huh?"

Few people did. Even Kane, who admired her strength and confidence so much. Ridley knew well he didn't realise how much of it was really just a tough outer shell, developed and hardened, over the years, to protect her fragile core. Years before, her weakness had almost done her in, when she had nearly surrendered her mind, and her life, to the siren song of drug addiction. Her mind's own defence mechanism had begun to form that shell. Like the scales of a fish, at first, light and flexible, just enough to protect her tender centre from the ravages of addiction and turn her life around. After that, her armour continued to thicken. Her addictive personality latched onto it, finding a new obsession to replace the old one. Her outer shell continued to harden, too, until it had become unyielding and inflexible.

She had become a warrior.

However, when that shell had begun to crack under the

weight of Mount Kailash, her mind, which had been so solidly protected for so long, had become vulnerable. She had been beaten, shot and nearly killed by the Korean gangster Do-Hyun Kim. Ultimately her toughness had triumphed. She had left him broken, most likely perished amid a human inferno.

She had won, but at what cost?

Alex Ridley was starting to doubt herself.

Chapter Two

It was the middle of the day as Kim approached the border checkpoint. Two men with rifles manned the crossing, their breath visible in the high-altitude air. They pointed their weapons at Kim's van as he rolled to a stop in front of the barricade. One of the soldiers kept his rifle levelled at Kim while the other moved to the driver side of the van.

Cold air blasted Kim's face when he rolled the window down. The border guard was just starting to open his mouth to speak when Kim barked in Mandarin, "Get Captain Chang! Now!"

The young soldier scowled, irritated at being given orders by someone who was obviously not military, and not even Chinese. He knew a Korean when he saw one. Yet the look on Kim's face would bear no argument. Additionally, his invocation of Captain Chang Zhu's name meant that he had friends in high places, at least in this lonely outpost.

The soldier stepped away and headed for the commander's hut, grumbling, and nodding at the other guard as he went. Kim noticed the barrel of the other guard's rifle had dropped somewhat, though he still held it at the ready.

After a few minutes the first soldier returned, trailing hurriedly behind Captain Chang, who was buttoning his coat as he walked. Kim rolled the window down a little further as Chang stepped up, yelling in Mandarin, "What the hell is it with you people? Don't you know this crossing is closed?"

Kim ignored the question. "The other group, the people I came through with the other day. Have they passed back through yet?"

Chang stood up straighter, trying to assert his position of authority, though it was difficult as he was looking up at Kim who was still seated in the van.

"Earlier this morning," he said.

"How many were they?" Kim asked.

Chang shrugged. "Who knows? I charge by the carload, not by the head. There were two vans, and both were quite full."

Shit, Kim thought. "Exactly how long ago?" he asked again.

Chang looked at his watch, and nodded. "About six hours. More or less."

Kim looked straight ahead, out the windshield towards the vast, barren wastelands of eastern Kashmir. *I'm gaining on them*, he mused. He was also well aware that if they made it out of the mountains before him, they'd be gone, lost within the vast multitude of the Indian population. "Open the gate!" he yelled, and began rolling up the window.

Chang barked some order in Mandarin that Kim didn't recognise. The two soldiers lifted their rifles, pointing their barrels straight at him. He took his hand off the window roller and looked over at Chang, who had a stern grin on his face.

Then Kim rolled the window back down. "What the fuck now?"

Chang nodded towards the barricade. "You cross, you pay," he said simply.

"Are you fucking kidding me?" Kim spat. He pointed in the direction of India, where the other group had been heading. "Didn't they already pay? I am with them!"

Chang shook his head. "They paid for two cars, not three. You must pay for this one."

Kim couldn't believe it. The amount of business he had done with this man over the years had earned Chang a small fortune. But he wasn't carrying a bundle of cash at the moment, nor did he have the time to argue about it. He felt the weight of the 9mm pistol in his belt. He looked at the rifles pointed at him. He had no choice. He turned to Chang.

"General Shengmin will hear about this. As soon as I can get a mobile phone signal."

Kim watched Chang's face closely. At first the man's eyes narrowed slightly. Then they opened wide. Finally, after a moment of hesitation, he laughed, nodding. "Well played, Mr. Kim," he said, and waved at the guards to open the barricade.

Chapter Three

"Hey!" Kayla said, adding a snap of her fingers. "Earth to Alex? See? This is exactly what I'm talking about."

Ridley was relieved when the waiter showed up with Kayla's beer, saving her from further scrutiny.

"On second thoughts," Kayla continued, grinning and hoisting her tall, frosty glass, "*this* is what I'm talking about!"

Several beers later, the mood had lightened. The afternoon came; with it more sunshine and several more patrons to the McLlo Bar's rooftop patio. They discreetly gave the two conversing women their space and relative privacy.

"How long will you stay? I mean, stay here in India?" Ridley asked.

Kayla shook her head. "Honestly, I'm not quite sure," she said. "I'm still, trying to decide what my future holds. I'm not due back in Sydney until next month, if at all. I... um... well, never mind. What about you?"

Ridley looked out past the railing of the patio. "Hiram is due back in England soon. I... I might stay here a little while longer."

Kayla's face brightened. "Here in Mcleodganj?"

"Well... no. Not exactly. I was thinking of heading south, down to... probably Mumbai."

"Mumbai?" Kayla asked, her eyes narrowing slightly.

"Yeah. Isn't that where you were staying? I mean... you know, before all this?" Ridley's gaze settled on Kayla.

Kayla nodded. "Yeah? I was thinking of heading back there myself. Wait..." Kayla paused, eyeballing Ridley suspiciously. "No way! You're thinking of going after them, aren't you?" Ridley glanced away.

Have I really become so easy to read? Only to someone as perceptive as Kayla, she hoped. Instead of answering the question, she said, matter-of-factly, "Could you identify them? Those men... the bastards who took you?"

Kayla exploded with excitement. "You're fucking right I could! That's exactly why I was heading back there!"

Ridley's heart sank. That is not what she wanted to hear. "Sweetie, do you understand how dangerous that would be?"

Kayla frowned. "Do you? I can take care of myself."

Ridley didn't doubt that. She knew that the younger woman, as beautiful as she was, was also an expert martial artist. Like Ridley, Kayla held a black belt in tae-kwon-do, a fact as surprising as it had been fun to learn of. They had lightly sparred together each morning since their return, as part of Ridley's physical therapy. The caliber of men she would be dealing with in Mumbai, however, was almost more than she could handle herself. Ridley knew of nobody tougher than she herself was. She admired Kayla's enthusiasm. However, she feared her new friend might be getting in over her head.

"I won't allow it," Ridley said firmly.

Kayla smirked. "I'm going, simple as that," Kayla

replied, just as determined. "With or without you. But I suggest we work together, if you've got the same taste for revenge I have."

Ridley sighed. She knew she was beaten. However, she had to correct Kayla on one point. "I'm not in it for revenge, not really. I got mine, against Do-Hyun Kim, who's probably lying dead back there in those godforsaken caves. So, this isn't personal. Not to me. I need to bring down the traffickers, simply to put them out of business. Plus, I want to save some girls from the same fate that awaited you and me, up there in that damned cave."

With both women now on the same page, they spent the rest of the afternoon devising a plan.

A few days later, Hiram Kane and Ridley lingered outside the security checkpoint of the international flights terminal at Indira Gandhi International Airport.

"Are you sure you're going to be okay here by yourself? I mean, your wounds are still healing." Kane touched the side of Ridley's face, tenderly running a finger over the stitches on her cheek.

Ridley looked at him, mock surprise on her face. "Hiram Kane, you know me better than that. At least, I hope you do."

Kane did know better than that. If anyone could take care of herself, it was Alex Ridley. She knew he loved her for it, though it never seemed to trump his inclination to be protective. He glanced over his shoulder at the people moving through security. She knew he would have to get into that queue soon if he were to make his flight to London for an important meeting the next day. Ridley and Kane frequently travelled separately, their varied interests and endeavours not always aligning perfectly.

"You're right, I do," Kane said. "But… Just once I'd like to be your knight in shining armour."

Ridley laughed. "And me, the damsel in distress?"

Kane grinned, seemingly at the absurdity of the thought.

"I'll be in good hands," she told him. "The yogini in Rishikesh are the best in India, and likely the world. I'll heal faster there. Besides, a little bit of clean living will do me some good while I'm convalescing. I'll catch up with you soon enough back in England."

Ridley didn't know if Kane was convinced. It didn't matter, as he was out of time to question her. She nodded up at the departures board. "You need to get going, Hiram. I'll be fine. But you need to move your arse."

Kane nodded, accepting she was right, so he took her in his arms and hugged her tight.

Moments later, Ridley was waving at Kane one last time before he ducked out of site into the terminal. As soon as he was gone, she turned around and saw Kayla Stone appear from around a corner. Kayla hurried towards her, towing both of their travel bags.

"So… he's still buying the yoga retreat thing?" Kayla asked as she walked up.

"Hook and line," Ridley confirmed. "Probably not the sinker too, though." She took her luggage from Kayla, and together they turned and walked towards the domestic flights terminal.

"I just don't understand why you have to be so secretive about it," Kayla said as they weaved through the throngs of tourists, pilgrims and businessmen.

Ridley walked in silence for a moment, and then said,

"It's hard to explain. Hiram is... he's a *good* man. The best man I've ever known, to be honest. And he loves me. Sometimes though, what's even more important to me is that he respects me the way I respect him." She turned and looked at Kayla. "Do you understand?"

Kayla shrugged. "Sure. We all want respect. What's that got to do with this, though? I mean, taking out the trash is surely something he would respect, isn't it?"

Ridley grinned. "Yeah, he would. In fact, if he knew what we were up to, he'd be right here with us. Therein lies the problem."

"How is that a problem? You said yourself these guys are the worst of the worst, and we're probably already in over our heads. Shouldn't we use all the help we can get? Especially from someone like Hiram?"

Ridley sighed. "That's part of the problem. Like I said, Hiram is good. Too good, sometimes, at times like this. He's an idealist. He doesn't believe in weapons, and is sometimes hesitant in the use of force. Though believe me, he's more than capable, when push comes to shove."

"Sounds like the kind of guy we need right now?"

Ridley shook her head. "These are bad guys, Kayla. The worst. We can't treat these bastards with kid gloves. We can't wait for them to act first, in order to justify what we need to do. We have to get down and dirty. We have to be like them. Become them."

Kayla slowly nodded. "I think I see. You don't know if Hiram would stoop that low."

"Oh, I know he would, if he knew I were in danger. He would do whatever it took. If he knew what I was up to— what you and I are planning on doing, what we're willing to do, to get this done—I'm afraid I could lose something that means more to me than just about anything."

Kayla waited for her friend to complete the thought. After half a minute passed with no reply, she asked, "What could that possibly be, that you're so afraid of losing?"

Ridley looked down, at the mirror-polished tiles that passed beneath their feet as they walked. Finally she said, almost inaudibly, "His respect."

Chapter Four

Kim pulled into the tiny dusty town of Mood while the sun was still high over the Indus River Valley, illuminating a palette of pinks and yellows, and a green serpentine ribbon that marked the river's course. All Kim could see was red.

The door of the Good Mood Guest House flew open, and Kim strode in like a typhoon, red face raging, black hair disheveled. He stumbled over a chair as he crossed the small room that passed as a reception area. In anger, he picked it up and hurled it against the nearest wall, knocking a painting of a Himalayan sunset off the wall.

"Amit! Where the fuck is Amit!" he yelled in his broken English.

A small face appeared from behind the door to the back room. "Mr. Amit is at Food In Mood," she explained in a meek voice, referencing the humble restaurant. "He's making lunch for guests."

"Get him!" Kim yelled. "Now!" he added, as his fist slammed down on to the registration counter. The girl disappeared. Kim hurried out the door towards the cottage that his associate Chan Lee used as a drop point.

That fucking traitor, Kim thought. *I'll kill him too if I ever see him again.*

Kim was pushing the bed aside to reveal the trap door, when Amit hurried into the room, his belly jiggling and his jowls sweating. "Mr. Kim! Back so soon, isn't it so?"

Kim glared at him. "Chan Lee," he said. "And the English couple. The German kid. Have they been back through here?"

The short round man shook his head back and forth vigorously, his jowls jiggling even more. "No, Mr. Kim! I have not seen them since they left!"

The Korean gangster nodded. They were smarter than to have stopped here for even a quick rest. Which meant that he probably wouldn't be able to catch them in the mountains, not before they were able to melt into the higher population centres of the foothills and lowlands.

Fuck!

Yet, had he lost them entirely? Maybe not. At least, not that bitch Alex Ridley. In their short time together, he had gotten to know her up close and personal. Fighting is one of the most intimate acts between two people, second only to fucking. Being locked into a contest of life and death brings you closer to your enemy, not farther away. And he knew the whore, now. They had danced. And while she may have won that round, this was not over yet. Not over by a long shot!

Something had been needling him ever since he had kidnapped her, over on the Tibetan side of the border. She had been defiant from the beginning. A worthy adversary. He admired her for that. It was a shame he had to kill her. Yet, he could no more stop himself from killing her than he could stop a river from flowing. The laws of the universe were absolute.

However, know her, he did. And what had been eating at him finally came into his full consciousness: she was more like him than unlike him.

She might not admit that, he thought. *Of course she wouldn't, the self-righteous bitch.* Yet she was a killer, deep down. He knew it. She was single-minded, just like he was. Once her mind wrapped its claws around something, it would not let go. Just like his mind. She would be tenacious in pursuing it, steamrolling anything that got in her way. He knew this, because what he realised was that she was just like him.

Kim turned and looked at Amit. The short, rotund man was just standing there, shaking and sweating. Wringing his hands. "The slavers," Kim said, more calmly. "They come through here too, I know they do. Who are they?"

Amit's mouth hung open. "Sl... slavers?"

"Yes, goddammit! Human traffickers! Sex slaves! Chan Lee and I aren't the only ones who move inventory up and down this godforsaken road. Who are they?"

"I-I-I don't—"

Kim's palm slapped Amit across the face, firm and stinging. Not hard enough to knock him out, but enough to send a message. Tears began to well in his eyes, though somehow Amit managed to keep control of himself. After a moment, his breath stopped hitching.

He looked down, and said, "There is one. A very large man. Muslim. His name is Alli. Azim Alli." Amit looked away in shame.

Now we're getting somewhere, Kim thought. He recognised the man from Amit's description. They had crossed paths before, probably at Kailash. "Is he the boss? Does he work alone? Where's he from?"

"He... he is in charge when he comes through. He usually has one or two men with him, depending on the vehicles they are driving. But he is the boss. At least, he is over those guys."

"Who does he answer to?"

Amit shook his head, trying to remember. "I do not know. Not for sure. I have never heard Azim mention a name. I have overheard him say some things, while eating with his boys. Yes, yes, he does make reference to someone higher up. Someone he answers to."

"I need a name!" Kim growled, winding his arm up to deliver another blow.

Amit shifted his gaze from the floor, to the ceiling, and back to the floor again. Finally he said, "I do not know a name! He calls him something strange. Like a bird, or something... "

"A bird? Like a parrot?"

"No! Something powerful. Menacing."

"Like a hawk? An eagle? Vulture?"

"That is it!" Amit cried, a grin spreading across his plump face. "Yes, yes that is him! The Vulture! Oh, and they are from Mumbai, I think. Azim Alli is from there. I would guess that is where this 'Vulture' is too."

Mumbai, Kim thought. That's as good a lead as any. No doubt the Ridley bitch would figure that out too. Though, he could imagine her methods might be sweeter than his own. That's where she would be headed. He was sure of it now.

He looked down at the trap door. "Key!" he barked.

Amit glanced at the padlock on the hasp and began wringing his hands again. "That is... Mr. Chan Lee's storeroom!"

Kim raised the gun and pointed it at Amit's face. "Key,"

he repeated, somewhat calmer this time. Amit knew calm men were often more dangerous than frantic men.

Amit stuffed his hand into his pocket and produced a ring with about a dozen keys on it. He clumsily fumbled through them looking for the right one, then dropped the whole mess on the floor with a loud jingle. Kim sighed as Amit bent over, wheezing from his over-taxed lungs, and picked up the key ring. This time he found the correct one quickly, removed it from the ring and offered it to Kim.

"Open it," Kim demanded.

After a slight hesitation, Amit knelt, his breath rasping as he did so, and worked the key into the lock. After some persuasion, the lock clicked open. Amit looked up.

The butt of the gun met Amit's temple with terrible force, and his unconscious body slumped over onto the floor. Kim knelt next to him to check for a pulse. Satisfied that there wasn't one, he rolled the dumpy body out of the way, opened the trap door and climbed down into the basement.

Kim scanned the shelves for what he needed. A couple of boxes of 9mm rounds to replenish his pistol. There was a crate of old Chinese Type 79 submachine guns, probably PLA surplus headed to Afghanistan. He opened the lid and grabbed one for himself, along with several boxes of 7.62 x 25mm Tokarev ammunition for it. Grenades might also come in handy, so he helped himself to a couple each of fragmentary and smoke grenades.

Kim looked around the room and found a black canvas gear bag, into which he stuffed his selections. As he reached for the ladder to climb out, he spied a shelf full of narcotics. Figuring he might need to replenish his supply, he added a brick of Nepalese hashish and a kilo of Afghan heroin. Who knew when he might have another chance to stock up?

After he clambered out of the basement, he rolled Amit's lifeless body over and dumped it unceremoniously into the hole. Then he closed the door, replaced the lock, scooted the bed back into place and left the room. Kim stayed in cover as he worked his way back to the van, where he climbed back inside and quietly drove away from the otherwise insignificant town of Mood, his own mood marginally better.

Chapter Five

Mumbai, India. The most populous city in the second most populous country on Earth. Over 21 million people from all walks of life, from all of the world's major religions, from every caste and strata of India's economic and social scale. One could easily get lost among the multitude. Or simply blend in.

Ivory Tiger Trading Company occupied a dilapidated warehouse in a blighted section of old Mumbai. The business that occupied the complex of rusty, corrugated tin buildings and cracked concrete walls was anything but dilapidated. It was a thriving, lucrative enterprise. Judging by the low volume of shipping containers and delivery vans that moved token loads of Chinese shoes, Malaysian textiles and domestic manufactured goods, it might seem as if *Ivory Tiger* was doing just about as well as any other business that still clung to life in this worn out section of town: barely getting by. That appearance was intentional.

Behind the peeling paint of a barbed wire-topped sliding gate, inside a similarly-appearing run-down building on the edge of the complex, was a well-kept garage of polished floors, climate-controlled air and stainless-steel walls. No less of a space would be worthy of its occupant.

As the door slid silently shut behind him, The Vulture stepped out of the back seat of the Bentley Flying Spur W12 S. He straightened the creases on his ivory-white Armani suit and looked around at the space. Satisfied that everything was in order, he strode towards the exit door at the back of the garage. Nandu, The Vulture's driver and bodyguard, shut the Bentley's rear cabin door with a soft click and followed his boss at a tactical yet respectful distance. Without a word, they exited through a fortified door and stepped into another world.

Prabhaker Das had grown up in a privileged family, enjoyed a top-notch education, and had been making his mark on the legitimate side of the Indian business sector. He had become The Vulture when he'd discovered how lucrative the illegitimate side could be. He had started in the prostitution business by forcing a female client that owed him money to sell herself to pay her account. Those humble beginnings had led to his control of prostitution in some of the wealthy tourist areas of South Mumbai. His territory had remained comparatively small, however, as he had soon after found an even more lucrative pursuit: human trafficking.

Over the years, the capture and transport of human livestock had far eclipsed his modest prostitution ring. He had held onto his prostitution ring, partly out of nostalgia, and partly because he enjoyed it. He couldn't deny that the money and power that flowed through these warehouses, from the product that he brought to market, had captured most of his attention in recent years.

The Vulture and Nandu made their way through a

sequence of mostly-empty warehouses. A few pallets of goods were scattered here and there, with the occasional forklifts moving crates around like rats scurrying about with some prized scrap of food. In one of the warehouses, a bay door was open. A van was backed up to the loading dock. A worker, standing next to the open door with a hand truck laden with crates, looked up as the two men passed. The Vulture nodded curtly and continued on.

They finally came to Warehouse J-3, nestled deep in the centre of the compound. A pair of dock workers stood at the door. Though they dressed the part, these were no ordinary dock workers. A trained eye might notice the bulge of a handgun at each man's waist. Also, each man had a hardened demeanour that spoke more to cracking heads than driving forklifts. As The Vulture approached, one of the guards unlocked the door and held it open for the two men to pass. Nandu heard the door shut behind him and the lock click into place.

Another set of locked doors and guards—these with automatic rifles held at the ready—brought them to the centre of The Vulture's primary enterprise. As before, one of the guards unlocked the door, and The Vulture stepped through, followed by Nandu.

Inside, yet another guard joined them, and shadowed The Vulture as he made his way along a row of holding cells that lined one of the walls. Each cell consisted of rusted chain link stretched across galvanised poles that were anchored into the concrete, similar to the kennels at an animal shelter. The space smelled faintly of shit and disinfectant.

The Vulture, Nandu and the guard stepped from cell to cell, inspecting the inventory. At each stop, The Vulture would appraise the livestock within. Sometimes he would consult the notes hanging on a clipboard near each cell's door. Nandu watched as The Vulture's head nodded slightly in confirmation of each piece of information he read.

Even after several years in The Vulture's service, this place still freaked Nandu out. The muffled cries of the prisoners still annoyed him. Though each was bound and gagged, the incessant moaning of the weakest ones still grated on his ears like fingernails on a chalkboard. He peered through the wire at the young girl in cell 14. She wasn't crying, thankfully. But she was looking at him, hatred in her eyes as she sat on the tattered old couch cushion that served as the cell's only furnishing. She was pretty, or would have been if her hair weren't matted, her face wasn't smeared with dirt and her eyes weren't so puffy. Her green eyes and long red hair would fetch a good price at market. Nandu moved away and followed The Vulture to the next cell.

"This one smells like shit," The Vulture stated, turning to the guard who was walking next to him. "Have that bucket changed. I will not have my goods spoiled." The guard nodded nervously and hurried off to find whoever had failed to empty the shit bucket.

Ten minutes later, they had made their way through the room. "This group is almost ready," he told the guard. "We have a few more spaces to fill, and they'll be ready to ship. Azim is working on that now. It could take a couple of days. See that they're fed and watered."

Just then the door banged open at the other end of the room. The Vulture looked up to see his right-hand man hurrying across the room. Azim Alli was one of The Vulture's 'couriers,' assisting with the capture and transport of inventory to market. He had recently returned from a delivery of livestock to the marketplace up in the mountains of Tibet. For the last few days he had been working on building inventory for the next shipment. Azim was built like a Brahma bull, yet he moved with speed and grace as he caught up to The Vulture.

"We've got a problem," Azim said between heavy breaths.

They retreated to an office that occupied a built-in space at the rear of the warehouse. Nandu and the guard waited outside as Azim and The Vulture stepped into the office and closed the door.

Azim pulled a handkerchief from his pocket and swabbed his sweaty brow, fixing his gaze on his boss's. "Kailash," he said. "It's all gone."

Chapter Six

"What do you mean, gone?" The Vulture asked. "Mountains don't just disappear."

Azim shook his head vigorously. "No, no… the market, the exchange that is—was—housed there. In the caves below. It's all gone. Everyone's dead up there."

The Vulture stared at Azim in disbelief. The exchange under Kailash had been the most lucrative market for their goods. The commerce they had conducted through there over the years had made him rich. Azim had just returned from there, only days before, with no report of any impending problem. "Explain," he said. His tone was chillingly calm.

Azim waited for a moment as he caught his breath, then he began to explain the phone call he had just received from Captain Chang up at the Chinese border. Chang kept Azim informed of the comings and goings through the checkpoint, via a sat phone that Azim had provided. Chang had felt compelled to call and inform him of an oddity. There had been a large group of Western women being escorted back through the checkpoint in the opposite direction from their original passage. That returning group was followed a few hours later by the Korean smuggler who had been with several of the people in the first group, on their way into Tibet.

The Vulture was silent as he listened to the details, nodding here and there in recognition of certain salient points.

"Chang was suspicious. So, he called over to his contact under the mountain. He couldn't reach anyone," Azim told his boss. "Next, he called the military base that lies twenty or so miles beyond the caves and left a message for one of his own men who had headed over there hours before to pick up supplies. When the soldier he had dispatched called him back, Chang ordered him to make the short detour up to the caverns on his way back to the border, to take a look around. Chang said this was one of his trusted men, who he keeps greased and loyal."

The Vulture continued to listen in silence. His eyes hardly twitched.

"When the man finally returned to Chang at the border checkpoint, his report was astonishing. The caves were empty... of living people, that is. There were plenty of dead ones. Mostly Chinese military, some who looked like private contractors, a few who looked like ordinary businessmen or government officials. As best he could tell, there had been a fight. And a fire. Some of the men had been shot, others beaten. Most had been burned to death."

A small refrigerator sitting along the back wall of the office hummed to life. It was the only sound in the room for several moments. Finally, The Vulture asked, "What of the inventory that had been there?"

"No sign of them," Azim replied.

The Vulture settled into a desk chair, lost in thought. The loss of livestock wouldn't be a cost to him, as ownership of the inventory he had sent up to Kailash had already been transferred, and he had already received payment. A creepy smile began to form on his face.

"Boss?" Azim prompted. "So, what do we do now?" He swept his arm out, gesturing towards the open space of the warehouse beyond the office wall. "What are we going to do with all this inventory? Kailash was our market—this is a disaster!"

The Vulture turned his eyes up towards him, which Azim immediately regretted. Those eyes. He never could figure out the thoughts hiding behind them. "Disaster?" The Vulture asked. "You see, my dear Azim Alli, that has always been the problem with you. Your narrow mind. You fail to see the bigger picture." The Vulture stood and walked over to the office window and looked out into the warehouse. "You have other... skills... which make you valuable to me. That's why I pay you to act, not to think. So, I suggest you leave the thinking to me. In this situation, I think that no, this is not a disaster at all." He turned and looked Azim in the eyes. "It's an opportunity."

"Opportunity?"

"Of course. We've been getting fat and lazy. Complacent with these easy pickings. This situation forces us out of our comfort zone. Into being more aggressive. Taking chances. More risks, perhaps. However, the rewards could be so much more. I've been thinking of this day for some time. Though I wasn't quite ready to make a move yet, I have been working on what comes next. I've already developed some contacts. We just need to speed up the timeline."

"Contacts?" Azim asked. "Where?"

"Everywhere! The demand for our product is global. It's

time we reached beyond southern Asia. In fact, as soon as we have this shipment rounded up and ready to package, I'll be sending you out to negotiate with some potential prospects. We'll start with Europe and North Africa. I already have things rolling in Italy and Morocco."

"Europe? Africa?" Azim asked, as if he had never heard of those two continents. "We can't drive there! That will require ships… "

"Like I said, do not worry about those details. Let me worry about them. You just concentrate on filling the quota and making sure everything here continues to run smoothly."

Chapter Seven

Alex Ridley stood on the steps of the Crescenzo Building in the bustling, modern Bandra-Kurla section of Mumbai, leaning against a railing and sipping a coffee from the Starbucks inside. *They're everywhere now,* she thought, longing for the relative peace and slower pace of northern India. Not that her recent history there was indicative.

The street in front of her was a tangled mass of cars and trucks, and a swarm of tiny black-and-yellow three-wheeled motorised rickshaws. Across the street, beyond the steaming, relentless mayhem, was a huge, perfectly circular swatch of manicured green turf. It was the home of Mumbai's Cricket Club, one of the many vestiges of English colonial rule. She had never been much of a fan herself, preferring martial arts and individual athletics over team sports. Even though the field was currently empty of players, however, it made her think of home. She wondered what Hiram was doing now, back in the English countryside.

"Got it!" she heard Kayla call out behind her, as she

burst from the glass door of the massive high-rise, waving a small blue booklet in the air.

Ridley raised an eyebrow. *This girl never ceases to amaze,* she thought. "You do have friends in high places, it seems."

"Not me, for the tenth time," Kayla said as she punched Ridley playfully on the shoulder. "I'm just a beach bum. Uncle Leo does carry some weight!"

Kayla had called him from Mcleodganj to ask for help, leaving out most of the details as to why she had needed what she now held in her hand. She had fled Mount Kailash with Ridley and the others, with only the clothes on her back. But she wasn't yet ready to alarm her family with the truth about how she had lost her passport. Leo Stone was a successful industrialist in Sydney, with several high-placed friends in Australian government. It had been a small favour to have a new passport delivered to the Australian Consulate-General's office in Mumbai, which was located high up in the building behind them. The envelope had also contained a prepaid ATM card for her to use until she could get her own credit cards replaced.

"I wish I had an uncle like that," Ridley mused as she dropped her empty cup into a waste bin and followed Kayla down the steps.

"You don't need one, you've got Hiram."

They flagged down a rickshaw and climbed inside. "Juhu Beach," Ridley told the driver. "The Orchid, please."

"Yes, yes, right away, isn't it," the driver said as he steered out into into chaotic traffic. The small vehicle was surprisingly punchy and nimble, as the driver skilfully wove between larger vehicles to speed them across town.

Kayla and Ridley had much to talk about, but the proximity of the tiny vehicle's driver offered no privacy. Instead, they simply sat back and watched Mumbai pass by on either side. Ridley grinned at the way many Indians added 'isn't it?' to the end of sentences, as if a statement rather than a question. Soon the steel-and-glass opulence of Bandra-Kurla gave way to ramshackle slums of tin and tarps, then it was back to the wealthier neighbourhoods closer to the beach. The economic extremes of Mumbai were bewildering, flipping instantly between the two seemingly at each intersection they crossed, only to switch back again at the next. Ridley had read somewhere that Mumbai possessed the world's most expensive real estate. One minute, that was easy to believe. The next, almost impossible to grasp.

They pulled into the valet entrance of the Orchid Resort, and the driver accepted payment with a smile before speeding away to find his next fare. The girls had decided to stay at least one night at The Orchid once they reached Mumbai. They wanted—probably needed—to treat themselves to a day of comfort and rest before plunging into their work amid the gritty streets of Mumbai's dangerous underworld.

As they strolled through the lobby, Kayla spied a pair of fashionably-clad mannequins posing in a boutique window. Ridley caught her gaze.

"Go ahead," she said, "I'll get us checked in and meet you over there." Kayla nodded gratefully and veered towards the boutique's entrance.

Ridley had loaned Kayla some clothes to tide her over after they had come down from the mountains. They fitted her okay, though a little tight around the chest and bum for Kayla's athletic build. She had been looking forward to visiting a well-stocked shop to start rebuilding her wardrobe. The boutique didn't disappoint.

Kayla was holding a sheer evening gown against her body and gazing into the full-length mirror when Ridley joined her in the boutique. "That looks like play, not work," Ridley said as she veered towards the racks of more casual apparel.

"Don't be so sure," Kayla said. "I've been thinking about ways to get to these guys..."

An hour later, the women finally made their way to the elevators which would take them to their room. Each woman's arms were now laden with shopping bags from the hotel's fancy store. Ridley had needed some new clothes as well, both for the covert work they would be engaging in, and for general use.

After getting settled in, they decided they needed a workout, to get their blood pumping after the long trip to Mumbai. "I saw a dojang on our way here," Kayla mentioned. "It wasn't too far, just a quick walk or jog." Ridley had learned back in McLeodganj that Kayla shared her passion for tae-kwon-do.

"We probably shouldn't," Ridley replied. "Two white chics in a local dojang will stick out. I know we do anyhow, anywhere we go in this city other than the tourist haunts. Probably best not to flaunt it. Don't they have a gym or a workout room here? In the hotel?"

Kayla checked the guest information booklet on the nightstand and confirmed there was indeed a small gym, on the ground floor near the swimming pool. She and Kayla changed into suitable workout gear and headed down.

The gym turned out to be more than they had hoped for, with well-equipped areas for free weights, Nautilus machines and even a large, padded tumbling area that would suffice for sparring. Best of all, they had the place to themselves as it was both midweek and midday.

Ridley and Kayla split up to each pursue her own normal warm-up and workout routines. Kayla began with a battery of stretches, then moved to the free weights to pump iron. Ridley spent half her time practicing yoga before moving to the exercise machines for a cardio workout. An hour later, they met back on the tumbling pad to spar.

After a few warm-up rounds of one-, two- and three-step sparring, the girls began an intense session of *kyorugi*, free sparring. They quickly learned of each other's strengths. Ridley's speed, Kayla's powerful accuracy.

When they were finished, Kayla suggested cooling off in the pool. They had brought their new swimsuits down from the room in their gym bag. Ridley thoroughly agreed. She had peeked out through the gym's plate glass windows to confirm there was a full-service cabana bar out in the pool area.

The hotel was posh enough to have private changing rooms, and Ridley had made it into her swimsuit and out to the pool first. After a quick swim the length of the pool, she had scrambled out, stepped over to the bar and ordered an Old Fashioned. The bartender raised an eyebrow at her order, perhaps expecting a margarita or some fruity beach-inspired drink. Nevertheless, he turned around, reached for a rocks glass and an orange, and somehow produced a bottle of Blanton's Single Barrel. He then spent the next few minutes making the best Old Fashioned Ridley had tasted since she and Hiram were in Kentucky for the Derby a few years before.

She had her drink in hand when she heard a splash behind her and turned around to see Kayla working her backstroke towards the far end of the pool. Ridley located a pair of lounge chairs sitting in the afternoon's dwindling sunlight and took a seat. She sipped the Old Fashioned as she watched her new friend swim back and forth, the length of the pool a half dozen times, using a different stroke on each pass.

When she was finally finished, Kayla paddled over to a ladder near where Ridley was lounging and called out to the bartender. "I'll have what she's having!"

Ridley raised her empty glass and added, "Make it two!"

As Kayla climbed out of the pool, Ridley couldn't help but stare. The Australian was magnificent in her two-piece swimsuit. Tall and well-toned, the sunlight glinted off beads of water as they trailed down her body, her curves steering their course.

"Take a picture, it'll last longer," Kayla teased, as she walked over and eased herself down into the lounge chair next to Ridley.

"Sorry, I didn't mean to stare," Ridley said, rolling her eyes and looking away.

"Shut up, you did too," Kayla replied, a mischievous grin on her face. "And don't apologise. I'm used to people looking at me. I don't mind it." She turned to look at Ridley. "When it's the right person, I even kind of like it."

Ridley looked back into her eyes only for a moment, not sure if either holding her gaze or looking away might send the wrong message. She was saved by the bartender walking up with their drinks. "Two Old Fashioneds," he announced as he set the glasses down on the table between them, then walked away.

Kayla watched him go. "He's kind of cute, too," she said, watching until he disappeared behind the bar.

Ridley laughed and dismissed her with a wave as she picked up her fresh drink.

"So, what's this?" Kayla asked, as she reached for hers and took a sip. "Oohh... that's strong. But tasty!"

"It's an American concoction," Ridley explained. "After

all these years they still haven't quite gotten beer right. But they know a thing or two about whiskey, even if their bourbon is a bit, well, utilitarian. At least they don't smoke their malt with that damned peat moss." She savoured a sip of her own drink. "It's almost a crime to mix this Blanton's into a drink, but I do love a good Old Fashioned."

Kayla shrugged. "I don't know what any of that means. But this is good. I just better not have very many of them." She winked at Ridley. "They taste like trouble!"

Chapter Eight

"Back in this shit hole," Do-Hyun Kim mumbled to himself as he crossed over the Ulhas River into Mumbai proper. It had taken him three days to drive there from the Tibetan highlands, though he had made several stops along the way.

His first stop had been in Pathankot, as he had come out of the mountains into the foothills of northwest India. He was physically wasted and needed to rest, so he had rented a room in a cheap hotel and slept for a few hours. He woke up refreshed and recharged. His injuries still throbbed, but handfuls of painkillers had dulled the pain somewhat. After a breakfast of *chole bhature* he was ready to get back on the road.

At the city of Amritsar, Kim ditched the van he had been driving, leaving it with an arms dealer acquaintance, who he knew from moving guns through the nearby border into Pakistan. The van was too traceable, and too recognisable, especially to his prey. So, he searched the middle-class suburbs of the city for a suitable replacement.

He settled on a four-year-old Tata Safari SUV. It was

plain enough to pass unnoticed in most places, with a coating of mud and dust to dull the forest green paint of its exterior. The vehicle had four doors with lots of cargo space, and darkened windows, all of which would come in handy. He had honed his car thieving skills while growing up on the streets of Seoul, and he was able to jimmy the door lock, break the steering lockout and hot-wire the ignition in under twenty seconds. Then he briefly scoured the next neighbourhood over for a car with which to switch the registration plates, before getting back on the road to Mumbai.

Kim had briefly considered heading back to Mcleodganj to stalk the Ridley bitch there. He ultimately decided against it, as that town was a few hours out of his way, and he wasn't sure she would still be there. From what he had learned in Mood, however, he was sure as shit she would show up in Mumbai. He knew that in his gut. In every ache and pain in his battered body, he knew it.

So, he had driven on, down the length of India, scooping handfuls of *Punjabi tadka* into his mouth, washing it down with litres of Thumbs-Up cola. The drive would take a few days. He felt better knowing he had his Daewoo K5 handgun on him as well as the cache of hardware he had brought from Mood. Had he taken a flight to Mumbai, it would have been impossible to bring the weapons with him.

The delayed timing of his arrival in Mumbai would not be an issue, Kim had reasoned. The bitch would undoubtedly take at least a few days to see after her friends before setting out on what he assumed was her crusade for revenge or justice. He had come to believe she wouldn't just leave India. Kim believed she wasn't built that way, he felt sure. He'd seen it in her eyes. Still, he might even beat her to Mumbai, and even if he was wrong about Ridley, either way, she had a date with destiny.

Ridley had humiliated him in front of those soldiers in the caves beneath Mount Kailash. It didn't matter that they were all dead now. He wasn't. And the sting of that humiliation eclipsed even the physical pain that still lingered from the wounds she had inflicted on him.

Regardless who made it to Mumbai first, Kim had a date with Ridley, it was inevitable. It was a date he was very much looking forward to.

Kim continued down the Eastern Expressway into the heart of Mumbai. Soon the expressway transitioned into inner Mumbai's network of elevated "flyovers," which Kim was thankful for as he looked down into the narrow, congested streets below.

Mumbai was still largely foreign to Kim, having come here only when necessary over the course of business. Most of his interests had been based in Delhi and northern India. In those areas, he would have known which cages to rattle, which strings to pull, which rats to ferret out of their holes in order to get the answers he needed. In Mumbai, his resources were quite diminished, by comparison. He wasn't completely without ideas on where to go first. So, he exited the expressway and made his way into the ancient, narrow streets of Kamathipura, near the southern end of Mumbai.

The press of humanity was nearly suffocating, teeming within narrow canyons formed by the tall, dilapidated buildings that dated back to British colonial times. Kim carefully navigated the Tata through the masses of people and vehicles until he got lucky. A couple of tuk-tuks pulled away from the kerb directly ahead of him, leaving barely enough room to shoehorn the SUV into a parking spot. Though the vehicle was old, it was unusual for the area. Kim noticed a pair of skinny youths in ill-fitting clothes leaning against a nearby stall, eyeing him as he climbed out. He reached into his pocket, pulled out a 10-rupee coin, and flipped it in their direction. One of the boys caught it in mid-air.

"There's another for each of you if the car is here when I return," Kim said, as he nodded at the SUV. The boys just stood there, stone-faced, then turned to watch as Kim made his way down the crowded sidewalk.

Kim made his way deeper into the Grant Road area of Kamathipura, the heart of Mumbai's declining red-light district. Despite some mild gentrification in recent years, here and there prostitutes still stood outside of the few remaining brothels. They posed provocatively in crop tops and low-slung skirts, baring their midriffs to passers-by. Kim had no interest in them as he shouldered past and ducked into a doorway adorned with a simple lotus flower symbol overhead.

One of the women outside cried out in protest, yet Kim continued through the narrow corridor, past several doors on either side, and burst through the last door at the end of the hall, emerging into a cramped office. A small man with acne scars on his face and Coke bottle glasses looked up from where he sat at the desk. When he spotted Kim, he bolted out of his chair towards a second door at the back of the room.

"I caught you, you rat," Kim growled as he grabbed the back of the man's shirt, stopping his forward progress just short of the door.

"What do you want?" the rat whined.

"Same as always," Kim said. "Information."

"You said we were through, after last time!"

Kim shoved the man forward, bashing his head into the door he had been so desperately trying to reach. There was an audible crunch as his glasses shattered. They fell to the floor when Kim pulled his head back and turned him around. His nose was bleeding and looked to be broken. Several small cuts marked his face from the shattered glasses.

"That was last time," Kim said. "This is now." He shoved the rat back towards the desk, where he stumbled but managed to land back in his chair. Kim stood over him, his knuckles pressed down onto the surface of the desk as he stared down into the rat's reddening eyes. "Is there a problem with that?"

"I... I, um... I guess not. No problem. What kind of information?"

"I'm looking for someone."

The rat let out an almost inaudible half laugh. "Good luck," he said, sweeping his arms out grandly. "This is Mumbai, isn't it? Easier to look for a specific grain of sand on a—"

The blow was swift and heavy as Kim's fist connected with the side of the rat's face. The small man's head swivelled to an unnatural angle as blood and spittle sprayed from his face to decorate the girlie posters that adorned the wall next to the desk.

"I don't have time for that," Kim said as he massaged his sore knuckles with his other hand. "Of course it's a big city. But it's a small world, in case you haven't heard. Anybody can be found. Every town has a way, has that someone who can find anyone. I need you to tell me who that is. Here and now. I have no more time for bullshit. Frankly, neither do you. The next thing out of your mouth better be something helpful, or it'll be your smashed teeth that emerge."

The rat looked up at him, still reeling from the blow.

Blood dribbled from his mouth. Tears streamed from his eyes. He began to lurch, and Kim thought he was about to throw up. Then the man opened his mouth and spit two teeth out onto the desk.

Kim looked down at them, then back at the rat. He chuckled, then said, "Okay, not helpful but I'll give you a pass on that one. Now, tell me something I can use, or learn what happens when you're no longer useful."

The rat began to speak, swallowed, and tried again. What came out was just a mumble. Kim could barely hear him. "His... his name is Chota. He can find any... anybody. Everybody uses him, even rival gangs to find each other's people. If anybody can find your mark, he can."

Kim stood up, slightly more relaxed. "Now we're getting somewhere. How do I get ahold of this '*Chota*'? Where is he?"

"Not far," the rat said. He turned his head and spat, a globule of blood and mucus landing in the wastebasket with a wet splash. "Over on Lamington Road, only a couple of blocks away. White Tiger Electronics. Go to the back and tell them you want to see The Governor."

"Is that Chota? Is he The Governor?"

"No, it is just a code. If they think you are legit, they will send you into the back, where some guys will ask you some questions before taking you in to see Chota."

"What kind of questions?"

The rat shook his head. "All I can say is, if you question them the same way you question me, you might not get very far."

Ten minutes later, Kim stood across Lamington Road from the White Tiger Electronics shop, smoking a cigarette. It looked just like the dozen other mobile phone and electronics shops that lined this section of the road. A narrow storefront, its windows crammed full of radio, cellular and other electronics equipment, with brightly-coloured, garish signs declaring the *Best Deals in Mumbai.*

Kim watched for twenty minutes as pedestrians passed back and forth in front of the place. Occasionally, one would step inside, to emerge a few minutes later carrying a small box or shopping bag. It looked normal, and not any different than the other shops on the street.

Satisfied, Kim flicked his cigarette butt into the gutter and stepped off the kerb to cross the street. A bell above the door chimed as he stepped into White Tiger Electronics.

Chapter Nine

They clinked their glasses, and Ridley exhaled as they laid back on the loungers to relax and talk strategy about bringing down the human trafficking ring that had swept Kayla off to Mount Kailash. During their trip down from Delhi, the women had concluded they would need to infiltrate the organisation from the inside. Kayla had proposed using herself as bait, in order to get re-abducted. Ridley had been vehemently opposed to the idea, but on further examination, she'd had to admit it was probably their best option.

"I won't have you in there without some insurance," Ridley said. "This Azim fellow, the man who took you to Tibet. What do we know about him, if anything?"

"He's ruthless, for one," Kayla said. "During the trip north, he murdered a woman on the side of the road because she had fallen and injured her face. To them she was merely damaged goods." Kayla shuddered, and took another sip of her cocktail. "Then he turned and shot the guy who had caused the accident, who had 'damaged the goods.' It was one of his own men."

Ridley reached out, placed her hand over Kayla's and squeezed it gently. "He's finished," she told her, looking into her eyes. "You and me, we're going to finish him. The rest of his organisation, too."

Kayla nodded. "There is another," she said quietly. "Someone Azim answers to. I don't know his name, I only ever heard him referred to as 'sir.' Well-mannered. Composed. And always impeccably dressed. The one time I glanced into his eyes, I only saw death. I think he was the main man in charge."

Ridley paused for a few moments to let that sink in. "What else do you know? Anything about their location?"

"It was a run-down old warehouse. There are a million of those here. I only saw it from the inside, where they kept us in the cages. Bastards. We were always blindfolded whenever they moved us around."

"Did you overhear anything that might help us?" Ridley asked. "Any pieces of conversation that might help us locate this arsehole?"

Kayla thought about it for a few moments. "He spoke on the phone often, usually very quietly, so even those around him couldn't hear. I did catch a few bits and pieces, mostly about prostitution. I guess they're involved in that somehow too. I assume abducting and selling us isn't the only way they're into using and manipulating women. I was thinking about that myself. That might be a way in."

Ridley nodded. She knew that brothels in Mumbai were, if not exactly legal, at least left alone by the authorities. Those would be the more legitimate side of the industry. However, in almost every country there also existed a black market. Wherever there was a black market for sex, there were men running it. "Did you ever overhear any locations mentioned? In conjunction with the prostitution?"

"Mmm... I don't think so. It was mostly just barking out orders or telling whoever was on the other end of the line to 'deal with it'." Kayla paused and took another sip of her drink, as she gazed out over the pool, past the beach and towards the setting sun. "Wait a sec," she said excitedly. "There was one time, right before they loaded us all into the truck for the drive north, the boss guy had gotten into a heated argument with someone on the phone. It was in some other language, Arabic maybe, so I didn't really understand it. After throwing his phone against the wall he turned to one of his henchmen and yelled, in English, 'Get over to the Neptune and straighten that bitch out, now!' Or something like that."

"The Neptune?" Ridley asked. "What's that? A brothel?"

Kayla shook her head. "Hell if I know."

Ridley picked up her phone and brought up the web browser. "Well, let's see." She typed in 'Mumbai brothel Neptune' and hit enter. The search results that came up offered little help. "There's nothing under those exact search terms. Plenty about brothels in Mumbai though. Looks like they're all down around Kamathipura."

Kayla shook her head. "No, it wouldn't be any of those. Those are the sort of legit ones. These guys only deal in illegal activity. Not enough money in anything the government only gives a nod and a wink at. What else does it say under Neptune?"

"Hmm... let's see here... Neptune Financial Services, Neptune Gyro—idiots don't realise he was a Roman god, not Greek—let's see, Neptune Auto Sales, Neptune Bar, Neptune Shipping—"

"Wait," Kayla broke in. "Neptune Bar?"

"Yeah, hang on, let me go back. It's, umm... looks like

it's a hotel bar. Inside the Pantheon Hotel. Looks like some swanky place over in Bandra-Kurla."

"We were just there!" Kayla said eagerly.

"We were," Ridley agreed, more subdued because she was lost in thought. "It's very close to where we were today, that's right." She clicked through to the Pantheon Hotel's website and found a page dedicated to the Neptune Bar. There was a photo gallery intended to impress upon would-be patrons how much excitement they would be having in the hotel bar during their stay at the Pantheon.

"Swanky indeed," Ridley mumbled as she scrolled through the photos. "The place is pretty upscale. Ocean and Roman-themed decor everywhere. Patrons all dressed to the nines. Cocktail waitresses and bartenders in togas."

"Doesn't sound much like a brothel," Kayla mused.

"No, it doesn't. It is exactly the kind of place where a high-end call girl might hang out though, trying to catch the eye of some rich traveling dignitary or businessman. That might be our way in, through the back door, to get some insurance before you go in through the front door."

"Okay, we're going," Kayla said suddenly, bolting up out of her lounge chair. "Come on, we can't just lay around here all night. We've got work to do."

"We do," Ridley said. "I agree, but first I think we need to base ourselves closer to the action."

Chapter Ten

Two men stood behind a counter at the back of the shop. The small one said, "Welcome to White Tiger! Can I interest you in the new iPhone?" The other man, who was much larger, stood silent, appraising Kim. There was just a hint of a tattoo showing above the man's shirt collar. He was about two inches taller than Kim, and stocky. The embroidered "White Tiger Electronics" logo on his shirt was distorted where the fabric stretched tightly over swollen pectoral muscles.

Kim paused inside the entryway and looked around the shop. The display in the storefront window had mostly contained cellular phones and other consumer electronics. Once inside, he saw that the store also catered to a more specialised segment of the electronics market. Kim recognised closed-circuit security camera systems and other electronic surveillance hardware. He nodded as he walked forward and stepped right up to the larger of the two, the man with the pecs, who had not spoken.

"I want to see The Governor."

Pecs looked Kim up and down. "He is not here."

Shit, Kim thought. He didn't know what to say next, or if he should just start beating and shooting his way in. Before he did so, he thought he'd give it one more try. "I want to see The Governor," he repeated.

Pecs did not move or say anything for half a minute, his eyes glassy as he stared Kim in the face. Finally, he turned and walked to a door behind him and knocked twice. The door opened, and he turned back to Kim, sneering. "Follow me."

Kim looked up at the camera above the door as he stepped through, locking eyes briefly with whoever might be watching. He followed Pecs into the back room and felt the cold hard circle of a gun barrel against his neck as soon as he passed the threshold. "Hands up!" The order came in English with an Arabic accent.

Kim complied. He wasn't alarmed. This was standard security for anyone in this Chota fellow's line of work. He raised his hands above his head as the door clicked shut behind him. He turned around in place when he was ordered to do so; he saw that the man with the gun was smaller than Pecs but had a deadly, serious look about him.

The Arab held his gun to Kim's face as Pecs stepped back and frisked him up and down. He pulled the Daewoo K5 from Kim's waistband and dropped it onto a nearby table. He tossed Kim's wallet after it. Pecs pulled the small wad of bills and coins from one pocket, Kim's phone from the other, and placed them all on the table with his other things. When he was finished, he stepped back, then crossed his arms and waited.

"What do you want?" the Arab asked, almost politely, as he held the gun pointed at Kim's left eye.

"I want to see The Governor," Kim said for the third time.

"You can cut that shit out now," the Arab said, as the barrel of his gun drifted over towards Kim's right eye. "You are here to see Chota. Why?"

"I'm looking for someone. I have been told Chota can find people."

The gun barrel shifted back to Kim's left eye. "Told by who?"

Kim hesitated. He wasn't sure whether to rat out the rat to these guys. The little guy had proven useful over the years, even if he sometimes had to turn the screws to get what he wanted. On the other hand, he was done with him, for now. Ridley was his primary concern. "I don't know his name," he said finally. "He's behind the door with the lotus flower, here in Grant Road."

The Arab nodded slowly. "Who are you? Who are you with?"

"My name is Kim." He saw no reason to lie about that. "I am not with anybody. I'm a merchant, a trader. I'm not from here, as you have probably worked out. I work mostly up north, along the border."

The Arab nodded towards the table where Kim's effects had been piled up. "Information is not free, Mr. Kim. How were you expecting to pay for it? With a few rupees?"

"I've got money. I can transfer it instantly, with my phone. Whatever Chota wants. Rupees, dollars, Bitcoin."

"Ten thousand," the Arab said, deadpan.

"What? Ten thousand what?"

"Dollars. Right now. That's the price of information."

Kim looked over at Pecs, and back at the Arab. "Are you serious? Ten grand, and you don't even know what I'm going to ask or who I need to locate?"

The Arab shrugged. "It is a flat fee. Take it or leave it."

It didn't take Kim long to make his decision. After all, ten grand wasn't really that much money. "Okay, I will need my phone."

Pecs picked up the phone and handed it to Kim. The Arab reached into his jacket, pulled out a card and handed that to Kim too, all without taking the gun off of him. The barrel was now pointed at his throat.

Kim looked down at the card. It had a series of numbers printed on it, nothing else. Kim recognised them as international routing and account numbers. He sighed and hit the home button on his phone.

A few minutes later, something in the Arab's pocket beeped. He pulled an electronic device out and looked at the small screen on it, then slid it back into his pocket. "Okay, it is your lucky day," he said. "Chota will see you now. Leave your phone here."

Pecs opened the back door of the room and stood aside. Kim looked at him, then at the Arab, dropped his phone back on the table and stepped through the door.

The heat was stifling inside the small room at the back of the White Tiger Electronics shop, despite the fans and air conditioners that droned loudly in the small space. Pecs had waited outside, but the Arab had followed Kim inside. He kept his gun drawn, though he now held it more loosely, only pointed vaguely in Kim's direction.

Kim looked around the room. It was dimly lit, with a bank of computer monitors and the status lights of several racks of servers providing most of the illumination. At the centre of it all, an ordinary looking Indian man wearing thick glasses sat at a workstation, surrounded by keyboards and monitors.

STEVEN MOORE

The man looked up at Kim, stared at him for a few seconds, then said, "I am Chota. Who are you looking for?"

Chapter Eleven

Azim Alli steered his Mercedes-Benz SUV towards the night life district of the south end of Mumbai, in order to check up on his networks. He managed both the trafficking and prostitution segments of The Vulture's sprawling enterprise, but they endeavoured to keep the two ventures separated, both geographically and financially. Their high-end call girls worked the city's luxury hotels and bars, servicing wealthy businessmen and government officials. For trafficking, their targets were young, oblivious foreign women who frequented the livelier night clubs in the tourist districts. That's where Azim was tonight.

Azim was born into a poor family in northwestern India, close to the Pakistan border. Life had always been tense in that region, due to decades of international tension between two nuclear powers. Things had become even more tense during the West's so-called War on Terror, when anyone who looked, talked and worshipped like Azim became the subject of scrutiny.

Azim and his brother, Tariq, had cried the day their

father left to fight in the resistance. "Do not fear, my sons," he told them as he packed his meagre supplies into an old canvas tote. "We all have a purpose greater than ourselves. If I do not see you again in this life, have no fear, for I will see you in the next one."

The boys had run out of the shack following him, as he strode towards the dusty old Mahindra pickup truck where his fellow recruits waited for him. They had each latched onto a leg, begging him not to go. Azim remembered looking up and seeing tears welling in his father's eyes.

"My sons, your time has not yet come. Keep in your hearts the words from the Holy Quran. *'Fight in the cause of Allah those who fight you, but do not transgress limits; for Allah loveth not transgressors. And slay them wherever ye catch them, and turn them out from where they have turned you out; for tumult and oppression are worse than slaughter.'*" Then he had pulled away from them and hopped into the back of the truck. Azim remembered watching him discreetly wipe a tear from his cheek as the truck drove away.

Their mother had watched it all from the door of their home, standing stoically while tears streamed down her cheeks. She had not been supportive of her husband's decision to join the Jihad a half a continent away. Nevertheless, their diminished family prayed each day without fail for his safe return.

Which never happened. There had never been any official word of his fate after that. His letters home soon thinned out, each one laden with apologies for not writing more often. As well, there were explanations that he was doing God's work and that they were too busy, or that they were operating in areas too remote to keep in regular contact. Eventually, the letters stopped altogether. She never learned what really happened to him. Whenever she would read of a battle or skirmish in the mountains of Afghanistan, she would shiver.

Life was tough with their father gone. Azim and Tariq helped their mother however they could. Ultimately, they grew older and were clever enough to hold various jobs to ease the family's burden. Tariq became increasingly agitated over the years, spending more and more time at the mosque, until one day he, too, left. He had told their mother that he would go and seek their father, or perhaps he would find the same glory he had. Their mother had cried again, that day. Azim had not. He had seen enough. He had cried enough.

The next day, Azim also left, but not to the killing fields of Afghanistan or Arabia. He headed south, into the heart of India, to make something of himself. He had told his mother he would send her money when he could. That had been fifteen years ago, and he had indeed made something of himself. Now he had two daughters of his own that were his whole world.

Neither Azim nor his mother had ever heard from Tariq again. Azim had kept his promise and sent money home regularly so that his mother might live more comfortably, if not happily, in her latter years.

He had bounced around in the Mumbai underworld for a time, learning to pick pockets and hotwire cars. It wasn't until he had caught the eye of Prabhaker Das, who he would come to know simply as "The Vulture", that his fortune began to change. Azim had been working as a "spotter" for a southern Mumbai gang, one of the street kids who would stalk young, attractive, foreign female tourists as potential targets for the gang's abduction and human-trafficking racket. He would hand over these tips to the "feeders," who were older than he but still young, in their late teens or early twenties. Feeders were handsome and smooth-talking. They would move in and woo the targets, take them to parties and supply them with drugs under the auspices of just having a good time.

In truth, the feeders' job was far more sinister than that. Once the targets were vulnerable, meaning they had let down their guard and opened up to the feeders' charms, and perhaps become a soft target due to alcohol or narcotics intoxication, the "trash collectors" stepped up. These were the guys who actually moved in and abducted the girls off the street, out of bars or through the back doors at house parties. They were swift, brutal and efficient at what they were doing. It had been the logical next step for Azim Alli, who lacked both the looks or the charm to work as one of the feeders.

It would be years before The Vulture even noticed him, though Azim was working within his own organisation. An unusually large shipment of girls was being sent north to the markets up in the mountains, and they were in need of an extra "courier". These were the men who transported the inventory, and Azim quickly showed a proficiency at it. Before long, he had become The Vulture's number one courier, his most trusted associate in the transportation of his valuable goods.

As he moved through the streets in the sleek black Mercedes, Azim could see his younger self on nearly every street corner. He recognised the spotters who now worked for him. There was young Abrar, leaning against a wall behind a potted palm tree outside the Flamingo Club, his face partially illuminated by the pink glow of the neon signs above him. A little further on, he saw Yashir stealthily following a group of young Western girls down the side-walk. Neither noticed him, but he saw them. Perhaps one day each of them would rise to power, as he had, within The Vulture's organisation.

Azim thought of his own daughter, Yasmine, his Little Flower, who was at this moment sleeping safely in her bed. She would never know the sacrifices her father had been making so that she could grow up and lead a better life, without pain and misery. Azim was aware of the irony; that he cherished his own daughter, yet had no qualms about abducting and forcing other men's daughters into a lifetime of misery and servitude. It did not matter. They were not his daughters. Their fathers were foreigners from some far away land, who worshipped a corrupted version of God, and had nothing but contempt for his. Fuck them. They meant nothing to him.

Even the one from his most recent delivery. The feisty one. What had her name been? *Kayla,* he thought he recalled. He had admired her, her determination and defiance. Yet, she had been delivered, just like the others, into the caves beneath Mount Kailash.

Azim snapped out of his daydreaming. *Kailash!* Had the Kayla woman had something to do with the disaster that had happened up there? Surely not. It would have required a team of highly-trained operatives to have pulled that off. Still, the Kayla woman had been a fighter. A survivor. He wondered.

Chapter Twelve

"Jot gat-eon ssi-bal-nom-a!" Kim yelled out the window as he rolled past a heavily laden delivery truck. *Fucking prick of a bastard!*

The driver had finally pulled the truck to the side after an agonisingly slow traverse up Juhu Tara Road. Kim then sped the final few hundred yards and jerked the wheel of the Tata Safari to swing it violently off the street into the valet entrance of the Orchid Resort.

Traffic had been murderously heavy, taking him nearly an hour to travel across Mumbai, from Kamathipura to Juhu Beach. He had left Chota's electronics shop without knowing what to expect from what had been a strange visit. Chota had asked him a few questions—it had taken only a couple to tell him what little he knew about Alex Ridley— and then dismissed Kim with a wave of his hand. The thug with the pistol had then ushered him back into the ante-room, handed over his things and then escorted him all the way out the front door to the street.

"So, what now?" Kim had asked, irritated. "How long

66

does something like this take? I gave you guys ten fucking grand, and you just shoo me out after a couple of questions?"

"Chota will call you when he has a location."

"That's it? When? Ten minutes? Next week? Chinese fucking New Year?"

The thug had frowned, growing impatient. "Chota works on his time, not yours. Have no fear. He is efficient. You will get what you need. Now leave. Get out of here before we cancel the contract and charge you a nuisance fee."

Kim's blood had been boiling by that point. No one talked to him like that. But he needed the information more than he needed to preserve his pride, so he'd held his tongue and stormed off down the street. He had found the Tata where he'd left it, with the pair of youths still leaning against a nearby wall. They put their hands out to collect their fee. Kim merely flipped them his middle finger as he slid behind the wheel, fired it up and pulled away in a squeal of tyres.

In the end, it had taken Chota less than half an hour to get Kim a location. Kim's phone had rung while he was standing at a garish red food vending cart on the edge of Kamathipura waiting for his frankie roll. The number didn't show up on his screen. The caller was described only as "Private." Only a couple of people had that number.

"She has checked into the Orchid Resort in Juhu," he had heard Chota say over the line, without greeting or salutation.

"When? What else can you tell me?"

"Today. Only a few hours ago. Suite 412. That is all the information you have paid for." The line went dead. Chota was gone.

Kim hadn't waited for his food, even though he had

already forked over a handful of rupees for it. He had hopped back into the Tata and sped away, just as the frankie vendor was leaning out of the window with his order of spicy tandoori chicken rolled in a crisp, hot *chapati*.

Kim felt as if he had finally arrived. He could almost taste his revenge.

"You cannot park here sir; this is valet only!" the regally clad attendant had said as soon as Kim exited the car.

"I'll only be a minute!" Kim roared as he hurried past, through the ornate glass doors and into the air-conditioned lobby of the hotel.

"Can I help you?" asked the fresh-faced clerk as Kim strode towards the registration desk.

He had already spied the property map sitting on the countertop, his eyes zeroing in on the location of his prey. Room 412 was an Executive Suite. Fourth floor, beach side. *Rich bitch,* Kim mused, before he looked up and smiled. "I'm meeting my party in the bar," he said, almost politely.

"Very well. Through those doors and to your left."

Kim followed the clerk's directions but detoured to the right after passing through the doors, towards a bank of lifts. He caught one of the lift doors just before it whooshed shut, stepped inside and thumbed the button for the fourth floor.

When he exited the lift, he looked in each direction down long hallways, then focused on a plaque on the wall which indicated rooms 402-424 were to the left. He found the bitch's room halfway down the hall. Out of habit he tried the handle, knowing it would be locked. The door had a keycard locking mechanism. Kim backed away and again looked in each direction, not finding what he was looking for.

The emergency stairwells were located at the end of

each hallway, so Kim moved quickly towards the nearest one and took the stairs down one flight to the third floor. He emerged from the stairwell; there it was, just what he was looking for.

The housekeeping cart was parked outside of a suite only three doors down. Its laundry baskets bulged with removed bedclothes, and spray-bottles of cleaning agents hung along one side. The room's door was propped open, and Kim could hear activity from inside. He crept to the side of the door and waited, his back tucked as close as possible to the wall.

He heard the maid's humming before he saw her, some light, airy tune he didn't recognise. Kim checked the hallway in both directions to make sure it was still empty. Then the maid stepped out of the doorway and over to the cart.

Kim moved swiftly into position behind her, placed his arm around her neck and choked her to unconsciousness. As she slumped into his arms, he took one more look in each direction to confirm nobody had seen, and then dragged her limp body backwards into the suite, kicking the door closed behind him. He continued to hold the choke until he was sure she was dead. He checked for a pulse just to be certain, then let her body fall unceremoniously to the tiled floor. The maid's master key card dangled from a lanyard around her neck. Kim removed it and stuffed it in his pocket, returned to the hallway, pushed the cart into the suite and closed the door. He retreated down the hallway to the stairwell and returned to the fourth floor.

Kim's plan was simple: let himself into Ridley's room and kill her. Only then would he worry about how to get away unnoticed. If she weren't there he would lie in wait. He pulled out his handgun, slipped the key card into the lock, listened for the click of the locking mechanism and burst through the door, sweeping the room with his weapon.

What he hadn't planned on was finding the room empty and already made up for its next guest, as if the bitch had never even been there. Chota had come so highly recommended, and his entire operation seemed so legitimate, Kim had been confident in the information provided. Now? Perhaps now he would have to pay Chota a second visit, this time as a disgruntled customer. That would have to wait until after he had found and dealt with Ridley.

On his way back to the car, Kim passed back through the hotel lobby. As he crossed in front of the registration desk, a thought came to mind and he detoured towards the desk.

"May I help you?" the young clerk asked him for the second time.

Kim smiled. It almost hurt his face to do so. "Yes, if you could, please. I'm still waiting for my party, over in the bar. Can you ring her room for me? Tell her I'm waiting. I tried her cell and it goes straight to voicemail. She probably left it charging."

"Of course. Room number?"

"It's 412. Executive Suite."

The clerk turned to her computer screen. Kim heard her fingers clicking away at a keyboard, somewhere below the countertop. He watched her face as her brow furrowed, then her smile turned into a frown.

"I am sorry, sir, do you have the guest's name?"

"Of course. Alex Ridley. She checked in earlier today."

The clerk nodded and continued tapping keys. "Mmm. Yes, I see now. She did indeed check in. But… it looks like she then checked out, only a few hours later… about an hour and a half ago."

"She checked out? Why? Where did she go?"

The clerk shook her head. "Who knows? We pride ourselves on our customer service, but perhaps we fell short of her expectations in some way? I do not see any notes in her customer file."

Kim looked up at the ceiling, as if the answers he sought were written up there. *Chota had been right, after all.*

He was just thinking of what to do next when the clerk offered, "Perhaps the bellhop might know something?"

Kim turned and looked through the large, plate-glass doors at the small man in the ridiculous costume, standing outside next to the bell desk waiting for his next tip. "Thank you," he told the clerk. "You've been helpful." As Kim turned away from the clerk, his smile melted away, letting his face settle into its usual grim countenance.

"You there!" Kim barked as he emerged from the hotel lobby, waving a crisp 1,000-rupee note at the bellhop.

The man glanced up, the irritated look on his face disappearing as soon as he saw the money in Kim's hand.

"Yes, sir, how may I be of assistance? May I call you a taxi?"

Kim shook his head. "No. There was a guest who checked out, over an hour ago. A woman, perhaps mixed-race, tall, slender, attractive in a severe sort of way. Long dark hair, maybe green eyes."

The bellhop nodded, holding out his hand. "I remember."

"Did you speak with her?" Kim asked as he placed the bill into his hand. "Did she say where she was going?"

The bellhop stuffed the bill into his pocket. "Sort of. They asked if I could recommend a guesthouse over by Dharavi." The bellhop shrugged at the idea of a well-heeled

Western woman choosing to leave the Orchid for the grimy slum.

Dharavi? What the fuck? Kim shook away the thought, as the 'why' was unimportant. "Where did you send them? Quickly!"

The bellhop held up his hands. "There are dozens of them over there. I suggested three or four they might check out, all close to each other. Old Bombay, King's Rest, Safe N' Sound… " Kim committed each of them to memory as the bellhop rattled the names off.

"Wait, did you say *they?* Someone was with her?" Kim asked.

"Yes, another Western girl. Younger than the dark-haired one, and blonde."

Who could that be? It didn't matter. If she were with Ridley, she was already as good as dead.

Chapter Thirteen

The King's Rest Guesthouse occupied the eighth floor of a crumbling high rise on the edge of the Dharavi slum. Ridley and Kayla's room was tiny, with two thin but comfortable sleeping mats, a cushioned bench, and a countertop with an electric kettle and a microwave that served as a kitchenette.

"It's a bit of a downgrade from the Orchid," Kayla admitted as she toured their new digs, which took all of ten seconds, while standing in the middle and turning in place.

Ridley nodded. "We're not here for drinks by the pool. We've got work to do and we need to get our heads in the game." She strode over to the room's single window and pulled the faded, flimsy and frayed curtain back. "This view helps with that."

Kayla joined her at the window and took in the sight. From eight floors up, a panoramic view to the north spread out before them. In the foreground, the ordered chaos of the Dharavi slum sprawled in every direction. Tightly packed, tin and plywood shacks were interspersed with blue tarps to form a curving, flowing checkerboard divided here and there by narrow lanes and alleys. It was nearing midnight. The hanging smoke from the dust and cook fires glowed eerily in the moonlight, and dimly lit the entire scene in shades of darkened pastels.

In the distance, across the vast sea of ramshackle buildings, stretched the darkness of the Mithi River and the mangrove forests that lined its banks. Beyond that, the bright lights of Bandra Kurla, rising like a beacon out of the darkness.

"Somewhere out there," Ridley said, gesturing towards the cityscape that lay before them, "is what we came here looking for. Our prey works in both of those worlds, among the rich and the poor. Wherever the hunt takes us, we will follow, and we will find them."

After leaving the pool, Ridley and Kayla had packed up their belongings and hastily left the opulence of the Orchid Hotel. A bellhop, who had helped them load their bags into a waiting taxi, had suggested several guesthouses that were close to Dharavi, but clean and safe. The King's Rest had been their first stop, and the bellhop had been right. Though the place proved to be only a caricature of its regal name, it was the perfect base for them to work out of, close to the Mumbai underground and worlds away from the luxury of Juhu Beach.

Ridley and Kayla each dressed in dark clothes, newly acquired from the Orchid's boutique. Kayla donned tight-fitting black leggings and a dark grey long-sleeve workout top, black trainers and a dark blue baseball cap. She tied her hair in a ponytail and pulled it through the adjustment hole in the back. Though she stuck out as a Westerner, she could be any tourist or traveling businesswoman out for a run or a quick trip to the cafe.

Ridley donned her new leathers, all black, cut tight, but flexible enough to allow movement. Sturdy boots completed the look. They reminded her of her riding gear back home, which made her wish she had her Triumph Daytona 675R with her now.

The women needed to get a feel for the city, at ground level, before diving headlong into the hunt for Azim Alli. They had decided to spend their first night in their new location scouting the area, keeping an ear to the ground and seeing what they could find out, if anything.

"We need weapons, too," Ridley added. "Perhaps we'll find some out there, if we poke around enough. By the way, leave your ID here," she advised.

"Good call," Kayla agreed, remembering the last time she had left a Mumbai guesthouse at night, carrying her passport. "I'm starving," she stated as they descended the steps from their room to the street below.

"Me too," Ridley concurred. "It's been a while since we've eaten anything." On the street at the base of the old high-rise, a number of street vendors sold a bewildering variety of food, all of which smelled heavenly. Even at this late hour, the street was alive with vendors and their hungry patrons.

They settled on a toothless old woman selling plain-looking, but mouthwateringly aromatic, *vada pav*. The crone reverently placed a pair of crusty rolls onto each paper plate, cut them in half and stuffed a freshly fried potato dumpling within each. Next, she ladled spicy coconut chutney into small plastic cups and placed them onto each plate. As she handed the plates over, the women returned her smile, tipped her well and then strolled down the street to eat their meals.

"My god, it's so simple but so good," Kayla said between mouthfuls.

Ridley could only nod, chewing vigorously as she finished the last of her *vada pav.* When she had finally swallowed her last bite, she dropped the plate into a nearby rubbish bin. "Okay," she said, her tone now serious, "we're fuelled up. No excuses. Let's go."

Chapter Fourteen

Ridley directed Kayla to cross the street, to shadow her position by about fifty yards, to stay visually separated but to watch Ridley's back and to keep a wider view of the street in front and behind them.

"You'll want to stay as incognito as possible, without looking in any way suspicious," Ridley told her. "If I stop, you figure out a pretence to stop as well. Chat with a street vendor or act as if you're tying your shoelace. Anything. Just keep an eye on me without directly staring."

"What if you get into trouble?"

Ridley grinned. "I can handle quite a lot of trouble myself, lovey. If I really do need backup, I promise you'll be the first to know it."

"Okay, but what are we looking for?"

Ridley had turned to look at the labyrinth of ramshackle huts and shacks spread out before them. "The key into any city's criminal underworld is the same in every country. You follow the drugs."

Within twenty minutes, Ridley had grown comfortable

with Kayla's shadowing. She had tested her with several counter-surveillance manoeuvres—doubling back, ducking through doors to emerge from different ones—and had found that the younger woman was a quick study and adapted to it well. She was smart, as well as tough. A natural for this work. Ridley decided to put their little two-person team to a bigger test.

They had been working their way along Mahatma Gandhi Road, one of the wider thoroughfares that ran through the southern edge of Dhavari. They were yet to plunge into the narrow alleyways of the slum proper. Ridley unbuttoned her jacket and mussed up her hair, in an effort to look as much like a partying foreigner as possible, despite her clothes being not quite appropriate for the task... and admittedly, she also being a little old for it.

She spotted a young man pushing a cart laden with plastic waste, apparently heading to one of the area's large recycling centres. Ridley shoved her hands into her pockets and strode up to him, looking around nervously.

"Hey! Hey, young man... yeah, you. Got a second?"

The boy stopped pushing his cart and looked Ridley up and down. "You shouldn't be here," he said simply, and, Ridley thought, honestly. "It is not safe, this time of night, especially for someone like you."

The young man turned back towards his pushcart to continue on his way. Ridley put a hand on his shoulder. "Please," she said, "I can take care of myself. I just need to find someone."

The man turned back to her. "Who are you looking for?"

"Umm... no one in particular," she said, continuing to look around, feigning anxiety as she spoke to him. "Just someone who can, you know, sell me something. You know, to party with. Maybe a little H. Or anything, really. I just need something to take the edge off so my friends and I can enjoy our stay here in your beautiful city."

"Yeah, right." The young man laughed and looked around at the slum that surrounded them on all sides. "Okay, though. You see that pottery shop, two alleys down, on the right? Go there, and turn right, into the alleyway."

"Okay," Ridley said. "Yeah, that sounds good. What then?"

The man eyed her for a moment, then shook his head, and said, "Keep going, deeper into Dharavi, along that alley. About a hundred yards in, you will find the shop of an old man who repairs bicycles. It will be closed right now, but you will know it from the bicycle parts lying around. Just past that is an even narrower alley, on the left. There, or maybe just a few yards into that small alley, you will find Jeter. He is about my age, but you will know him by his hair. It's all white, like he has seen a ghost."

"Okay, okay, yeah, he sounds like the kind of guy I need. Jeter, the kid with the white hair. Thanks man, you're a life saver."

The trash collector's face turned grave. "Do not go any further down that second alley," he warned her. "It is not safe. Not for someone like you. Find Jeter, get what you need, and get the hell out of there. Go back to your hotel or wherever you are staying." With that, the man turned back to his cart, groaned as he gave it an initial shove to get it moving and hustled down the street.

Ridley watched him go, until he was out of sight around a bend in the road. Then she turned and spotted Kayla, under a streetlamp about fifty yards away, acting as if she were removing something nasty from the bottom of her shoe. *Good girl,* Ridley thought, and turned to head towards the pottery shop.

Once she'd arrived at the pottery shop, Ridley kept up her wayward tourist act by looking around in affected bewilderment, before turning and plunging down the alley into the heart of the Dharavi slum.

Chapter Fifteen

Korean gangster Do-Hyun Kim was making his way to each of the nearby guesthouses suggested by the bellhop at the Orchid Hotel. They had been easy to find using the mapping app in his phone.

He had checked them in order of proximity, not the order in which they had been listed for him. First up was the Safe N' Sound Guesthouse, which occupied a series of rusty, re-purposed metal ocean containers, stacked two high, on a busy corner at the edge of the slum. He had observed the place from across the alley for ten minutes, with no sign of the Ridley bitch or the mysterious woman she was now traveling with. He had needed a closer look, so he strode up to the proprietor, whose humble registration office occupied a partitioned end of one of the adjoining containers, beneath a plywood sign that read "Stay Safe N' Sound in Dharavi!" in brightly coloured, hand-painted letters.

The proprietor hadn't been readily amenable to sharing his guest's information, so Kim had softened him up a bit with a punch to the gut. After recovering his breath, the man had changed his attitude and personally showed Kim the occupants of his ten rooms, one by one. Four were empty. Two were occupied by sleeping, single men. Three by couples, and one by a pair of older, sweaty Western men engaged in sex, who quickly hid under their blanket when Kim had burst through the door. The Safe N' Sound was a bust.

When he arrived at the location for the Old Bombay Guesthouse, on the edge of the slum near the Sion train station, he found an empty, dilapidated two-storey building with a sign outside that read "Closed for Renovations. Come See Us This Summer!" The faded paint looked to have been several years old. *The bellhop needs to update his information,* Kim thought, irritated.

When he finally reached the King's Rest, Kim stood across the street and looked skyward, at the crumbling old high-rise that rose before him. There were no exterior signs indicating a guesthouse, though the street in front was alive with locals, foreigners, hawkers and beggars. He crossed the street, pushed past the crowd, and slipped through the double doors that served as the building's ground-floor entrance. Inside, several hawkers had set up their stalls to either side of a doorway that led, as the sign over it announced, to the "STAIRS." On both sides of the room, obscured by vendors and their wares, were the boarded-up remnants of the elevator doors that had once moved people swiftly, if not reliably, to the floors above.

Kim caught the eye of an old woman weaving baskets near the entrance door. She had stacks of them arrayed around her, with hand-written prices affixed to each of them with Post-It notes.

"I'm looking for the King's Rest Guesthouse. Is it here?"

The woman shrugged. She may have been deaf. She

pointed to a spot on the wall behind where Kim was standing. He turned around and saw a metal-framed signboard with "The Nehru Building" printed at the top, "DIREC-TORY" beneath that, and a series of engraved metal placards arranged below, bearing the names of various tenants.

Kim found the guesthouse listed in between a dentistry firm and a block of residential apartments. According to the directory, the King's Rest occupied the entire eighth floor. Kim turned, hustled through the door to the stairwell and started climbing.

A modest yet well-maintained reception area occupied most of the eighth-floor landing, with the words "King's Rest" carefully painted across the back wall. An attractive young southeast Asian woman with a nose ring and purple hair sat on a stool behind the counter. She looked up from her phone when Kim approached from the stairway.

"Welcome to King's Rest," she said. "How long will you stay?" She finished with a wide smile of perfect, white teeth.

Kim's heart sank only a little, as he lamented that he might have to knock some of those out to get the information he needed. It was a shame, as she reminded him of a girlfriend he had left behind years ago back in Seoul.

Kim was in luck. Once he'd pulled out a few bills the girl dropped all pretence of protecting her guests' privacy. She readily confirmed that a woman matching Alex Ridley's description had checked into the guesthouse only a couple of hours ago. "With a young, yellow-haired female guest," she had added with a wink.

A guest? Kim thought, intrigued. "Are they still here?"

"Not sure," the girl replied. "Some guest use other stair at back of building to come and go. It is faster. We have no camera, so I no see."

She smiled coyly when Kim asked if he could see inside their room. "You want I show you?"

"If I could just borrow the key for a few minutes, I'll look myself. I wouldn't want to drag you away from your post. There's another thousand in it for you," he said as he pulled another bill from his pocket.

The girl stuck out her lower lip and feigned pouting. "No customer this late," she lamented. "No excitement. But here, Mister Man." She pushed the tarnished brass key across the counter and snatched the bill from Kim's hand. "You go now. Be quick, in case guest come back!"

The Nehru Building was tall but narrow, so it turned out the single floor occupied by the King's Rest Guesthouse was actually quite small. Only twelve rooms, situated six on each side of a central hallway. Kim located Ridley's room at the northeast corner of the building. He drew his pistol, slipped the key in the lock and burst in.

"Shit!" he muttered when he found the room empty and realised he'd likely just missed his mark once again. This time his luck was marginally better, as the Ridley woman was indeed still checked in here and her things were still in the room. And yes, there were two travel bags, each sitting on one of the two sleeping mats, their zippers open with a few clothing items spilled out.

Also, on each sleeping mat was a small pile of personal belongings from each woman. Pocket contents. A phone, a small purse containing a few cards and money, ID cards, passports. Kim picked up Ridley's first and flipped through it before tossing it back onto the pile.

When he picked up the other passport and opened it, he let out a low whistle. "Kayla Stone, what is a beauty like you doing in a place like this, with the likes of her?" Then it came to him. She was just the type to have been snatched off the street and put up for auction, up at Mount Kailash. She had been there too. "Miss Stone, you have no idea what you have gotten yourself into. Soon you will be just as dead as your new friend."

Kim took another look around the room, wondering what to do next. Should he simply wait for them? Would the receptionist tip them off? He thought not, but he had no way of knowing how long they would be out. They had obviously recently left. Whatever they were up to, they could be out all night.

Kim stepped over to the room's single window and pulled back the curtain. Below him spread the jumbled mass of the Dharavi slum, faintly illuminated by moonlight and a few working streetlights. "Alex fucking Ridley," he said to the empty room. "And Kayla motherfucking Stone. What in the world are you two looking for down in that festering shit hole?"

Kim decided to wait and ambush the two women when they returned. He could take care of both of them quickly and cleanly. Then again, it might be better to tie them up and have a little fun for a while, before breaking their necks. He would have to be careful. He knew how dangerous Alex Ridley could be. On second thoughts, maybe he would just punch her ticket immediately; he'd save the Stone bitch for his extracurricular activity.

Either way, he couldn't leave the Tata where he had parked it, in a marked loading zone. He would need to go down and move it or risk unnecessary attention from the police. He looked around the room to make sure everything was still in place, as he had found it. In the highly unlikely scenario that the women would beat him back to the room, he didn't want to broadcast that someone had been here.

Satisfied, he slipped out the door and re-locked it, using

the key the cute registrations clerk had loaned him. He would have to take care of her as well. She would be a loose end. Perhaps, Kim mused, he might have a little fun with her, too, before dispatching her. Kim glanced down the hallway towards where the reception desk sat, just around a corner. Then he smiled, turned around and headed for the emergency stairway at the other end of the hall.

When Kim emerged on the ground floor, the emergency exit had deposited him at the back of the building. He carefully worked his way around its perimeter, to the front, weaving through piles of refuse and makeshift dwellings which had been thrown up against the sides of the building.

Before stepping out onto the sidewalk at the front of the building, Kim stayed in cover long enough to watch the Tata for a few minutes. There it was, still parked haphazardly in the loading zone. He hadn't expected to be there long when he had hastily parked it. There were no signs of Ridley or the Stone woman, and the SUV appeared undisturbed. Satisfied, he quickly made his way towards it and slipped the key into the lock.

"Stop what you are doing!"

Kim froze. The order was yelled out from directly behind him. It was accompanied by the pounding of boots and the clicking of weapons.

"Put your hands up! Mumbai Police!"

Fuck!

Chapter Sixteen

Though the alleys were mostly dark and sparsely populated at this time of night, a few vendors and residents were awake. They were either milling about or sitting in front of their hovels, enjoying the cool night air before the sun came back up on another day of arduous toil. A few stared, but most paid Ridley no attention at all as she made her way deeper into the slum. She checked behind her to see that Kayla had made the turn. She spotted her there, at the mouth of the alley, admiring some crockery at the potter's stall.

Up ahead, Ridley saw light reflected off chrome; she knew it was the bicycle repair shop the young man had told her about. As she drew closer, she saw a stack of bicycle frames in various states of disassembly. Chrome fenders and handlebars, spoked wheels, a bucket filled with greasy roller chains, and an enormous pile of rubber bicycle tyres of varying size and vintage. As the man had predicted, the shop was currently closed, with a blue nylon tarp pulled down across the front of the stall, behind the stacks of parts.

Ridley glanced towards the other side of the lane and saw the opening of a narrow alley, right where the kid had said it would be. She kept her head down and passed by the alley, only stealing a quick glance into it as she passed by.

That one glance was enough. He was there. Jeter. She had seen him leaning against the side of a shack that formed one wall of the alleyway. He had been looking down into his phone, the glow from the screen lighting his face and the shock of white hair on his head. Jeter, the ghost.

She continued beyond the narrow passage, found a dark corner to back into, and peeked out into the alley to look for Kayla. There she was, still a few yards from the bicycle shop. Ridley stepped out into the alley so she knew Kayla could see her.

When she had Kayla's attention, she pointed at the bicycle shop, then at the opening of the narrow alley across from it. Next, she pointed at herself and then back at the alley. Then she pointed at Kayla, and held up her hands, palms out. Finally, she pointed at her own eyes with two fingers, then at Kayla, then at the mouth of the alley. *I will be in there. You stay put. Keep an eye on the alley.*

Kayla nodded her understanding and gave her a thumbs up for good luck, before melting into the shadows on her side of the narrow street.

Ridley took another look at the opening of the alley where Jeter was located, then turned around and headed farther into the slum. She kept her eye on the shacks along the same side of the lane as the passage where Jeter was posted, until she found what she was looking for. In between two of the makeshift dwellings was a gap barely wide enough to fit through sideways. The foul smell of raw sewage emanated from the gap. Indeed, there was a small, trickling stream of runoff flowing at the base of the passage to where it joined with a wide gutter in the middle of the main alleyway. Ridley noticed that a series of steppingstones had been placed within the gap so that people could shimmy through without stepping into the sewage.

She stole a quick look down each direction of the alley and, satisfied that nobody was watching, plunged into the narrow gap.

Chapter Seventeen

The plywood wall of a second-hand clothing vendor's shack pressed in on Ridley from one side. Corrugated tin lined the other. Barely enough light filtered down into the narrow passage from the city glow above for her to make out each of the steppingstones that led down the centre of the cramped alley. The stones showed up as faintly lighter splotches against the dark, polluted water that flowed around and between them. She carefully stepped from stone to stone, working her way deeper into the labyrinth.

The passage eventually widened slightly, before ending at another alleyway that ran perpendicular to it. She knew that this new lane would run directly past the passage where Jeter plied his trade, a few yards to the left, forming a rectangle whose perimeter she was traversing.

The alley was empty, almost. This seemed to be more of a residential section of the slum, rather than commercial, with most of its residents likely asleep inside their humble homes. Ridley could make out the faint sounds of conversation, off to the left, punctuated by the occasional laugh.

She carefully looked around the corner and plotted a route through the shadows along the near side of the alley; then, she began to make her way towards the voices. The conversation grew louder as she drew near, until she could make out the words. She found cover behind a stack of cardboard boxes labeled "Made in China," only a few feet away from the men who were talking. She worked her way into a position that offered a slim view between the stacked boxes to observe them.

There were two men. Both appeared to be in their late twenties. Though their faces were angled away from her, she saw that one of them had a serious acne problem. The side of his face she could see was covered with pimples and scars. They were seated on folding chairs, their legs splayed out lazily. Ridley could just about make out the darkened opening of the alley beyond them. Jeter would be stationed somewhere up through that passage.

"Aliah's okay," she heard the one with the pimples say. "Just a bit plain for me. Now, if you want sexy, Priyanka is hard to beat."

There was a plastic shipping crate sitting on the ground between the two men, serving as a table. On it were an old tin can being used as an ashtray and several empty Daredevil beer bottles. Each of the two men had a half-empty bottle in one hand and a cigarette in the other. Sitting on the ground next to the makeshift table sat a black nylon duffel bag. *Bingo.*

Although she could hear them now, Ridley hadn't paid much attention to their conversation. They were only bull-shitting about Bollywood stars and which ones they wanted to fuck. Nothing tactically important.

"Sunny Leone?" the second man said. When he leaned forward in his seat, she could see the logo for the local pro football club on his shirt. "Of course she's hot, she's a fucking porn star. It kind of doesn't count."

They continued like this for several minutes, until Ridley heard a shuffle coming from the small alleyway just beyond them. She tensed as she saw both men stand. Pimples pulled a semi-automatic pistol from somewhere inside his jacket, though he held it low, at his side.

And there he was. Jeter came bounding around the corner, a shit-eating grin plastered across his face. "Three this time!" he said excitedly as he walked up. He handed Pimples a stack of bills, while the man in the football shirt bent down and reached into the duffel bag, producing a fistful of small, clear plastic envelopes full of product.

"Good work," Football said as he handed Jeter the drugs. "Keep it up." Jeter gave them a salute as he backed away, then turned and hustled back through the narrow passage.

The two men sat back down and picked up their beer bottles. "Seems kind of slow tonight anyhow," Pimples said.

"Yeah, kind of," Football answered, before steering the conversation back to its earlier subject matter. "That Nargis Fakhri though. Now there's an arse that won't quit."

Ridley heard their beer bottles clink together in agreement, and knew it was time to act. She silently backed away from her hiding place and retreated a couple of yards back down the alley. Then she again unfastened the top few buttons on her leather jacket, revealing the swell of her breasts against her tight shirt beneath. She unclipped her hair and let it fall to her shoulders. When she was ready, she started stumbling forward.

"Oh shit, this doesn't look right," she said out loud as she weaved her way from side to side, stumbling down the alley. The two men jumped to their feet and turned to face her just as she came into view. The one with the pistol instantly drew his weapon.

"Oh, hey, boys!" Ridley said, intentionally slurring her sultry English accent. "Am I glad to see you! This fucking place is like a ghost town… not a soul in sight to help a poor girl find her way out."

"Stop right there!" Pimples ordered. He had hauled his gun back out, but had not levelled it in Ridley's direction, yet. She didn't comply. Instead, she continued forward.

"My god is that beer? Could I have one? Pretty please? I'm so parched! No telling what I'd do for a beer!"

The two men looked at each other. Then Pimples turned back to her. "Get the fuck out of here, bitch, before we just have our way with you. Go back the way you came."

"Oh now, hang on a second," Football said, his voice dripping with mock sympathy. "Can't you see, the nice woman is thirsty?" He turned to Ridley and eyed her up and down. "I think we could spare a beer. She looks a bit overheated too, don't you think? She might want to take that jacket off and cool down."

Ridley smiled. "Well, it is just a wee bit warm out," she purred, as she stumbled another step forward while fumbling with the last few buttons of the jacket.

The two men had stepped a few feet apart, perhaps unconsciously flanking her. Ridley wasn't worried. They were moving right where she wanted them. She shuffled another step forward as she slid the jacket from her shoulders and let it fall to the ground. Pimples now held the gun loosely at his side, though he had moved to her right as she approached. Football had reached down to pick up a fresh beer, had popped the top and was reaching out to hand it to Ridley, a grin splashed a mile wide across his face.

"Oh my god that looks delicious!" she squealed drunkenly as she reached for the beer. Pimples had moved in closer on her opposite side.

Just before her hand closed around the neck of the bottle, Ridley rotated her wrist to grab the bottle by the neck with an upside-down fist. The initial reaction from Football was a look of surprise on his face. It was already too late.

Ridley's drunken steps were replaced by precise footwork as she planted her feet and bent her legs slightly, to lower her centre of gravity, as she wound up for her next move. By now, the beer bottle had started its circular flight at the end of her arm, most of the beer staying contained within by centrifugal force. Some escaped and sprayed in an arc as she spun.

Ridley had rotated her hips in the direction of her motion, ahead of her upper torso, to slingshot her arm and shoulders around at lightning speed. In a split second, the bottle had traveled almost 180 degrees, from Football's hand on one side, to its impending impact with the other man's face on the opposite side of the arc.

Pimples had no time to react. His gun hand had barely twitched. The barrel of the weapon had risen only a few inches by the time the beer bottle, with most of its 500 millilitres of extra-strong lager still inside, impacted the side of his head with an audible crunch.

The bottle shattered, as did the man's eye socket, in an explosion of beer, blood and glass. Pimple's body went limp, his grip on the gun loosened and it fell to the ground with a thump. Next, his knees unbuckled and his body began to fall like an imploding skyscraper.

Ridley had loosened her grip on the bottle's neck as impact was made, to avoid cutting her own hand. She was left slightly off-balance by the follow-through, however, as her body required another half-revolution to halt its inertia. By then, Football had wizened up and decided to join the party. He drew a knife from his pocket, a tactical folder with a nasty looking tanto-style blade.

"Oh, you fucking bitch," he growled. "I am going to carve you up—"

Ridley came to a stop, transitioning effortlessly into a fighting stance, one foot forward, one back, perfectly balanced and ready to strike.

Football lunged with the knife. He may as well have been in slow motion. Ridley's reflexes reacted at the first sign of movement, her forward hand sweeping inside of the attacker's, blocking his slash with her forearm against his wrist. She shifted her weight to her back foot as her front foot came up lightning fast to strike the man in his side.

He let out an audible "oof!" and staggered backward. The knife clattered to the ground.

Ridley shifted her weight forward and leapt into a spinning kick, her boot connecting with the side of the man's skull. He dropped, unconscious, next to his friend as Ridley landed back on her feet. She knelt beside each of the men and frisked them for weapons, finding no more. She looked around and spotted the gun Pimples had wielded. She picked it up and inspected it. It was a Chinese Type 54 9mm. She checked the magazine and saw nine rounds with one already in the chamber.

"It'll have to do," she mumbled to herself. She spotted the knife that Football had dropped. She snatched that up too, folded the blade shut and slipped it into her pocket. Lastly she grabbed her jacket, dusted it off and shrugged it back on.

She still needed that beer though; that part of her little show hadn't been a lie. She glanced at the table and saw there was one bottle left, unopened. She scooped it up, popped the top and downed half the bottle in one long, satisfying draft. Then she stepped over to the two drug dealers and poured the remainder of the cold beer over their faces. They woke up sputtering beer and blood.

"One move and you're both dead. Don't even fucking try me." She racked the slide on the pistol, ejecting the unfired round and catching it in her other hand as a fresh one slammed home. The manoeuvre was unnecessary, but it got their attention.

They both shook their heads as if to clear the cobwebs out, and looked at her.

"That's right, boys. Remember me?"

Pimples seemed to have lost any fight he'd had in him. Football remained defiant. "You are fucking dead, you know that? Even though you are holding that gun, you are dead."

"Whatever you say, tough guy. But if I read this right, you two bozos are dead, too. I'm going to walk out of here with that bag full of shit over there. You two are going to sound like idiots when you try to explain what happened to it. Am I right?"

Football shook his head in disbelief. After a defeated sigh, he conceded, "We are all dead."

Chapter Eighteen

"What is this about?" Kim asked for at least the tenth time.

The police officers riding with him in the back of the vehicle offered no explanation. Not that he needed one. He had been sloppy with the maid, back at the Orchid Hotel. He had done a piss-poor job of concealing her body, and an even worse job of trying to hide his own identity. His mug was probably all over the security cameras at that damned place. Not to mention the receptionist, and the bellhop who he had spoken to, who could have pointed the cops in the right direction.

Fuck! he thought again. Not for the first time, he had let his bloodlust overrule common sense.

The metal cuffs bit into his wrists behind his back. He was chained to a railing at the back of the bench, in a way that made it impossible to sit comfortably. Kim looked around at the three men seated beside and opposite him on the benches. They wore the paramilitary uniforms of Force One, the elite S.W.A.T. team of the Mumbai Police. Force One had been established in the wake of the deadly

97

Mumbai terror attacks of 2008. Each man was heavily armed, with a Glock 17 in his sidearm holsters, as well as shoulder-slung MP5 submachine guns, every one of of which was pointed directly at Kim. The men wore masks which mostly concealed their faces, but their eyes were cold and business-like.

They had taken him down swiftly as he stepped up to the Tata SUV. The team had been professional and efficient, sweeping him up, disarming and restraining him, and then loading him into the back of the crazy-looking Mahindra Marksman. The armoured vehicle had seemed to have come from out of nowhere. The entire episode had lasted mere seconds.

Of course, the Tata was being towed to some police impound facility, he was sure of it. It would be searched. The weapons and narcotics that would be found inside it wouldn't help his case. Though he had to admit, they couldn't actually make it much worse either, compared to murder.

This wasn't Do-Hyun Kim's first encounter with the law. He had been in a few tight spots over the years. Those had usually been in areas where he had more contacts to lean on. Up in Delhi, and the parts of northwestern India where he mostly operated. Down here in Mumbai he was poorly connected. Yet, he did not panic. This was merely a new problem that needed to be solved. Kim closed his eyes and tried to concentrate on how to get himself out of this situation.

They had driven north, to the shiny new buildings of Force One headquarters, situated among the leafy green environs of the Aarey Colony section of Goregaon. The Marksman armoured vehicle pulled into an underground garage, where Kim was unloaded, hustled through several checkpoints, then deposited into a high security holding cell.

Do they treat every murder with such force? he wondered. Homicide was a serious charge, but surely the anti-terrorism unit wasn't mobilised for every incident, was it? He filed that question away for further consideration. On top of that, they hadn't done anything in the way of "booking" him into detention. Something was up.

Kim sat on a bench in the holding cell for what must have been a couple of hours. He wasn't sure, because there were no clocks on the walls, his watch and phone had been taken from him, and there was no one to question. He heard the occasional sounds from far off: the closing of a door, or faint, unintelligible snippets of conversation. The hum of an air-conditioning unit he wasn't benefitting from.

Finally, someone came to collect him. Three men with submachine guns escorted him from the cell, down a series of hallways, and into a small interrogation room. He was seated in a chair on one side of a table, a chain connected from his wrists to an eyebolt embedded into the floor. The guards exited, though Kim knew he was being watched. The large, mirrored wall on one side of the room was obviously made of two-way mirrors. A series of cameras were mounted in the high corners of the room.

Kim almost grinned. *Show time!*

Chapter Nineteen

"So, here's what's going to happen," Alex Ridley told the two drug dealers, who were sprawled on the ground before her. "I've got no interest in you, nor what's in the bag. All I want is information. Well, this is a bonus I have to admit," she said as she held up the gun. "I'll be keeping it. What I really need out of you two idiots is some intel. Play nice and you will walk out of here in one piece. Continue to play nice, and you will even get your bag of candy back before anyone asks you where it went. Understand?"

"Sounds like a fairy tale," Football said.

"Maybe it is, maybe it isn't. You've got no choice, either way. You fuck this up, you'll die either by my hand or theirs, whoever *they* are. However, if you play it cool, all of this could go away within a day or two. Got it?"

The beaten drug dealer who had offered the beer looked up into her eyes, held her gaze for a moment, and slowly nodded his assent.

Ridley inclined her head towards the other man. "What about him?"

Pimples nodded too, without looking up.

"Okay, now we're getting somewhere." She reached behind her and grabbed one of the chairs the two men had been sitting on. She dragged it over and sat down directly in front of the two men, but outside of their reach in case either of them tried something. "Now, listen. I don't give a fuck about what you guys and your bosses are up to. I could not care less about the shit in that bag. I'm more interested in prostitution in this town."

Both men looked up at her, surprise on their faces. "Whores?" said the beer man.

Ridley nodded. "Yes. But not the ones that operate out in the open, down in the red-light district. I want to know who runs the black-market sex trade here. Street hookers? High-end call girls?"

The men looked at each other, then back at Ridley. "There are only three, really. They control the pussy market for the whole city. They are much worse than us, and our boss. They are ruthless. Those are guys you really do not want to fuck with."

"Try me."

"None of this comes back on us? Or our boss?"

"I don't even know who the fuck your boss is. And I don't want to know. Now, the pimps. Who are they?"

After a moment, Pimples seemed to debate whether to say anything. He finally spoke. "Th-the guy who runs the north part of town is Punjabi, a gangster from up north. His name is—"

"That's not who I'm looking for. Next?"

"Well, there is a small-time guy who mostly operates around the port, and the south end of the island. I think they call him Rajiv something."

"The third one?"

"He is the biggest one," Football chimed in. "He controls all the prostitution in this area, across the river from here, and all the way down to the red-light district at Grant Road. Nobody knows his real name. People know him as the..." He paused, glancing at his mate, eyes wide and jaw set firm.

After a moment his mate nodded.

'People call him 'The Vulture.' We do not even know what he looks like."

"So, if nobody's ever seen him, who does the dirty work for him?"

Pimples sighed, then said, "His main man is this big *katwa*—I mean Muslim—who goes by the name Azim, or something like that. I do not know any more about him. Except that I have heard he is a cold-blooded killer. You should steer clear of that one."

"Does he have girls here in Dharavi?"

"Well, kind of. Some of them live here but they do not work here. They cater to more of an upper-class clientele."

"So, where do they work?"

Football inclined his head in a generally northern direction. "Over there, across the river," he said. "In Bandra-Kurla, at the bars inside the fancy hotels."

"Like The Neptune Bar? At The Pantheon hotel?"

Both men stared at her, puzzled. "How did you know?" Pimples asked.

"Just a lucky guess, but thanks for verifying it. Next question, what do you know about this Buzzard or Vulture or whoever he is? What about his ties to human trafficking?"

The men looked at each other again, then turned their eyes down, away from Ridley. They said nothing.

"Come on now, I already know they're into it. But I need some details; how does it work?" Ridley lifted the gun and pointed it straight at Football's face. It was Pimples who spoke first.

"Yeah, yeah, they are into that, too. I have a cousin who works for them, under Azim's network, as a spotter."

Ridley raised one eyebrow. "A spotter?"

"Yeah, they are teenagers, mostly boys, who watch the posh clubs where the tourists go, keeping an eye out for likely targets. He told me all about it over some beers one night—he is only fourteen so the alcohol really got his mouth going. He said he was hoping to move up in the organisation."

"Lovely," Ridley said. "So, these spotters find women to kidnap. What are they looking for?"

Pimples shrugged. "You know, hot girls. Big hair, big boobs. Western, white girls, mostly. They look for the easy targets. Girls who are drunk and either alone, or walking in quiet areas. Definitely not someone like you. Easy targets, you know?"

Ridley was finding it harder to hide her anger. But she managed to hold back the venom in her voice, as she needed this information more than she needed to take out her rage on these two idiots. "How do they do it?"

"They all have mobile phones. The spotters report to the feeders. These are the guys who move in for a closer look. If the girls fit the profile, they get closer, start talking to them, turning on the charm."

"So, you're saying these 'feeders' are older? Good looking?"

"Oh yeah, they are playboys. Dressed to impress, gold chains, you know. While they are getting to know the mark, they further assess if she will be an easy take. Then, if everything is a go, they summon the trash collectors."

Ridley bolted up out of her chair, the gun coming back

up. "Trash collectors?" she yelled, sweeping the gun from left to right, from Football to Pimples, and back again. The men each threw up their hands in surrender.

"That is what my cousin called them!" Pimples yelled. "We have nothing to do with them, honestly!"

Ridley knew he was right. Yet, she was becoming furious over what she was hearing. For the abductors to call themselves something so callous as 'trash collectors' had brought her to boiling point. Still, she needed the rest of the information, and forced herself to put her emotions aside, at least for a little longer.

"What do these trash collectors do? I assume they're the ones who move in and abduct the girls?"

Pimples nodded. "Yes, they are just thugs. Brutes. The feeder will lead the girl through a back door or to an alley behind the bar or club, looking for a place to make out or something. Then the trash collectors move in and sweep her up. Haul her away in a van."

"Where do they take them?"

Pimples shrugged. "Who knows? Honestly, my cousin did not know any more than that. They are very secretive."

Ridley was silent for a moment. She kept her eyes pinned on the two drug dealers, though her thoughts were drifting away. All this business about spotters, feeders, trash collectors… It rang true with what Kayla had said she could recall about her own abduction.

"This Azim," Ridley finally said. "You said your cousin works under his umbrella. Are there others like him? Like Azim? Who also work under The Vulture but operate their own networks to abduct girls?"

Pimples nodded. "Yes, it seemed that way. My cousin said they work by territory. He did not know how many territories there are, but he said the area covered by him and the others under Azim was mostly the clubs in the south end of town."

"Far away from Bandra-Kurla?"

"Yeah, it seems as if he keeps the two sides of his business separate."

"But others from The Vulture's organisation work the other parts of Mumbai?"

He nodded. "Wherever the kind of girls they are looking for hang out."

Ridley fell silent again, thinking. This information was invaluable. If it was accurate. After a moment, she looked back at the two men, still sitting on the ground, propped up on their elbows. "Okay, that's all I needed to know. However... I need one more thing from you." Her eyes were trained squarely on Pimples.

"Me? What now? My fucking first-born?"

Ridley gestured at his open jacket, and the strip of leather that was visible beneath. "I'll need that shoulder rig," she said, waving the gun slightly. "This thing might get heavy."

"Oh, for fuck's sake," Pimples said. But he weakly reached inside his jacket, unfastened a buckle and shrugged out of it. Then he pulled on the straps until the whole rig had slid out from under him and held it up.

Ridley saw that in addition to a form-fit holster, the rig also carried a pouch for a spare magazine, which appeared to be fully loaded. "Now pitch it over here. At my feet. Easy now."

The man complied. As the holster rig landed in the dust at her feet, Ridley heard footsteps from the direction of the narrow passage. She turned in time to see Jeter hurrying around the corner, another big smile on his face.

"Two more!" he sang out, before his eyes fell on the

scene in front of him. He froze in mid-step. Then he turned and bolted back into the passage like a rabbit down a hole.

Ridley stood up, with the gun in one hand and the holster rig dangling from the other. She backed away from the two men until her feet bumped into the black bag. Without taking her eyes or the gun off of them, she reached down and picked the bag up, slinging its strap over her shoulder.

"I think I've heard enough," she said. "I'm leaving, and I'm taking this with me. You'll get it back in two days, unless I find out you've told anyone about me. You can hold your bosses off that long."

"But... how will we get the bag back?"

"Jeter will have it. I'll find him. If you fuck up, the bag goes into the river. Then I come looking for you."

Ridley backed away, towards the narrow passage through which Jeter had disappeared. She kept her eyes and the gun trained on the drug dealers until she reached the passage. Then she turned and ducked into its shadows, then hurried through to the other side.

When she emerged across from the bicycle shop, she was not surprised to see Jeter sprawled out on the ground. He was crying, and holding his wrist as if it were broken. His white hair was a disheveled mess.

Kayla Stone was standing over him, smiling.

Chapter Twenty

They left Kim on ice for twenty minutes or so before someone finally came into the room to speak to him. The door clicked open and a tall, lean man in his late fifties strode into the room. He was wearing the khaki uniform of the Maharashtra State Police and carrying a manila envelope under one arm. He took a long look at Kim, then pulled out a chair on the opposite side of the table and sat down across from him. He lifted the flap of the folder and consulted the information contained within it one more time.

"My name is Sahm Malek. I am the Deputy Inspector General of Police, Force One. And you, sir, claim to be..."—Malek checked the information inside the folder once more—"Jang Jin-Seung," Malek finished with a dramatic roll of his eyes. "Would you care to tell me who you really are?"

Kim stayed silent for a moment, considering the police officer who sat in front of him. The man was not dressed the same as the commandos who had picked him up.

Instead, he wore the khaki uniform that was more common among the Mumbai police. He also wore a black beret, more reminiscent of the country's special operations forces, adorned with a Force One logo patch.

"My name is Jang Jin-Seung. I am an immigrant from South Korea. I have been a resident of India for nine years, though I do admit I'm a little bit out of my element here in Mumbai. I live in Delhi and am only visiting this city." Kim had drilled the details of his alias into his memory. Reciting the fictitious details came naturally to him. Though he was disappointed that, should he make it out of this bind, he would have to brush up on one of his alternate identities now that this one was used up.

"Do not bullshit me," Malek said coldly. "We already know everything about this 'Jang' alias. Post box in Delhi, supposedly works at a shipping company there. Which does exist, however no one there knows anything about Jang Jin-Seung or any other Korean immigrant. So, you can drop the story and come clean. Or rot behind bars in Arthur Road."

Kim's face was made of stone, but inside he winced at the mention of Mumbai's notorious central prison. "You have not even told me why you have arrested me yet," he said. "I have done nothing wrong."

Malek laughed. "Nothing? Are you serious?" He stood up from his chair and paced the room. "Let me start with an easy one. You know what we found in the car, right?"

Drugs? Guns? Kim thought. *Take your pick.* "Why don't you tell me."

The Force One officer shook his head. "No, no… no, you're not asking the questions here. Perhaps you need some more time to think about it. I will be back in one hour."

With that, Malek turned on his heel and strode towards the door through which he had entered.

Just before reaching the door, he detoured to the corner of the room, reached up, and pulled the power cable from the camera mounted there. Then he stepped to the other camera and did the same. Kim watched the small red power light blink out.

Malek turned towards the mirrored wall and made several hand gestures, finishing with a mock finger slash across the neck. Then he turned back towards Kim.

"There are eyes and ears everywhere, even in here. Some things are best kept private, at least for a time. So, now we are completely off the record, yes?"

Kim remained stone-faced.

Malek stepped back to the table and sat back into the chair. "I am who I told you I am. What I did not tell you is why we picked you up. This was not a normal police operation here in Mumbai." Malek pulled a pack of cheap, filterless cigarettes and offered the pack to Kim. "Charminar?"

What a ridiculous offer, Kim thought. With his hands cuffed behind his back, Malek would have had to light it and place it in his mouth for him. He declined with a curt shake of his head.

The officer leaned back in his chair and tapped a cigarette out for himself. "Do you know what Force One is?" he asked as he struck a match and lit up, puffing blue smoke to get it started.

The pungent sulphur of the match was quickly replaced by the heavy, smoky aroma of the roasted tobacco. Kim tried to push the craving out of his mind.

"Of course," Kim replied. "The elite counter-terrorism unit of the Maharashtra State Police. I read the papers."

Malek nodded, his face nearly obscured by a cloud of

smoke. "That is correct. We go after terrorists. The worst of the worst. Because we are the best of the best. We train and prepare for those events you have read about in your papers." Malek laughed, his breath swirling the smoke even more. "Of course, that is what the public is told. Do you know what we really do, Mr. Jang?"

Kim offered no reply.

"What we really do, mostly, is sit around all day on our arses. Waiting for something to happen. We do some drills now and then, keep up our physical training. But mostly, we sit around and talk bullshit. Smoking cigarettes, watching movies, fucking around. Every once in a while, in between the dry spells of keeping the people safe from terrorists, we get an unusual request. One such call came to me the other day. This time, from my own dear brother-in-law, back home in Amritsar. Does that shit-stain of a town ring a bell, Mr. Jang?"

It did. Still Kim stayed silent.

"I can see it does. In fact, I know it does, but I will get to that. So, my brother-in-law happens to be one of the deputy commissioners up there. One morning, one of his fellow commissioners just happened to be pulled over by a city cop for ignoring a traffic signal. The policeman would have simply sent this government official on his way, unmolested, upon learning who he was. Just as a matter of routine, before confronting the driver, the traffic cop called in the number plate."

Malek paused momentarily to savour his cigarette, regarding Kim through the smoke as he did. "By now, you know where this is going, Mr. Jang. You can guess that the number plate on the official's car was incorrect. Naturally, upon discovering this, that official started pulling whatever strings were available to him, to find out why. I will not bore you with the details, except to say that a traffic camera here in Mumbai happened to pick up the registration plate number that did belong to that official, after a quiet notification had gone out nationwide."

Kim was making his best effort to remain calm and silent, with no outward sign of reaction to anything he was hearing. But inside, he was now laughing. It took every ounce of willpower to resist bellowing out loud.

"You can imagine what came next," Malek continued. "Someone in Amritsar receives a report that the purloined number plate had been positively identified, all the way down in Mumbai. It also turns out that this particular deputy commissioner serves on several committees with another commissioner who just so happens to have a brother-in-law in Mumbai. And how very fortuitous, that this brother-in-law just happens to be a Deputy Inspector General in the city's elite counter-terrorism force, with a team of highly trained commandos at his disposal." He paused, analysing Kim's reaction. He saw none and continued.

"I suppose we were not doing anything anyhow. Sitting around picking our arses. So when the call came in, yes, we jumped right up. We were bored. It was not hard to locate the vehicle, after asking a few questions at the hotel where the traffic camera first pinged it. Now, here we are."

Kim was impressed at how quickly and efficiently the corrupt Indian politicians and police had acted. He was also angry at his own bad luck. Until he remembered that he didn't believe in luck, and that had to apply to bad luck as well as good. *Good luck is where preparation meets opportunity*, he thought. So, the flip-side, *bad luck*, must either be where opportunity meets ill-preparedness, or preparation never meets opportunity. In this case, he thought it must be the former. He had been ill-prepared for this contingency, and for that he silently cursed himself.

"I deny any wrongdoing," Kim said, finally. "I demand to speak with my advocate, now."

Malek shook his head. "Mr. Jang, you have not been listening. This operation was not authorised. You have not been arrested, officially. Your notions of justice and due process simply do not apply, I'm afraid."

"So you have kidnapped me."

"In a manner of speaking, that is correct. I prefer to say that we have temporarily detained you, pending further investigation. What we know so far of you, Mr. Jang, includes the commission of several serious crimes. Perhaps you can see the difficult position that puts us in."

"What happens next?"

"Well, that is entirely up to you, Mr. Jang. As soon as you decide to tell us who you really are, we can make that determination. In the meantime, my contacts from Amristar will be making their way here, in order to question you in person. Due to scheduling and travel, that may take a few days. It could even be a week."

Chapter Twenty-One

It was nearly three in the morning when Ridley and Kayla finally returned to their room at the King's Rest guesthouse.

"Someone has been here," Ridley stated after making a circuit of the tiny space.

Kayla turned around in place, surveying. "What makes you say that? Everything looks the same to me."

"Me too," Ridley replied. "I can't quite put my finger on it, but something seems out of place. All our things are still here, about where we left them. Something is ringing alarm bells in my mind."

"Maybe it was housekeeping."

Ridley laughed. "Here? Not likely."

"Should we ask the clerk?"

"I don't think so. Whoever got in here might have done so with her assistance. Maybe bribed her. We can't be sure."

"Well, who do you think it might be?"

Ridley considered this for a moment. "Most likely it's random. Someone followed us because we're foreign, and not poor. Maybe they left everything as it was to see what else we might bring back here, hedging on a better take if they waited another day."

"You don't think it could be Azim? Or somebody specifically looking for me? Or you?"

Ridley pondered that. Surely news of what had happened at Mount Kailash had reached the Mumbai underworld by now. Though, would anyone back here be anticipating the survivors returning to the scene of their own abduction? Most women would have caught the first flight home. Most women, but not Ridley or Kayla.

"I suppose it's possible," Ridley said after a few beats, "but I think that's less likely. We probably haven't been as careful as we should have been, but we haven't been that sloppy. Either way, I think we'd better move. Again."

"Where to? One of the other places the bellhop suggested?"

"No. Some place else entirely," Ridley said as she stepped towards the room's only window and pulled the near-worthless curtain aside. "We can't rule the bellhop out as part of the problem. Now that we know our next move, perhaps we should just head right over."

Kayla joined her at the window, where Ridley was gazing out across the cityscape, beyond the hovels of Dharavi, past the inky blackness of the Mithi River and towards the sparkling high rises of Bandra-Kurla, currently blazing with a million lights even at this hour.

They were thoroughly exhausted, having never even slept in their beds at either the guesthouse or the Orchid Hotel before that. Nevertheless, the women gathered up their things and left the King's Rest, exiting through the back stairway, away from prying eyes. They flagged down one of the few taxis operating at that time of the early morning; ten minutes later they were checking in at the Pantheon Hotel.

"International flights," Ridley said to the registration clerk. "They never arrive at a decent hour."

The clerk offered only a quick grunt in reply as he studied the computer monitor in front of him. "We're just about fully booked," he said. Ridley fixed him with unnerving stare, which did the trick. "Ahem, well, yes, I do have one room available, isn't it? It has only one bed, madams, very king size. But the sofas in our rooms are quite comfortable, if, you know, if you need it."

Ridley said the room would be fine and completed the registration process. Then the women took the elevator to their room, dropped their bags just inside the door, stripped to their underwear and collapsed onto the bed.

Neither would wake until almost noon.

Chapter Twenty-Two

Taara checked her face once more in the mirror. Her quick re-application where the drunk American had smeared her makeup was not perfect. It would have to do.

Seth, he had called himself. He had said he worked for a California software company that used call centres in India for customer service, and he was here to negotiate contracts. Or had that been last night's punter? What had been the name of that one? Nikolai? Caesar? She couldn't quite remember. They all sort of melted into one slimy, sleazy mess, over time. Men from all over the world, drunk on their own success, traveling and partying on their company expense accounts.

The American had become quite drunk on Dark & Stormy cocktails. He had spied her sipping one. She loved the sweetness of the dark rum combined with the snap of ginger beer. Hector, the toga-clad bartender, favoured her with easy pours, supplementing a portion of the rum with diet cola. That way, she might sip cocktails all night without getting too drunk. A mild intoxication? That was helpful in some ways, such as dulling the shame of renting her body to random men each and every night.

When Seth had walked up and taken command of the barstool next to her, he had barked out to the bartender, "Two more! Whatever this ravishing creature is drinking!" Hector had nodded and brought two of the drinks over, one for him with the usual pour, and one with Taara's special blend. I few rounds later he had made his move.

When he had leaned in to kiss her, she had discreetly turned her head so that he might plant it on her cheek, which she normally allowed, though she never kissed them fully on the mouth. It was part of the act. Part of the mating dance that turned curious prospects into paying customers.

However, rather than kissing her on the offered cheek, he had stuck his tongue out and licked the side of her face in one long, wet stroke. It was disgusting, like being slapped in the face with a cold, oily fish. Taara had recoiled in horror at first, looking at the American with shock on her face, before remembering to stay in character. Her job depended on it.

"They will do crazy things," Azim had told her several times. "Nasty things. And, you will do them, sweetling. You will perform these things with a smile on that pretty face of yours. Do you know why?"

Because... the customer is always right, she would answer. It was a mantra that he had beaten into her and the other girls over and over.

Thus, she had instantly wiped away her expression of shock in favour of a serviceable, if contrived, smile. "I'm sorry," she had said sweetly, trying to salvage the situation. "I just wasn't expecting that. Boy, you are a wild one."

"Fuck you, bitch," he had replied, his face now twisted

up in anger. "What, I ain't good enough to kiss a whore like you? Anyway, what the fuck is that on your face?" His mouth was convulsing in a gag reflex. "It tastes like licking chalk board!" He had swallowed the last of his drink in order to wash his mouth out, and stormed off towards the elevators, shaking his head.

She had invested an hour and a half of her precious time on him, all for naught. She had stifled a small giggle when she thought of him gagging on her makeup.

Wait! she thought, suddenly alarmed. *My makeup!* She had quickly run to the ladies restroom to inspect the damage.

His wet tongue had left the makeup on that side of her face a muddy mess; the bruising below her eye and to the side of her nose was showing through.

She had put so much effort into concealing the bruises Azim had dealt her a few nights prior, when she had asked for the night off in order to tend to her sick mother. There was nothing she could do about the swelling other than an ice pack and ibuprofen. Thankfully, it had mostly subsided over the last couple of days. The bruising had proven more stubborn.

Taara slipped her small makeup case back into her clutch and left the restroom.

Chapter Twenty-Three

It was Ridley who opened her eyes first, becoming instantly alert, as was her custom. She lay still, unmoving. Despite the blackout drapes on the enormous plate glass window, daylight sneaking around the edges dimly lit the room. Kayla's back was to her, a couple of feet away on the enormous king bed. She was still asleep, softly snoring in rhythm with the slight rise and fall of her torso.

The younger woman's long blonde hair spilled across the pillow and comforter, reaching out towards Ridley like tendrils of golden smoke. The rest of Kayla's body stretched across her field of vision like a distant mountain range. Kayla's muscular shoulder formed the high point of that landscape, which gently tapered down along her ribs to the narrow valley of her waist. Another peak rose after that, the smooth, round swell of her hip, followed by another gentle decline along her thighs to the foothills of her calves and feet.

Not for the first time, Ridley caught herself struggling between seeing the woman before her as the perfect womanly specimen she had become, and the young, inno-cent girl she had been until recently. What was she doing, allowing this innocent, sweet young woman to travel down this dark road with her?

By all accounts, Kayla was one of the strongest women Ridley had ever encountered. Not only in terms of physical strength, though she was well endowed with that too. But in her strength of will. And in the power she had over people. Power over their minds, their hearts, and certainly their desires. She was Aphrodite, in the flesh.

And now I'm using her, Ridley thought bitterly, *as a tool, as bait, in my own crusade. I am corrupting this perfect, beautiful person.*

In her mind's eye she saw Kayla turn towards her on the bed and lock eyes. *Be careful who you think is using who,* her imagined version of Kayla said. *I'm on my own crusade. But I'm glad we're here, together.*

"Hey, wake up, sleepyhead," Kayla called from behind her.

"Huh? Wha—" Ridley slurred as her eyes snapped open. She sat up and looked around. Kayla was standing at the edge of the bed, stretching.

"I think you were dreaming," Kayla said. "You were mumbling in your sleep."

"I was not. Wait, really? About what?"

"I couldn't make it out, but it was soft, and sounded nice. I hope it was a happy dream. What was it about?"

What had it been about? Even now it was fading into noth-ingness; only vague, conflicted remembrances of comfort and shame remained. "I... I don't remember," Ridley said honestly. "I usually can't. It was probably about Hiram. I miss him. A lot."

Kayla's face brightened in a wide smile. "That's so sweet. I can't wait until I have that with someone."

Oh, you will, Ridley thought, as she watched her disappear into the bathroom. *You definitely will.*

Ridley and Kayla spent the rest of the day recharging. They ordered lunch from room service and followed it with another nap.

Late in the afternoon Kayla asked if Ridley would like to go to work out. "This place has an incredible gym," she said, flipping through the guest services notebook.

"We had better not," Ridley said. "We need to try our best not to show our faces around here, for now."

"Oh yeah," Kayla conceded. She sounded disappointed. "I guess you're right."

However, they did need to go out, to run some errands in preparation for the evening's operation. They both donned their most forgettable clothes, left the room and took the stairs to the ground floor. There, they slipped out discreetly through the parking garage into the street.

They had located a fashion boutique online, which was only a couple of blocks away. Ridley left Kayla in the evening wear section as she herself browsed active wear. Thirty minutes later, they had both made their purchases and stopped at an Italian restaurant for dinner.

"Oh my, you don't know how badly I want pizza!" Kayla squealed. "Not want, need. I need pizzzzaaaaa."

Sufficiently sated by the surprisingly good food, it was well after dark when they returned to their room at The Pantheon. They took turns in the bathroom, getting ready for the evening. Ridley went first, emerging twenty minutes later showered, shampooed and wearing a smart-looking business suit that consisted of a dark grey knee-length skirt and a matching blazer over a white chiffon blouse.

"Ooh, hot for teacher!" Kayla teased as she stepped into the bathroom.

Nearly an hour later Kayla emerged from the bathroom and asked, "How do I look?"

Ridley had been busy adjusting the straps of the shoulder holster she had purloined from the drug dealer. When she turned around and saw her friend standing before her, her jaw dropped. For a long moment she said nothing.

"Is it... too much? Do you think?"

Ridley finally snapped out of it, giving her head a quick shake to clear her mind. "It's, umm... yeah. I think it'll work."

The tiny red dress was nearly as revealing as the bathing suit that had left Ridley speechless at the Orchid's pool the previous day. It featured a deep, draped halter neckline in the front that plunged to her navel, revealing the cleft of Kayla's cleavage and toned abs. It didn't cover much below that, either, with the hem stopping at the upper thigh, showcasing her long, muscular legs.

Kayla turned in place and looked back over her shoulder at Ridley. "You don't think it's a bit, I don't know, over the top?"

Ridley admired Kayla's muscular back, generously revealed by the dress's backless cut, which scooped to just above the swell of her arse. An arse which itself was accentuated by the thin, clingy material of the dress. Ridley knew she herself looked good for her age, but could feel a hint of unbidden jealousy as she struggled to tear her eyes away.

"Yeah," she said, before clearing her throat and continuing. "I think that's what we're looking for. It will definitely catch every eye in the room. Hopefully including the ones we're interested in."

"I thought these would go nice with it," Kayla continued as she reached into the bag she had brought from the boutique. She produced a pair of gold, rhinestone-covered platform Mary Jane pumps and proceeded to put them on.

"For heaven's sake you're already tall," Ridley said in mock protest. "How high are those heels anyhow?"

"Only about four inches," she replied. "Besides, they help accentuate the calves, and my butt."

As if you needed any more help in that department, Ridley thought. "How can you even walk in those things?"

"Practice. I've done a bit of clubbing, you know. Don't worry though. If for some reason we need to run, I'm kicking these off and hauling arse barefoot." Kayla glanced towards the nightstand, where the knife Ridley had taken from the dealers and given to her, was sitting. "My only worry is I've no place to conceal a weapon."

"That's why I'll be keeping a close eye on you," Ridley replied. "Discreetly, from a distance."

Chapter Twenty-Four

Ridley watched the room from her seat in a high-backed booth in a dark corner of The Neptune Bar. The room was ornately decorated with a sea-inspired motif. Several large pillars in the centre of the room were sculpted to look like a dense kelp forest, willowing up towards the ceiling where the kelp leaves spread out as if on the surface of the ocean. The ceiling itself was back-lit in a moving, flowing pattern to mimic the dappled light of waves on the surface. They had carried the theme into the smallest details; even the skewers holding condiments in their cocktails were shaped like tiny tridents.

The oceanic theme was broken up here and there by Romanesque architecture, such as marble-looking columns and archways, which carried throughout the rest of The Pantheon Hotel. Staff uniforms within The Neptune Bar were also Roman-inspired, with the bartenders and wait staff wearing pristine white togas. Ridley doubted whether the actual Romans of antiquity had fashioned their garments from such small swatches of material.

Kayla had entered the room ten minutes after her, as they had planned. Ridley had swept the room, assessing each patron as a possible threat or asset. The Neptune Bar was still only about half full, but she guessed it would fill up more as the hour grew late.

Ridley had noted the dark-skinned beauty in the green sequinned evening dress who had been consorting with the drunk businessman at the bar. She had marked her as a likely prostitute, along with one other candidate who had been working the far side of the room. They were definitely in the right place.

Not long after she arrived, Ridley heard an angry voice, rising over the pounding beat of the monotonous house music. She turned in time to see the drunk businessman stand up from his stool, yell at the prostitute in the green dress and storm out of the room. A moment later the woman had hurried into the ladies bathroom.

When Kayla entered the room, it was almost like when the saloon's piano player stops in an old western movie. Everyone turned to see what the big deal was, what everyone else was staring at. And their eyes lingered. Ridley couldn't blame them. She was almost helpless to look away herself. She watched as Kayla strode in, clad in her barely-there red mini-dress and sparkling shoes. She found a seat at the bar and ordered a drink. Ridley saw her glance around the room a couple of times, as any vendor looking for her next customer might. If she'd spotted her friend, she hadn't shown it. The bartender soon returned with her drink.

"I'll be damned," Ridley said, barely in a whisper. Even from a distance she could see the bartender had brought Kayla's drink in a short, squat rocks glass. There was a single, jumbo-sized ice cube in it, surrounded by amber liquid. She could barely make out the twist of orange peel added for garnish.

Ridley looked forlornly down at her own drink, a Blue Hawaiian, which she had ordered more as a cover than out of any craving. It was a sad mix of pineapple juice, vodka, the world's most lifeless sour mix, and blue curaçao, a liqueur with an interesting history but ruined by electric blue food colouring. The result was a sickly-sweet, ridiculous mess. She had merely seen others enjoying them, so she had ordered one too. "When in Rome," Ridley mumbled as she sipped. *Or Mumbai...*

A flash of light caught her attention. She turned in time to see the ladies' room door closing behind the pretty young woman in the green dress, who was returning to the bar. She seemed to have left whatever had been bothering her behind. She walked back to her post at the bar with her chin up and her chest out. Ridley noted the concerned look on the bartender's face as he exchanged a few words with her.

They're friends, she thought. *He looks after her.*

Ridley watched as several men approached Kayla. She smiled broadly, talked and laughed with each of them. But, each left within a minute or two. She was following the plan. Do not let any one prospective client monopolise her time. Always be looking for the bigger whale. Hope someone notices, and alerts Azim's people.

This had been going on for less than an hour when Ridley noted that the woman in the green dress had been watching Kayla. She saw nothing abnormal about that. Surely prostitutes could spot their competitors. She went on red alert when she saw the woman slide off of her barstool and start walking in Kayla's direction.

Ridley quickly scanned the room for other movement in

Kayla's direction as her hand subconsciously drifted towards the Type 54 sitting in its holster underneath her suit jacket. She noted no other suspicious movement, which would indicate the woman was working with a team. She was going in alone. Ridley watched from across the room as the woman approached Kayla, took a seat on the barstool next to her and leaned in as if having a private conversation.

Chapter Twenty-Five

Kayla had marked the striking, dark-skinned beauty as one of the room's working prostitutes from the moment she had emerged from the ladies room, shortly after she herself had arrived. She had also marked Alex Ridley, discreetly posted in a booth on the far side of the room. Though she was unarmed and almost naked herself, knowing Ridley was watching over her made her feel a lot safer.

She had witnessed several short conversations between the woman in the green dress and male patrons. The poorer and more "local" they looked, the shorter the conversation. She had been holding out for bigger fish. She had caught Kayla off guard when she abruptly got up and walked over, taking the seat right next to her.

"It is not safe for you here, sweetheart," the woman said to Kayla as she leaned in.

"It's a free country, sister. I'm just trying to make a living. Just like you."

The woman half-laughed. "You are not just like me. You are nothing like me. But I know one thing about you. You are in over your head. I know you are not a pro. I've been watching you. If you want to try your hand at hooking, I will say this… this is not the place to start out."

Kayla turned towards her and looked her in the eyes. *Alright, I'll roll with that opening,* she thought. "And why not, sister? Think I don't have what it takes?" She wiggled her body slightly, as if to prove her point.

"This is not amateur hour!" the woman hissed. "It is not safe here! Don't you see? It is not me you should be afraid of. Or Stella over there dancing with that Englishman."

"Then what's the problem?"

The woman looked around the room once more and leaned in closer. "It is our boss. The men we work for. This is *territory,* don't you see? This bar, this hotel—all of Bandra-Kurla. They will beat the shit out of you for working here. Or worse!"

Kayla sensed it was time to change tactics. Perhaps this woman could provide the information they needed. It was worth a shot. She touched the woman on the hand. "What if I'm a customer?"

"A… a customer?"

"Yes, a customer. A John. Or Jane, or whatever you would call it. A client."

The woman looked at Kayla for a moment, then leaned back, her eyes scanning her up and down. "Are you a cop?"

"Do you see any place I could hide a gun? Or even a wire? No, I'm not a cop. However, I would like to buy an hour or two of your time. Or the whole night, if that's what it takes."

The woman looked Kayla up and down again. "I… do not do women, sweetheart."

Kayla smiled. "You don't have to *do* me. I just want to talk. Seriously. As you've noticed, I could use some advice about all this. What do you say? I'll pay you for the night, and we just talk? Over coffee?"

The woman studied Kayla's face, as if looking for any trace of malice in it. Finally she looked around the room, and then back to Kayla. "My name is Taara. I know a place."

Chapter Twenty-Six

Dante's was a 24-hour diner just over the river, in Kurla West. "It is far enough away that we will not be spotted by the wrong people," Taara had said. "They have some booths in the back for extra privacy."

Kayla had hailed a cab at the street; it was still early enough in the evening that they were readily available on the busy streets of Bandra-Kurla. The two had ridden mostly in silence for the short ride over the bridge into the older section of Mumbai.

"Just coffee for me," Taara had told the waitress, and Kayla echoed her order. Taara had been right; the booth at the far back of the restaurant did indeed afford some privacy, with high backs and no view inside from the street. Just about the only patrons who could see back into the booth, without being too obvious, were those seated in the last two stools along the counter. And that's where Ridley had taken up position only a few minutes after Kayla and Taara had been seated.

"So... You want to get into hooking," Taara said,

followed by a sigh. "I do not recommend it. It can be bad for your health." She gestured down towards Kayla's body, of which everything below her spectacular display of cleavage was below the tabletop, out of view. "You have certainly got the assets for it though. Physically, that is."

Kayla nodded, as shyly as she could manage. "I know there are risks, Taara," she said as the waitress brought their coffees. She waited until she left before continuing. "I'm not naive. I also know there is decent money to be made, if you're careful."

"Oh, there is a lot of money in it. A lot changes hands, though you would be surprised how little of it you actually get to keep."

"I'm not surprised. I know the pimps run the show out here."

Taara laughed. "They do not call themselves that here, darling. You had better not, either. Unless you would like that pretty face rearranged for you. Here they are just 'handlers'. And they are brutal. I did not quite understand how brutal, until it was too late." Taara reached up and touched her face absently. "Like I said, choose a different line of work. You will live longer. And happier."

Kayla glanced across the room at Ridley. She saw her nod, almost imperceptibly, though it didn't even appear she was looking at her.

"Taara, do you mind if I call my friend over? She's cool."

Taara looked up, her eyes wide. "What? Is this a setup?" She looked wildly around, leaning over to see past the booth's tall seat-back.

"No, no, no. It's nothing like that. She's my friend. You will like her. Neither of us are cops, and I promise, neither of us want to do you any harm whatsoever."

"Did you lie to me?" Taara said, anger in her voice. "Are you really even looking into getting into hooking? Was that a lie?"

Kayla sat back, her face turning serious. "Of course it was a lie, Taara. I didn't really come here for that. I came here to find your boss. But I found you, instead."

"My boss? What for?"

Kayla shook her head. "I can't say more, not on my own. If you'll let my friend join us, we can talk all about it. Yes, we're still paying for your time."

"Which one is she?" Taara said, turning again to look out into the dining room. "The one in the headscarf? She is looking this way."

"No. My friend's name is Alex. That's her in the business suit, there on the stool."

Ridley was studying a menu or handbill that had been lying on the counter, while sipping her coffee. She gave no outward sign that she was even aware of Kayla and Taara.

Taara turned back around and slumped into her seat. "Okay. She can come over."

Kayla nodded, and Ridley slid off of her stool and walked over. Kayla scooted across the bench seat, and Ridley slid in next to her.

"Alex," Kayla said, "this is Taara."

Ridley looked the woman over, at first studying her with furrowed brows. Then her face softened, and she offered a smile. "Hello Taara. Thank you for talking to us."

"Do not thank me yet. You might not get the information you are seeking. But my time costs the same, regardless."

Ridley nodded. "We understand. We can pay now, up front, if you'd like."

"Later," Taara said. "We do not know how long this will take, yet. I will trust you until then."

"Okay, that's a start. Good."

"Why don't you start by telling me who you are, before you begin asking questions?"

Ridley and Kayla exchanged glances. Kayla decided to take a chance. "I think it's best not to give our names, yet. I can tell you what happened to me. Jesus, was it only two weeks ago?" Kayla looked up at the ceiling and shook her head. Ridley placed a hand over Kayla's.

"It's alright," Ridley said. "Go on."

Kayla inhaled, then let her breath out slowly. She nodded. "Two weeks ago, I was kidnapped, out of a club, here in Mumbai. I was beaten, drugged, and transported to a remote location in the mountains up in Tibet. I was not the only one. A whole van full of women and girls were taken, along with me. There were more already there when we arrived. It was a marketplace, and we were the livestock. We were being sold into slavery. Sexual slavery, most likely."

Kayla had laid it out quickly, without beating around the bush. Taara's mouth hung open. "My God," she whispered, and slumped back into her seat.

Kayla nodded. "But, I survived, along with the women who were there with me. By sheer luck, and by the will of this amazing woman sitting next to me, and her friends. Alex was among the women there to be trafficked. My luck was that someone had made the mistake of abducting her, too."

Taara was listening intently. Kayla saw a tear stream down her cheek. "I think I know where this is going," she said.

Kayla nodded again. "Yes, I think you do. My abductor, the man who abducted me, enslaved me, and trafficked me into a faraway land to be auctioned off to the highest bidder... "

"Was my boss," Taara finished. Tears now streamed freely down her cheeks. "Azim."

"Yes," Ridley said, speaking for the first time since Kayla began her story. "Azim Alli. Your boss. Your... handler, as you say. He does more than just handle the prostitutes in this part of Mumbai. He also abducts women—foreign tourists, mostly—and sells them like livestock. Like slaves."

Taara hung her head, shaking it back and forth, crying. "I am... I am sorry. So, so sorry."

Kayla reached across the table and touched Taara's hand, enclosing it within her own. "No, Taara, it's not your fault. You have nothing to do with it. We're here for Azim, not you."

Taara looked up, her makeup a mess. "You do not understand. I am sorry, because I knew about it. I knew, and all I did was look the other way."

"You knew this was going on?" Ridley said sharply, a hint of anger in her voice.

Taara looked at her, her eyes pleading for forgiveness. "Only the rumours I heard. They sounded correct, knowing those people like I do. I knew it was true. I believe they allowed those rumours to circulate, among us working girls. They made us think that we were the lucky ones. At least we got to go home to our families when our work was finished."

Taara was openly sobbing now, almost uncontrollably. Ridley glanced around the room, to see if anyone could hear them. So far, it appeared no one had; the view of Taara and Kayla was mostly obscured by the high seat-back of the booth.

"Kayla and I came very close to never getting to see our families again," Ridley said coldly. "Who knows how many came before us, who weren't so lucky. Hundreds? Thousands? Where are those women now? How many of them are still alive, living in servitude? How many have died, their families still with no clue as to whatever happened to them?"

"Alex," Kayla said. "She's not them."

Ridley turned on Kayla, ready to press the attack. When she saw her friend, however, who had been with her there in the shadows of Kailash, even though they were not yet friends—she understood her clearly, and realised that Kayla was right. It was time to move forward, not look back.

They they had a job to do. A job that would require setting emotion aside, for a time, and focusing on the task.

With a long sigh, Ridley let out the breath she'd been holding, and her face softened. She turned to Taara, and placed her hand over Kayla's, which already covered Taara's. "Kayla's right," she said. "You're not them. You are also a victim, in a way. We have that in common. We are sisters."

Taara looked up. "Sisters? Yes, I suppose we are, in a way."

Chapter Twenty-Seven

"He beats you up," Ridley observed. It wasn't a question.

Taara looked away instinctively, preparing to deny it. Then her hand returned to her face, where her tears had re-smudged her makeup, the bruises around her eye again showing through.

"Yes," she said quietly. "He does. We all get beaten, it seems, whenever it is our turn. Azim is a violent man. When he is away, his people do it for him. But he is the worst." Taara looked up at Kayla and Ridley, each in turn. "You cannot beat him, though! He is powerful, and has many men at his disposal. Evil men with cruel weapons and no honour. Even worse than that, he is part of a much bigger orhanisation. Azim has a boss, too. I hear that one is a very evil man."

"The Vulture?" Ridley asked.

Taara's eyes grew wide. "You know of this man?"

"Only by reputation. Yes, we know of him. Don't worry about me and Kayla. We can take care of ourselves.

However, we lack information. That's why we have come to you. Can you help us?"

"I will help however I can," Taara said, glancing nervously around, her eyes darting back and forth. "But I must think of my own safety, too, and that of my family. They may be put in danger if I do anything to upset these men. Anyhow, I do not know how I can help. I do not know much about Azim, or the Vulture. They do not talk to us about such things."

"We won't ask you to do anything that would jeopardise you or your family," Ridley told her flatly. "You have my word on that. Really, all we need is information. Kayla and I will do the rest."

"The rest?" Taara asked. "What does that entail? If you kick that hornets' nest, it may make it worse for me and the others, whether you intended that or not."

Ridley leaned back against the seat and looked Taara in the eyes. "We're not just going to kick the nest, Taara. We're going to exterminate them."

Taara looked doubtful. "There are so many of them. They are well armed, well trained, and they are evil. I have just met you two... I am sorry... I fear for your safety... for your lives."

Kayla and Ridley stayed silent, letting Taara work her thoughts out. After a moment, she took the last sip from her coffee cup, set it down, and said, "God forgive me for telling you this. Azim... he has a daughter. She is his world. I have been around him when the girl has called him. He pauses what he is doing and takes the call, every time. I believe her name is Yasmine. For those few moments, Azim is a different man. Almost human, in the way he speaks with her. When he hangs up, the shadow falls back over his face and he is again the Azim that everyone knows and fears. If there is a chink in his armour, it is his love for his daughter." Taara looked down into her lap and said, again, "God help me."

Kayla looked at Ridley, who nodded back, gravely.

"Taara, we won't harm the child," Kayla said. "We promise. Right, Alex?"

Ridley hesitated for a beat, and then agreed. "Of course not. She is innocent in all of this. Though, perhaps we can use her as a means to get close to the father. Can you tell us where they live? Azim and his family?"

Taara shook her head. "They do not tell us such things. I have heard that he lives somewhere in the south end of Mumbai, probably Colaba, but that is only a guess."

"Is there anything else, anything at all, that you might have heard?"

Taara thought for a minute. "There really is not much to tell. I have only overheard a couple of those conversations. One time, it sounded as if he was soothing Yasmine after she had been reprimanded at school, for having dyed her hair some unusual colour. Green, I think."

"Green hair?" Ridley asked. "That is helpful."

"It might not be green now. In fact, it probably is not. It sounded as if it got her in trouble. Azim told her he would talk with the headmaster and work it out."

"Do you know what school it was?"

"No, I have no idea. Sorry. I had a sense that it was some private academy. Some place with more restrictions than public schools. You know, because the dyed hair was an issue."

Ridley nodded. "Yes, that's a fair assumption. If Azim is as you say, he would want the best for his girl, regardless of the cost. Kayla and I will do some research on private schools in the Colaba area."

"I'll get right on it," Kayla said. "Is there anything else you can tell us? Even the most insignificant piece of information might be helpful."

Taara thought hard few a seconds, then shook her head. "No, there is nothing else. Like I said, they are very secretive. They only speak to us to give us orders or to collect money. Or if any of us get out of line… then they…" Taara looked down at her lap, and muttered, "They punish us."

Ridley reached into her pocket for the money clip she kept there. "That reminds me… "

Taara held up her hands in protest. "No, I cannot take money from you. You have suffered so much at the hands of these people."

"A deal is a deal," Kayla said. "We owe you for your time."

"Keep your money. Perhaps that is the small way I can help in this."

Ridley was insistent. "You'll need to show your income for the time you have spent with us. I won't allow you to be short when they come to collect."

Taara reluctantly accepted the cash Ridley offered, along with a small scrap of paper on which she had written a phone number.

"That's the number for the phone I'm carrying. If you need us at all, or find yourself in trouble, call. Don't hesitate, just call. Do you understand?"

Taara nodded, her eyes wide with what looked like a mix of both fear and gratitude.

Kayla and Ridley bade Taara farewell and made their way back to their room at The Pantheon. They were careful to use the back entrance and to stay away from the busier corridors.

"We need to set a watch, from this moment on," Ridley

said, once they had settled back in. "I'll take the first shift. Things will get more dangerous the longer we're here and asking questions. In the morning we should move again. I feel as if we need to stay on the move, both for our safety, and because we're getting closer to the target."

Chapter Twenty-Eight

Ramanujan Secondary Academy occupied a tree-covered block in Colaba, near the southern tip of Mumbai. Though the area was densely populated, it wasn't as solidly covered with concrete and asphalt as the other areas of the city Ridley and Kayla had seen so far. Here there were plenty of trees, vegetation and even some pleasant open spaces, although limited.

The school sat behind a high brick wall, with wrought iron gates along the street on two sides, at ninety degrees to each other. Kayla and Ridley sat at a cafe across the street and halfway down the block, at an angle that afforded a view of both gates. The women were dressed casually, as expatriates enjoying the morning, sipping espresso and chatting. Behind their dark sunglasses, their eyes were trained on the school, and the students that were wandering towards it from every direction.

"Are you sure this is the place?" Ridley asked, not for the first time.

"No, I'm not sure," Kayla answered again. "Though I

think it's most likely, based on what little we know. It is a private school, in the general area, with enhanced security, and a mostly exclusive clientele. This place checked more of the boxes than any other. We've been over this before."

"I know. Sorry. It's just, not being certain, and not even really knowing what she looks like… "

"Well, we haven't seen any kids with green hair yet."

"Nor will we, most likely. Remember, she got in trouble for that. Surely it's been dyed back to her natural colour by now."

Ridley glanced at her watch. Five minutes until the start of classes. Surely Yasmine would already have arrived, if they were even in the right place. Only a few kids were still straggling in.

"Do you see that?" Kayla asked, suddenly excited. "Coming down Sommath, towards the school. They just passed behind that blue delivery van and should be back in view right about… now!"

Ridley nodded. "Yeah, that could be her. The defiant little thing." The women watched as a girl of about sixteen strolled up the street with a male friend. He was dressed casually, in street clothes. She was dressed in the smart-looking skirt and jacket that were the Ramanujan School's uniform. Her shoulder-length hair was dyed bright pink.

"I guess she told the school where they could shove it," Kayla said.

"Either that or Daddy Warbucks did."

The women continued to sip their coffee while watching the young couple approach the gate of the school, talking and smiling. When they reached the gate, they stopped and turned towards each other for a few final words. Then, the boy leaned in to place a discreet kiss on the girl's forehead, and the two parted. Just before she disappeared into the school's entrance, she turned and called out to him. He looked back. She mimed with a closed fist near the side of her face, her pinky extended towards her mouth, thumb extended to the ear. The universal sign for "call me."

The girl disappeared through the gate into the school grounds, and the boy turned on his heel and walked back the way from which they had come.

"Did you see that?" Ridley asked, not taking her eyes off the boy.

"Of course. What part?"

"What she did, there at the end."

Kayla thought a moment. "Oh shit. She has a phone!"

Ridley began sliding out of her seat. "Correct. You know who has that number, right?"

Kayla gathered her things and hurried after Ridley, who was already making her way up the street. When Kayla caught up, Ridley said, "We're just out for a stroll. For now. We might have to transition into more of a surveillance mode. Depending on where he goes."

He was easy to follow, as he didn't appear to be in any sort of a hurry, just casually strolling along. The women followed at a discreet distance, making small talk about the weather.

At the next cross street, the boy turned right and walked the short distance to a commercial area where concrete buildings became more prevalent than the trees and foliage. While not as crowded as the slums and heavily trafficked commercial areas closer to the heart of Mumbai, the street was lined with well-kept storefronts, including restaurants, merchants of various goods, a plethora of coffee shops, and professional offices. There was an A-frame sign placed on the sidewalk out in front of one of the establishments, inviting patrons into the Galaxy Arcade. The boy opened the door and stepped inside.

"Do you think he made us?" Kayla asked, as the women slowed their pursuit, still half a block away from the arcade.

"Doubtful. He didn't seem too situationally aware. Probably just some privileged rich kid with nothing else to do until his girlfriend gets out of school. Dropping a few coins at an arcade seems about right. If not a bit outdated. I didn't think these places still existed."

"They're coming back," Kayla said. "Retro is cool again."

"Apparently."

"What do you think? We'd probably stick out like a sore thumb in there."

Ridley nodded. "I'm sure we will. In fact, I'm counting on it. Time to turn on the charm, sweetie."

Chapter Twenty-Nine

The garish neon signs above the bars and stores of Seoul's notorious Itaewon district made Do-Hyun's head ache. That, and the several bottles of soju he'd polished off at dinner with his friends. Well, they thought he was their friend, but Do-Hyun didn't think of them that way. Acquaintances at best. At worst, anoying losers whom he would use to his own ends and spit out when he no longer required them.

Because Do-Hyun Kim didn't need anyone. He was making his way in the world just fine without any help from others, and at 22, he was a man about town.

In fact, he thought of Itaewon as his town now. He'd joined a local low-level jopoj—*gang*—as a teenager and had caused a bit of a stir among members of the higher level Kkangpae—*mafia*—with rumours of his penchant for violence and disregard for the law. Do-Hyun knew those rumours, while inflated in no small part to him spreading them himself, weren't without some merit. Though, the truth was somewhat less impressive. Do-Hyun was tough, but he wasn't a great fighter. Hence, he tended to pick on those weaker than himself, and usually women. It was true that Do-Hyun had no issue beating and bullying women, especially when they spurned his advances. Which happened often... most of the time.

In fact, if he were pushed, he would have to admit he hated all women, and saw them as little more than something to be used and abused, and discarded like the trash they were. He knew the child psychologist he'd been assigned in his youth would have put these thoughts down to the mental abuse and neglect he'd suffered at the hands of his alcoholic single mother in the housing project where he'd grown up in the Sangkok suburb. His mother had disappeared one day and was never seen again. No one had questioned poor little fifteen-year-old Do-Hyun about it, which suited him just fine.

He stepped into a brightly lit convenience store, wincing at the blinding ovehead lights, and grabbed a bottle of water from one fridge and after a moment's consideration, he snagged a bottle of soju from another.

He threw the boy standing behind the counter some cash, and with a grunt, he stepped out once more into the unbearable humidity of a summer night in Seoul's rundown Itaewon district. Do-Hyun downed most of the water in one go, dumped the plastic bottle on the floor, and opened the soju, taking a long, deep gulp of the clear Korean national drink his mother had once guzzled, disguised as water. He glanced at his watch. It was 2:30 am and the roads and pavements were still teeming with the usual collection of partygoers, street vendors and US soldiers from the nearby Camp Humphreys military base.

Do-Hyun didn't like the Americans. He didn't like the way they strutted around as if they owned the place. In fact,

Do-Hyun was fixing for a fight, and knew just where to find it.

He finished the soju, then made his way up the stairs of Soul Train, a bar frequented by locals and expats alike, and popular for its live music. It was also notorious for fights, often involving US soldiers on leave and filling their boots before curfew. Turning on what he thought was his local charm, Do-Hyun got talking to one of the female soldiers. He didn't really expect success... not with an arrogant *waygookin*—foreigner. After his constant efforts to convince her into leaving the bar and going home with him, and after her persistent and desultory refusals, his drunkeness had overpowered his self control, and he pushed her over.

Unfortunately for him, and her, she had fallen and crashed into a table, sustaining a nasty gash on her face that spilled blood onto the tile floor. What happened next was a whirlwind of flying fists and brutal kicks, and although he got his wish for a fight with an American, it wasn't Do-Hyun acting as the aggressor. One of the woman's male soldier friends had seen Do-Hyun push her, and he reacted instantly, serving up justice and beating Do-Hyun senseless, leaving him in a heap in the corner of the bar, before making themselves scarce.

Do-Hyun was kicked out of Soul Train by the bouncers, and, sensibly for him, he took himself home, beaten, humbled, but in many ways, changed somehow.

It had been a low moment for Do-Hyun, and one that would set him on a path he hadn't planned on but one that he would come to enjoy and eventually thrive upon. From that moment, Do-Hyun's hatred of women grew to the point that he was soon engaged in one of the more nefarious aspects of Itaewon's after-dark scene: Prostitution.

In the jopok he'd joined, he became an enforcer for one

of the pimps, and revelled in his ability to frighten the women into working hard to find their next customer. He carried out his work in Itaewon's edgy and notorious back streets, an environment in which he thrived, among the whores and the lowlife bastards who used them. He was above all that, of course. He was not a lowlife, and relished his percieved power.

A promotion soon followed, and instead of acting as an enforcer, he became a pimp, in control of a specific section of Itaweon. As his reputation grew, so his thirst for power burgeoned along with it. But Do-Hyun became sloppy, and his self-control, already a weakness, began to crumble as even the whores he lorded over started mocking him and spurning his leering advances. One night he lost control completely. At knifepoint, he had led one of the whores into a dingy room of a cheap hotel they used for their business. Do-Hyun had demanded that she perform a specific sexual act on him, threatneing to ruin her face if she refused. Not only did she refuse, but she had mocked him, telling him she had heard from one of the other girls that his *eumgyeong*—penis—was no bigger than a mandu rice dumpling. By the time he had finished with her, she had suffered more than two-dozen stab wounds and her throat had been slit. He had also cut off one of her nipples.

Word soon got out to his bosses about what he'd done, and Do-Hyun had to go on the run. He understood his life was now forefeit, and if he stayed in Seoul, he wouldn't survive a month. He rounded up his meagre belongings, took a bus to the southern city of Busan, and caught a ferry to Fukuoka, Japan. There he sat tight, laying low for a bit while planning what to do. As an unknown foreigner in Japan, he was relatively anonymous, thus safe, and he quickly found his way into Fukuoka's seedy underworld, which he realised was no different to that in Seoul.

After a few years in that world, he'd made important contacts, and was soon running drugs between northern India and Japan, but over time, he found himself spending more and more time in cities like Delhi, where he was once more anonymous. He learned via the grapevine that not only were the Kkangpae still after him back in Seoul, but he was a wanted man to the Korean Police.

It meant he could never return to Korea, and it was even to risky to go back to Japan. Delhi became his home, and it wasn't long before he was working his way up through the ranks of the heinous underworld infrastructure of the weapons, drugs and ultimately, the human trafficking business.

It was thinking about how he had come to be laying on this flea-ridden mattress in this damp and dingy police cell that kept him awake at nights. Mistakes he'd made. Regrets he had. He couldn't deny there were many of both.

But one thing Do-Hyun Kim knew he would never regret was that, when he finally got out of this mess, and when he'd tracked down Alexandria fucking Ridley, he would take his sweet time destroying her in every way possible before he killed her.

Chapter Thirty

They quickly discussed their plan, and then walked the remaining half block to the arcade.

The interior room was long and narrow, with two aisles running between four rows of game consoles. Asteroids, Dig-Dug, Galaxian, Salamander, Ms. Pac Man. Ridley recognised many of them, from a distant past, including the sounds they made... a cocophony of familar beeps and dings. There was even a bank of pinball machines across the back wall. A clerk sat behind a low counter at the front, complete with a change machine. A door sat in between the pinball machines at the back, with a sign over it that had a bathrooms symbol, for those in the arcade for the long haul.

There were perhaps a half-dozen patrons in the place, including the rich boy who had been walking with Yasmine. None of the patrons looked up when Ridley and Kayla entered, as they were all engrossed in their games.

"Welcome to Galaxy Arcade!" the clerk said happily. "How many tokens would you like?"

Ridley gave him a few bills, which he exchanged for a

handful of game tokens. She gave half to Kayla and then stepped over to the Galaga console and fed it two tokens. Soon there were alien ships dancing across the screen in an unnaturally ordered formation; she was blasting them with tiny projectiles of light from her own ship, which maddeningly only moved in two directions.

The aliens were taking their toll, not so much because she hadn't played Galaga in over twenty-five years, but because she was mostly keeping an eye on Kayla; she had moved further down the aisle towards the boy, whose face was in the viewfinder of a game called BattleZone. Ridley watched as Kayla stopped at Centipede, two consoles away, and shoved in some tokens.

The annoying "GAME OVER" sound played, and Ridley looked down in time to see her last starship disintegrate from enemy fire. She dug two more tokens out of her pocket and slid them in. A new crop of alien ships materialised to rain extra terrestrial havoc down upon her.

Across the room, she noticed Kayla had rolled up her sleeves, removed the scrunchy that had been holding her hair in a bun, and undone the top few buttons on her shirt. She was standing at the Centipede game in a pose that exaggerated her arse, her back slightly arched, as she wiggled and squirmed while playing her game. *Like catnip for teenage boys,* Ridley thought, before noticing that her own attention had been distracted enough to have lost another starship. *Shit!*

She had two ships left, and the aliens were starting to break formation and dive-bomb her in squadrons of eight. She managed to take the first wave of them out while somehow keeping an eye on the events unfolding across the room.

The boy slapped the side of the BattleZone console in

anger, apparently having lost. Then he dug his phone out of his pocket to check the screen. He must have missed a call, so he tapped it and brought the phone up to his ear. Ridley saw Kayla glance in his direction. He looked at her, his eyes widening slightly as he took in the sight. He smiled at her and then returned his attention to the phone conversation.

Ridley heard the alarm that signalled one of the enemy ships had dropped into her zone and turned on its tractor beam. She looked at the screen just in time to see it sucking her second ship in and whisking it away. *Fuck.*

As her last ship was brought up to continue her battle with the alien fleet, she saw that the boy's conversation was winding down. He said his final words and hung up. She watched Kayla pour on the sugar, moving her body seductively, pointing at the Centipede game console. The boy glanced over at her and said a few words. Ridley thought she read "Want some help?" on his lips. Kayla nodded. Ridley grinned.

The boy placed the phone down on the surface of the BattleZone game and moved the two steps towards Kayla. *Good work, girl!* Ridley thought as her last ship was destroyed. She didn't even notice; she was already in action.

Ridley slapped the top of the Galaga console in mock frustration, turned on her heel, and headed towards the bathroom at the back, a route which would take her directly past Kayla and the boy.

"It is not really that hard," she heard him say as she walked past. "Keep an eye on the mushrooms, that is where they will turn."

BattleZone was only two consoles past Kayla's machine. Ridley adjusted her path slightly in order to sweep very close to it as she passed. And there it was, the boy's phone. Her hand darted out and snatched it as she passed, bringing it back in close to her body and out of sight from anyone else in the room.

"The damn thing moves so fast!" she heard Kayla whining behind her as she ducked into the bathroom.

Ridley looked at the phone. The screen was still active. She quickly touched it so it would stay that way. She navigated to the phone app and looked at the recent calls. The one he had just received was from someone named Kamesh. That couldn't be Yasmine, even under an alias, as she was still in class. Ridley quickly switched to the contacts app and searched for Yasmine. Nothing. No Yas, Yaz, or Jaz either. *Shit!*

She glanced at the door, hoping she wasn't out of time yet. Then she switched back to the phone app, and to its call log. She started scrolling backwards, looking only at the field for lengths of calls. Most were five minutes or less. She scrolled on, until... there, last night. A call at 9:14 PM, which lasted an hour and thirteen minutes. The call was from a *Meethi*. She scrolled further, to the night before last, and saw another call to the same recipient that had lasted an hour and twenty-seven minutes. That had to be her. She checked the contact, found the number and committed it to memory. Surely she was out of time by now.

Except that she wasn't. When Ridley stepped back into the arcade, the boy was now at the controls of Centipede, blasting away at the electronic creatures while Kayla squealed with delight. Ridley stealthily replaced the phone onto the BattleZone console as she passed it; then she smiled and winked at Kayla as she walked by her. *Mission accomplished.*

Five minutes later, Kayla joined her out on the sidewalk. "I had to see him through," Kayla said, grinning. "He was on a high score. It would have been rude to walk away."

Chapter Thirty-One

Abducting the girl had been the simple part of their plan. Much more problematic would be locating a suitable place to hold her. It would require privacy, which is almost impossible to find in a tightly packed city of over eighteen million people. A simple hotel or guesthouse room would not suffice, with its thin walls and shared entrance. It was a long drive the length of the peninsula, on highly congested roads, before one might find any empty land or remote spaces; every possible patch of inhabitable ground within the city that wasn't already developed was covered by the makeshift shanties of Mumbai's countless slums.

Ridley found what she was looking for during a driving tour of southern Mumbai in the hours after she and Kayla had hijacked Yasmine's phone number from Fravash at the arcade. Along the port area of the city's eastern shoreline sat a wide swathe of newly cleared ground. Several pieces of idle construction equipment were arrayed around the site, which must have been at least ten acres. A small cluster of portable offices and metal shipping containers was placed near the centre of the complex. Sturdy chain-link fences—that appeared to be at least ten feet high and topped with coils of barbed wire—surrounded the site.

Ridley had parked the car to walk the perimeter, finding three entrance gates, each padlocked. The one along the south end of the property was located along a narrow alley, partially concealed by enormous stacks of pre-cast concrete building blocks.

Every twenty yards or so, for the length of the fence, signs advised trespassers to keep out, under penalty of law. Beneath these were signs identifying the site as the *'Bay View Residential Projects, A Cooperative Effort of the Brihanmumbai Municipal Corporation and State of Maharashtra'*.

When she returned to the car, she asked Kayla to pull out her phone and do a search for whatever she could find about the Bay View Projects.

It only took her five minutes to find out. "Looks like they started construction two years ago," Kayla said as she scrolled through a recent news article on the *Times of India's* website. "Another of the city's efforts to relocate and house residents of the various slums around the area. Turns out this land was cheaper than some piece of ground up near downtown where they want to build more highway inter-changes to ease traffic congestion. They had funds appropri-ated to start the project, so they started by bulldozing a bunch of old wharfs and crumbling warehouses. Then they ran out of money and the funds for the next phases are tied up in political wrangling."

"Just like back home," Ridley said.

"Mine too. Happens everywhere. Anyhow, the project is not expected to get back on track for at least two years. So, the site has been sitting in limbo."

"It sounds perfect," Ridley said. "Let's come back tonight when it's dark and do some more reconnaissance."

"Sounds good," Kayla agreed, though her tone was less certain. "Besides, you need to get ready to make your call, Mrs. Guidance Counsellor."

They returned to the guesthouse in nearby Pathak Wadi, which had become their latest base of operations upon fleeing The Pantheon Hotel up in Bandra-Kurla. Each took a turn napping on the room's only bed, while the other kept watch. Ridley offered to let Kayla get some rest first, and after a brief argument the younger woman relented, and lay down. Ridley heard her soft snoring almost immediately after her head touched the pillow.

The room was tiny, with just a bed and a small, scarred wooden table and chair. There was a single window next to the room's door. Ridley pulled the chair over to it and sat down, at an angle that afforded her a narrow view between the edge of the window and the frayed hem of the curtain. She placed her elbows on her knees and lowered her chin to her laced-together fingers. And thought.

So far, their moves had mostly gone according to plan. It had seemed easy, so far. Perhaps too easy. Even that business with the drug dealers in Dharavi. So far, nothing had stood in their way.

Which made her nervous.

What had Mike Tyson once said? *Everyone has a plan,* she recalled inwardly, *"until they get punched in the mouth,"* she ended in a whisper.

The trick was to not get punched in the mouth. To anticipate your opponent's next move.

So, what have we missed? Anything?

She went over the plan once more in her mind. She and Kayla had talked about it for hours, looking at it from every angle, trying to find its strengths and weaknesses. While it was by no means the safest course of action, it was one they had agreed had the best chance to achieve their goal. Which was to infiltrate The Vulture's organisation and take it down from the inside.

To do that, Ridley had reluctantly agreed to let Kayla go back inside. To get herself re-abducted and taken back into the slave traffickers' inventory. This would lead them right into the heart of The Vulture's operation. They had devised a plan to put Kayla on display in some of the most likely abduction zones watched by The Vulture's network of spotters and feeders. They had to be careful to avoid those of Azim's part of the organisation, so that she wouldn't be recognised by her previous abductors. As bait, the tall, blonde and curvy Australian would once again be irresistible to the traffickers' network of spotters.

That was the part of the plan Kayla had insisted on; abducting Azim's daughter as insurance was the price Ridley had countered with. If everything went to shit, if they got punched in the mouth while carrying out their plans, the girl would be their last resort.

Later, while waiting to make the call to Yasmine, the girls talked about the other part of their plan; getting Kayla re-abducted. They decided to bait the traffickers at the bar they had learned about from the Dharavi drug dealers, once Yasmine was in their custody.

Ridley practiced for an hour before placing the call to Yasmine's phone.

Chapter Thirty-Two

Yasmine dropped her backpack on the floor in the entry hall and headed into the kitchen to look for a snack. She was still glowing from her walk home with Fravash. He had been so sweet and considerate these last few months. She had to admit he was growing on her.

"Your mother is at the shops, child," Khairiya said as she entered the kitchen. The old woman's apron was dusted with maida flour.

Typical, Yasmine thought, rolling her eyes. Her mother had no shortage of reasons to be out of the house lately. "Yes ma'am. I have to study anyway. I'll be up in my room."

"Very well. Take one of these *Balushahi,*" Khairiya said, gesturing towards a plate of sugary pastries sitting on the kitchen's butcher block centre island. "They are still warm."

"Oh, Khaki," Yasmine said, using the term of endearment she had known for the old woman since she was a baby. "You're going to make me fat!"

Khairiya frowned at her. "You could use a little more

meat on your bones, child. Soon boys will start to notice you. Boys like sturdy girls, not waifs."

If you only knew, Yasmine thought as she took a bite of the warm pastry.

"Dinner will be ready at six!" Khairiya called to her as she picked up her backpack and headed up the stairs. "Your father will be late again. He said to start without him."

Also typical, Yasmine thought as she continued up the stairs and down the hall to her room.

She set the remaining pastry down on the edge of her desk and collapsed onto her bed. Her books would have to wait. She just wanted to lie there for a moment, thinking about Frav.

At first, her father had not approved of him. He was considerably older than she was, already graduated from higher secondary. He wasn't working, but his family had money. The problem was that he was not a son of one of her father's business associates, which had made him suspicious. One day her father pulled Frav into his study and closed the door. They had been locked in there for almost an hour. When they emerged, her father announced that she would be allowed to continue to see him. Further, Frav would, henceforth, be responsible for escorting her to and from school each day, and wherever else she needed to go.

Yasmine was pleased with that arrangement, but Frav would dodge the subject whenever she asked him the details of that fateful conversation. Her father was likewise tight-lipped about the meeting, except to grunt "he knows what's at stake," on one of the occasions she had asked him.

Frav was certainly better company than the rotating cast of goons her father had assigned to escort her over the years, each new one as surly and impersonal as the last. In the months since, she had come to trust Frav, and was even starting to reciprocate his growing affection towards her.

When her phone rang, her heart leapt, thinking it must be him, though it was early still. He normally waited until after dinner to call so they could spend as long as they wanted—sometimes hours—just talking, learning about each other. And, she was almost afraid to admit, falling in love.

Of course, it couldn't be him calling. He had just brought her home from school. Maybe he was walking back to that video arcade he spent so much time at. That was one small character flaw, she had to admit. He should be working, or furthering his studies. However, it was endearing, somewhat, on the rare occasions she watched him play, the way his face would light up as he blasted aliens on those silly old arcade games.

She picked up her phone and looked at the screen. It wasn't a number in her contacts. Neither was it the annoying "No Caller ID" that usually denoted a spam caller.

"Hello? Who's calling?"

"Good evening Yasmine. I'm sorry to bother you after school," a polite-sounding woman with a refined, British-Indian accent said. *"I had sent an aide to your classroom at the end of last period, but she missed you."*

Yasmine sighed. She hated getting calls about school matters when she wasn't at school. This was *her* time they were intruding on. "I'm sorry, who is this?"

"Oh, my apology. This is Mrs. Kapoor, your guidance counsellor at Ramanujan Academy?"

"Umm… Okay. Yeah, I think I heard something about that." It was a lie. She hadn't heard anything about it, but only because she had not been paying much attention these past few weeks. Her head had been elsewhere.

"You should have. It was announced in the school bulletin that we would be assigning counsellors to all standard IX students this week, to help guide your academic and career paths through secondary and upper secondary."

"Oh, yeah that's right. It was in the bulletin," she told the lady on the phone. *I really should start reading those,* she thought.

"So, Yasmine, I have been assigned to you as your counsellor, and I wanted to jump right in to make sure we are not missing any opportunities for you. I have been holding brief initial meetings with each of my students this week. I did have an opening directly after classes this afternoon, but like I said, the aide just missed you in Mrs. Jindal's class."

"I'm sorry. I tend not to hang around after class is finished." *Duh.* She had more important things to do. Like walking home with Frav.

"Oh, that is quite alright. It was very short notice. But listen, I do have an opening in the morning, before school. Can you come in at seven a.m.?"

"Of course, but must it be that early? That's a whole hour before class." The truth was, she was usually up by 5:00 every morning anyhow. She wasn't sure whether Frav would be able to meet her early enough to escort her.

"I know it is. I have already scheduled someone for seven thirty though. I am leaving early in the afternoon for a conference at the Education Department uptown. After that I will be away from the school until next week. We need to get working on this soon, as there are some important core stream choices coming up. Can you make the seven a.m. appointment? It really would be for the best."

"Umm, I think I can. I'll try." She knew it was important. Her father was always insisting she take her education more seriously. "No, wait, I will make it," she said. She was a big girl now and could take care of herself. She wouldn't even inconvenience Frav about getting up early to escort her. "I will be there at seven."

"Excellent. Just come into the office and ask for me. They have installed me in an office in the south wing. An aide will escort you there."

"Okay. I will see you in the morning."

"Thank you, Yasmine. You have a very bright future. I look forward to helping guide you in the right direction."

"I hope so. Good night, Mrs. Kapoor."

"Good night, Yasmine."

Chapter Thirty-Three

Well after midnight, and now rested and ready for the next phase of their operation, Ridley and Kayla returned to the port area to further scout the construction site.

"Can you pick it?" Kayla asked, as they stood at the site's most concealed entry gate along the south perimeter.

Ridley hefted the large steel padlock, the heavy chain clinking softly against the gate. "I left my lock picks at home," she said, shaking her head in mock annoyance. "But I might be able to use these." She pulled an assortment of small metal strips from her pocket and displayed them in her palm.

"Hair pins?" Kayla asked, her doubt evident.

Ridley nodded. "They started out that way. However, while you were napping, I went to work with some pliers and a file, and fashioned some makeshift tumbler picks and a tension wrench. They should work. I just hope the metal is strong enough."

"How on earth did you know how to do that?" Kayla asked doubtfully.

"It's amazing what you can learn on Youtube," Ridley said, winking, before getting to work.

It turned out that her home-made kit worked just fine on the cheap Chinese padlock. It took her less than thirty seconds to pop the shackle open. The gate's rusty hinges let out a low moan as she eased it open.

"Follow me," Ridley said as she stepped through and jogged towards the collection of containers and portable buildings that were clustered at the centre of the site.

The two mobile office trailers didn't interest her. "Too many windows, not secure enough," Ridley explained as she walked past them. She looked around until she found one of the metal shipping containers at the centre of the complex, with its door-end mostly concealed by the other containers around it. This time, it took her over a minute to pick the lock. "Higher quality," she mumbled. "Probably Japanese."

When they pulled the doors open, they were greeted with a mostly-empty interior. Only a few crates of wooden grading stakes, small orange plastic flags and spools of surveyor's twine were stacked at the back of the container.

"I think we've found our spot," Ridley said, walking towards the back end of the container.

"I don't like it," Kayla replied matter-of-factly as she surveyed the space. "It's fucking barbaric, Alex. This isn't any better than what they did to us! And you want to imprison a *child* in here?"

Ridley turned at the sudden outburst, and saw Kayla in silhouette, framed by faint starlight reflecting off the waters of Mumbai Harbour into the square opening of the container. Without speaking, she walked back to her. She had to look up slightly, to see into the taller woman's eyes, and to see that she was crying. She put her arms around her friend and drew her tightly against her.

"Kayla, we've been over this," she said softly as they embraced. "Who knows how many women we can save from these animals. We have to speak to them in a language they can understand. Pay them in their own coin. The only difference is, we will not hurt her. Unfortunately, yes, we will have to restrain her for a while, and probably scare her. But you have my word; other than some, hopefully temporary, emotional scarring, the child will not be harmed."

Kayla was silent for a moment, but she returned Ridley's hug, wrapping her long arms around her. "Those scars are just as real, Alex. I will live with them for the rest of my life. So will Yasmine."

Ridley flinched at the mention of the girl's name. She pulled away from Kayla slightly, in order to see her face again. "So will I, sweetheart. I will never forgive those men for what they did to me up there. What they turned me into deep in those caves. What they're forcing me to do now. But, they did it. I simply can't walk away now. We have to do this, and this is the only way."

"Is it, though? The rest of our plan is sound. I'll be the bait, just like we planned. I'm fine with that, ready for it. I'm looking forward to going back in, even being re-abducted myself." Kayla broke eye contact, her eyelids fluttering as she looked away. "Because I will know you're out there," she said softly. "Watching over me. I've never met anyone like you, Alex. Who can do the things you can do. I know I will be safe."

Ridley's heart almost broke, at hearing that this woman had more faith in her than she had in herself. "I won't let them do anything to you, Kayla," she said. "In only a few weeks you've become my closest friend and confidante, after

Hiram. Honestly, you're probably even closer to me than he is in some ways, with what we have been through, and what we're getting ready to do. I can't lose you now. I won't."

Ridley relaxed her embrace and stepped back, keeping her eyes on Kayla. "That's exactly why we have to do this. We must take the girl. I refuse to send you into that snake pit without insurance, and she is our ultimate insurance."

Kayla nodded slowly in agreement. "I know. It just sucks." She cuffed a tear from her face with the back of her hand. "God forbid, what if something happens to me?"

There was a long silence before Ridley answered. "God forbid. But, I will let her go anyhow. It's not her fault."

Kayla sighed with relief and wiped away a stray tear.

Ridley shed a tear herself, but not because of what was happening. It was for lying to her friend.

Chapter Thirty-Four

"The inventory is still short," The Vulture growled, a trace of anger seeping into his normally-calm voice. He was standing in front of the last two holding pens, which stood empty, their gates hanging open.

"We should have the order filled by tonight," Azim said. The two stood together inside the large warehouse. The low sounds of whimpering, crying, even some light snoring, mingled together to give the room a background soundtrack of misery and despair.

The Vulture swivelled his head in Azim's direction and raised an eyebrow. "See that it does," he stated coldly, then turned and began walking towards the door that led to the small office at the end of the warehouse. "We have a lot to talk about. Our new friends have been making specific demands, as regards packaging and handling."

"I thought our terms were clear?" Azim queried, as he hurried to catch up to The Vulture's swift strides. "F.O.B. the container station at the dock?"

Azim's phone began to ring just as The Vulture was reaching for the doorknob. "They have some extra requirements," he said, turning back to look at Azim. "Certain medications and fortifications they would like administered to the livestock, prior to packaging for transport. To ensure delivery to the ports in North Africa and southern Europe with as little... spoilage... as possible."

The Vulture waited for a response, but Azim was staring at the screen on his phone. Azim knew that the boss had zero tolerance for personal matters intruding on business; when he saw the text on his screen and that it concerned Yasmine, he immediately excused himself and retreated a few steps to place the call.

The Vulture released his grip on the doorknob and stood, his arms folded across his chest, his eyes beginning to smoulder as he waited for Azim.

The text had been from Khairiya, the Allis' household maid. Azim called her back. "What is it? What about Yasmine?" he said immediately upon hearing the line connect.

"Mr. Alli, so sorry to trouble you at work. Yes, it is about Yasmine. There was a call this morning, here to the house phone. I was busy with the laundry, so I did not pick it up. The caller left a voice message. It was an automatic recording from Ramanujan Academy, advising that Yasmine had missed the register taking and was being charged with an unexcused absence. I thought I should call you, because that has never happened before."

"And Tahira?" Azim asked, referring to his wife. "Did you ask her?"

"I have not seen her this morning, Mr. Alli. She was out of the house by the time I arrived."

I could have guessed that, Azim thought. His wife had been making herself scarce the past few months. Perhaps that was another problem he might have time to look into after this current shipment was finally on its way. Yasmine was his little girl, his shining star. Anything having to do with her could not wait. Would never wait. "Thank you, Khairiya, I will look into it," he said, and clicked off.

Azim glanced in The Vulture's direction and saw that he was no longer there. He had stepped into the office. Azim winced at the thought, and then brought his phone back up to dial the Ramanujan school himself. The assistant head-master took his call personally, but only to tell him that Yasmine had not shown up for school that day. She had not made register in her first class, nor had any of her teachers seen her.

Azim hung up, then hurried over to the office door and stepped inside. The Vulture was seated at the desk, looking over some papers.

"I am going to need a couple of hours," Azim said.

"We are busy here. It can wait," The Vulture replied, in his calm but menacing tone.

"I am sorry boss, but with respect, no, it cannot."

The Vulture turned slowly, to fix Azim with his dead eyes.

"It is my daughter. Yasmine," Azim said. "She is missing."

The Vulture looked at him, unmoving, for what to Azim felt like years, his eyes never blinking. Finally, he said in emotionless monotone, "Go, then," before turning back to his papers.

Azim made several calls as he hurried through the long maze of empty warehouses to where his Mercedes was parked. Repeated calls to Yasmine's mobile phone went straight to voice mail. He was about to call Fravash next, but as he reached his car, he paused with his finger hovering over the call button.

Fravash, he thought. He had trusted that little son of a bitch with his daughter's safety. He had thought the boy was worthy of that trust, especially after their private conversation that day. Yet, something had always bothered him about that boy. Perhaps he had better treat him with caution.

Azim called Ravi and Bada, his top two men. They were his best "trash collectors," the men who specialised in abducting women out of nightclubs and off the streets. Ravi and Bada were effective, efficient and possessed the ability to be brutal if necessary. They frequently assisted Azim on other matters that might require a liberal application of muscle and malice. The two had been close by, making the rounds to their various contacts in the south end of Mumbai, in preparation for that evening's activities. Azim told them to head his way.

While they were en route, Azim pulled up the tracking app on his phone and activated the locating feature for the phone he had given Fravash that day long ago. The day he had brought the boy into his confidence under threat of death if he ever harmed his daughter, allowed her to be harmed, or failed to carry that phone at all times. Yasmine's phone also had the locating feature, but whoever had taken her must have either ditched the phone or shut it down, as the tracking app had failed to locate it.

Fravash's location had pinged at Leopold's Cafe, that historic restaurant and bar in upper Colaba. Azim immediately called Ravi and Bada to re-route them to that location, pick up Fravash, and bring him to his house.

They had showed up shortly after Azim had arrived at

home and told Khairiya to go to the market. The old house-
maid understood, picked up her handbag and left just as
Ravi and Bada were turning in to the carpark.

Chapter Thirty-Five

Yasmine sat on a stack of construction materials at the back of the storage container.

Her feet were still bound by the plastic ties the women had applied when they picked her up. Upon reaching the confines of the ocean container, Kayla had cut the ties that bound her hands behind her back, and re-tied them in front of her, so she could help herself to food and water. They had also removed the gag, after Yasmine indicated she understood by nodding that it would be put back on if she yelled or called out for help.

Early that morning, they had abducted her from the front garden of Ramanujan Academy, taking her down among the dense foliage that grew on the school's grounds between the perimeter wall and its main building. They had watched her come through the school's main gate on the east side of the complex. Ridley had stepped up behind her and placed her in a restraining hold while Kayla quickly slipped a gag over her head and into her mouth. Yasmine had struggled valiantly, but within seconds, the women had her fully restrained with plastic ties at her hands and feet, and a hood over her head. Then they had carried the still-struggling girl through the shrubbery to the school's little-used north gate and into the rented car they had left there.

The take-down had taken less than a minute. Kayla had protested the idea of placing the girl in the car's tiny boot for transport, but had relented when Ridley convinced her it was the only way to move her without being seen. The girl was only in there for about fifteen minutes as Ridley drove them to the shuttered construction site near the docks.

"You don't look like kidnappers," Yasmine said with admirable calmness, after finishing a bottle of water and dropping the empty container to the floor.

Ridley and Kayla stood just inside the closed door of the container, looking at her.

"We're not," Kayla said. "Not kidnappers."

"Oh yeah? Then what do you call it? Luring a young girl away from her security, bundling her up, then hauling her off to God knows where? Are you taking me on a field trip?"

Kayla shook her head. "Listen, everything's going to be okay. We're not going to hurt you. We just need to keep you here. For a while."

"Keep me here," Yasmine echoed. "I can't leave. Can't walk." She stuck her bound feet out towards the women, then held her tied hands up. "Hands bound. Sure seems like a kidnapping to me. Or abduction. Choose your word, it's the same thing. You know, you can go to jail for this. For a long time. They will throw away the key, too. You are not even from here. Wait until they hear about two white, Western women abducting a poor little Indian girl."

"Enough!" Ridley shouted, fixing her gaze on the girl.

"Do you think you know what abduction is? Do you? Really?"

"Alex," Kayla said gently.

Ridley held up a hand in Kayla's direction and continued walking towards Yasmine. "Being abducted is when they beat you, drug you, and throw you in a cage." She stopped when she was standing directly in front of Yasmine, her eyes locked on the girl's. "When they throw your beaten, drugged arse in the back of a fucking truck, with dozens of other girls—"

"Alexandria!"

"—and then haul you hundreds, perhaps thousands of miles away, to be poked, prodded, judged, and sold. To the highest fucking bidder!"

Yasmine's eyes had grown wide. A tear had formed at the corner of one, as she leaned away from the woman's anger.

"Alex, stop it!" Kayla pleaded.

But Ridley continued, bearing down on the girl. "Then you're hauled, like cattle, to the highest bidder's personal prison, to be fucked, and sucked, and beaten, and shat on—"

"Alex!" Kayla grabbed her by the arm and spun her around. Kayla could see the rage in her eyes, as she pleaded, "Please, Alex. The girl is innocent! You promised we wouldn't abuse her!"

Kayla started to weep. Some of the fire in Ridley's eyes began to fade away. Finally, she dropped her head, stepped around Kayla and walked towards the door of the container. When she reached it, she turned around and saw Kayla, standing there wiping her eyes, while the young girl cowered where she sat on the stack of construction materials.

"That's what abduction is, Yasmine," Ridley said, her voice calm now, though hoarse with emotion. "That's what people like your father do. Not us."

Ridley pushed the heavy door open and stepped outside, closing it softly behind her.

Chapter Thirty-Six

Fravash doubled over from the blow to his gut, gasping for the wind that had been knocked out of him. Blood and saliva hung from his mouth in long ropes.

Azim Alli stepped back after delivering the punch, massaging his knuckles which had smarted from a first punch to the jaw. He'd thought a blow to the boy's belly would be softer on his fist. He had been wrong. The boy's stomach was rigid and rock hard, like punching a stone wall.

It only made Azim angrier. "How did you lose her?!" he roared.

The boy wavered, his chest hitching as he fought to breathe. He managed to straighten, air finally wheezing through his lungs. He looked around the room, his eyes still dazed.

They were in the underground carport beneath Azim's condo. Though real estate was prohibitively expensive in Mumbai, especially in the exclusive sections of Colaba,

Azim's property was rare in that it boasted a spacious, two-car garage.

Azim's long, black Mercedes GLS filled one side of the space, with its limo-dark windows, 20-inch wheels and low-profile tyres. The other side of the garage was empty, its immaculate floor and walls almost sterile, except for Azim, Fravash and the two henchmen who stood behind him, glowering with menace.

"Why don't you go over it one more time, then," Azim said. He had heard the boy's story half a dozen times already. Each time it was the same; it hadn't wavered. But there must be something he was missing.

Ravi found a folding chair somewhere and placed it behind Fravash. Bada grabbed the boy by the shoulder and jerked him backward until he stumbled and sat down in the chair with a thump.

Frav shook his head, snot now flowing from his nose and mingling with the blood trickling from his mouth. "I told you, I do not know where she is. Like I have already said, when we talked last night, the last thing she said was that she had to go to school early this morning, to meet with her counsellor."

"The school told me that is bullshit. They do not assign guidance counsellors yet, not in Yasmine's grade."

"I… I know, I know it is bullshit. I know now, anyway. But, that is what she said. She actually sounded a little excited about it. I told her I would show up here at six-thirty to walk her there, and she told me no. She said she would be fine, that she would see me after school."

"She is not allowed to make that decision!" Azim roared.

"I know!" Frav replied. "I was insistent! But she was adamant. Some crap about being grown up and able to take care of herself. You know how she is! I love that about her. Yet, I know my duty. The promise I made to you."

"You promised to keep her safe! On your life!"

Frav sobbed uncontrollably, the tears now rolling down his face, mixing with the snot, blood and saliva. "I know, I promised. I swear, I did everything I could, even though she insisted. I showed up here, at six-thirty as promised. She told me to go home. I did not, even though she was starting to get angry."

"You followed her?"

"Of course I did! I tailed her all the way there."

"You saw her go inside?"

"Yes sir, I watched her walk through the gate. Just like I do every day, even though I was a few yards behind her."

"From that distance did you observe anything unusual? Anybody else following or watching her?"

Fravash had answered "no" to that question several times already. However, he thought it prudent to at least pause and think about it one more time, before shaking his head again. "No, sir, nothing. There were very few people on the street that early. Nobody was paying any attention to her. Please, Mr. Alli, listen, we are wasting time here! I have told you everything I know. We need to get out there! We need to find her!"

Azim paused his pacing and looked at the boy. "Oh, we will be. Soon enough. When I am convinced we know everything there is to learn from the last person who saw her." Azim resumed his pacing, back and forth, four steps in one direction, turn, four steps back, repeat.

"You have been with her every day, outside of school and this house. Have you observed anything unusual?"

"No. Nothing at all. I walk her to school. I walk her

home. Every day. We talk on the phone each night, usually. You know that."

Azim nodded. "What about you? The rest of the time, when you are not with her? Have you noticed anything weird? Anyone following you? Anything at all that seemed unusual in any way?"

Frav wiped his face with the back of his arm. It came away slick with his various bodily fluids. "No, not really. I live a boring life, not like you guys. I get up in the morning, come here to meet Yas, walk her to school. Then I just goof off for a while, maybe get some lunch, kill time until she gets out of school. Then I walk her home. Those two events, only about twenty minutes each time, are the highlight of my day. The rest is really kind of boring, except when we talk on the phone."

Azim had heard all this before. He was just about to the point of thinking they would get nothing more out of the boy that was useful. He looked at the poor excuse for a man, hunched over in the chair, sobbing and dripping everything from snot to blood onto his garage floor. Azim looked up, past Fravash, to Ravi, who stood behind him. He was about to incline his head in Ravi's direction when a thought occurred to him. He paused, and looked back down at Frav.

"What do you do when you, as you say, 'goof off'?"

Frav looked up. "I don't know, whatever. Go to the record store, listen to new music. Sometimes I go to the arcade. Or the cinema. Sometimes I will just sit in a coffee shop and read the papers."

Azim nodded. "Most recently? Where did you go, when you were goofing off? Start with yesterday and work backwards."

"Well, yesterday I dropped Yasmine off at school, just

like normal. Then I... let me see... first I went to the arcade for an hour or so, and then walked down to Starbucks."

"Slow down a bit. The arcade? What is that?"

"You know, Galaxy Arcade, over on Captain Prakash? They have all these antique video games, you know, from back in the eighties and nineties? From before I was born, but surely you remember those."

"We didn't have these 'games' where I grew up," Azim said with contempt. "So, you were in there for an hour or so? Did anything unusual happen?"

"Not really. There are usually only a few players in there, mid-morning. Nerds, mostly."

"Just a room full of nerds playing video games, then?"

"Well, there was an attractive woman in there, for a short time. I suppose that was unusual; the place is usually just full of boys and young men."

Azim immediately came to attention. "An attractive woman?" An alarm in the back of his mind immediately started pinging.

"Yeah, you know... It was nothing threatening or anything, but yeah, I guess that was unusual. Especially since it was a foreign woman."

The ping turned into a loud klaxon in Azim's mind. "An attractive foreign woman? In a retro video arcade in Mumbai? What did she look like?"

"She..." Frav cleared his throat. "She was very attractive, if you like Caucasian women. About my age, maybe a little bit older. Tall, with blonde hair, blue eyes, very shapely. Real Hollywood type."

Azim was beginning to see red at the edge of his vision. The alarm in his head was now blaring a steady, constant wail. "Did you speak to this woman? What was she doing?"

"Well, she was very nice. She was playing the game next

to me and kept losing. I offered to show her how. She seemed lonely, as friendly as she was, so I thought I would be nice and help her out. I played a few games, and then she left."

Azim's breathing quickened. Sweat began beading on his brow as his rage began to overtake him. "This woman! Did she give you her name? Say where she was from? Who was she?!"

Fravash's eyes had now grown wide, in reaction to Azim's visible rage. "She did not tell me her name, sir! Honest! I don't know who she was! Only that she had an Australian accent!"

Azim's vision went fully red as the alarm filled his mind with warning signs. *It was her! The Australian woman! Blonde, blue eyes, beautiful, shapely... Kayla? Kayla fucking Stone!*

While he retained his last vestige of control, Azim looked up again, past Fravash, to Ravi, who stood there, pulsating red in his field of vision. Azim nodded.

Ravi stepped up behind Fravash, slipped a garrotte down over the young man's head, pulled the thin steel wire tightly across his throat, and bore down on the ends. Fravash began to struggle, his legs kicking out violently while his eyes bulged and his face began to turn red, starved of air. After about thirty seconds, the boy's movement stilled, his eyes closed and his head lolled to one side. Ravi continued the hold for another full minute, then he loosened his grip. Fravash's body slumped to one side and fell off of the chair into a puddle of his own filth.

"Clean this fucking mess up," Azim ordered as he wiped his brow with a handkerchief. His vision was beginning to return to normal as he stepped around the dead boy. He slipped between Ravi and Bada and stepped towards the door that led from the garage into the condo.

"Then come and see me," he said, just before stepping through the door. "We have a problem."

Chapter Thirty-Seven

The deep breathing meditation techniques she usually relied on weren't working. She squeezed her eyes tighter, trying to let her mind empty of all the swirling thoughts that filled it, then she relaxed her eyelids, trying to release the tension building behind her eyes and on her forehead.

Ridley exhaled, and unfurled the fists she didn't realise she'd been clenching, noticing the white knuckles. "Jesus, Alex, get a grip."

She stood up from the huge wooden spool she had sat on, devoid of its cable, and inhaled through her nose again, held the breath for an eight-second count, then let it out slowly through pursed lips. It was an action she'd done many thousands of times in her life, but this time it wasn't serving its purpose, and she almost cried out in frustration. Placing both palms over her face, Ridley inhaled deeply again, and finally her mind began to free itself of the the clutter and the chaos that had resided there for the last ten minutes.

Now thinking clearly, she let her thoughts drift to Kim.

Ridley knew what she had to do if and when the chance came to finish Do-Hyun Kim. There would be no thought of her own revenge. No thought of the satisfaction she would get making him suffer as he had made her suffer, and had made countless other girls and young women suffer, worse fates than even Ridley herself had endured. The very worst kind. No, she couldn't let those kinds of thoughts impact her mission, which was very simple; to kill Kim and take down the others.

She would find Kim, and as soon as the moment presented itself, she would act swiftly and decisively, and shoot the bastard in the head. That would be revenge enough.

Ridley heard the door to the container open, and knew Kayla was coming out. She had to take control of her emotions, both for her own sake, and that of her friend. More than that though—much more than that—she had to focus on the task at hand, and losing control now was not going to benefit the women she was there to help. Not being in control led to a lack of clarity in her thought processes. That lack of clarity led to hasty judgments. That haste led to irrational decisions, which in turn led to mistakes which would put both themselves and the women she was determined to rescue in even more danger than they were already in. And that wasn't good for anyone.

Come on Alex. Keep it together. For yourself. For Kayla. For the dozens or hundreds or even thousands of girls and young women that you can help if you do this thing right.

She glanced to her left and saw Kayla closing the door behind her, and turned back towards the view of Mumbai Harbour. "You've got this," she whispered to herself, and

with another deep breath, she cosed her eyes just as Kayla
called out:

"Hey. Are you okay?"

Chapter Thirty-Eight

Yasmine was crying now, too.

Kayla stepped over to the pack of bottled waters they had brought, picked one up, opened the cap and took a long drink. When she was done, she looked at Yasmine.

"Please forgive her," she said to the girl. "She's been through a lot, and can get a little intense sometimes. I promise she means well."

"What… what did she mean?" Yasmine asked. "I mean, about my father?"

Of course, she doesn't know, Kayla thought. *How could she?* It would be a disservice to hide the facts from her now.

"Yasmine, what Alex said was true. I admit she could have been gentler with the information. Essentially, she's right."

"Abductions? Kidnapping? My own father?" Yasmine's eyes were wide in what must have been shock.

"You had no idea?"

Yasmine wiped her face with the back of her hand. "I mean, I know he does illegal things. I'm not blind. He always has these hard-looking men around him, and he has guns. I know he's obsessed with security, and I know he's been arrested several times. I just assumed it was drugs or smuggling or something." The girl paused and looked up at Kayla. "How would you know about this? That he abducts girls? Are you guys cops? You could be lying to me too! Everyone's always lying to me!"

Kayla placed a hand over the girl's bound hands. "Listen, sweetie. The reason Alex gets so emotional about this is… " She looked down, once more trying to fight back the tears. After a moment, she looked up again, into Yasmine's eyes, and continued. "It's because she was… well, both of us…" Kayla inhaled. "Both of us were abducted, Yasmine. Just like she said. Taken off the streets, caged, beaten, hauled away, and sold."

Yasmine started sobbing uncontrollably. Kayla opted to say nothing, letting the girl absorb what she had heard. She rubbed her shoulders to offer what comfort she could.

"I'm sorry," the girl mumbled between sobs.

"There's nothing for you to be sorry about," Kayla said. "I'm sorry you had to learn about it like this."

"I always knew he was a bad man. To others, anyway, to other bad men. He has always treated me like a princess."

"Well, other *girls*," Kayla said, "he treats like livestock. To be hunted, captured, bought and sold. Caged, beaten, abused in the most dreadful ways. That part is true. Alex and I know it, firsthand. We know it too well."

Yasmine cried for a few more minutes, until finally regaining her composure. "So you are going to kill him," she said. It wasn't a question.

Kayla looked down at her hands. Hands that had never spilled blood, despite her years of training in martial arts and extreme sports. Long, slender fingers, still tipped with the red, glamour-length nails she had applied for her hooker impersonation at The Neptune Bar. Could she kill with these hands? Would she? She thought back to her harrowing experience at the hands of the traffickers, and of its fiery conclusion under Mount Kailash. It seemed a lifetime ago now, though it had only been weeks.

Alex Ridley had been an unstoppable machine. Fearless, as she took the fight to their captors, dispatching them one by one with skill, until her final showdown with the Korean gangster who had abducted and took her to Kailash. Alex Ridley could turn her emotions on and off like a light switch, simply shutting them down whenever they might get in the way of what needed to be done. Kayla wondered if she herself could do that.

She pictured Azim Alli, Yasmine's father, as he stood on the side of the road to Tibet and shot a girl twice in the back of the head. She had been a fellow abductee and had been injured during a struggle with the guards. It had been an injury to her face, marring the beauty for which she had been captured. With her market value depleted, Azim had killed her, with less remorse than a rancher putting down a horse with a broken leg. Then he had killed the guard who had been responsible for damaging the goods.

Kayla looked back up at Yasmine. "We only want justice, sweetie. Not for ourselves, but for the hundreds of girls that came before us and are now lost. Lost to society, lost to their families."

Yasmine looked at her, her eyes puffy and red, but now dry. "If... if what you say is true, he has done such terrible things!"

"Our first priority," Kayla continued, "is to make sure no more girls are captured and doomed to the same fate. Unfortunately, your father is one of the major players in that trade. However, he's not our ultimate target. Your father has a boss, a man who goes by the nickname The Vulture. He is the kingpin of this operation. And yes, our friend out there does mean to see him die, and his network dismantled. Your father? Perhaps, for him, justice is best served by the authorities, with a fair trial."

Five minutes later, Kayla stepped out of the container and closed the door behind her. She looked to her left and saw Ridley sitting on a large spool that had once contained some sort of heavy-gauge cabling, leaning against the corrugated metal wall of one of the containers. Ridley's head was turned away, her eyes glued to a narrow view of the blue waters of Mumbai Harbour, visible between the closely stacked containers.

"Hey," Kayla called out. "Are you okay?"

Ridley turned towards her. "I'm fine. I'm... well, sorry I got a little testy in there."

Kayla acknowledged with a short nod. "I think she'll be okay. Yasmine, I mean. She's taking it pretty hard, learning what her father has been up to."

"What about you? Are you still okay? Are we good?"

Kayla smiled. "Of course. You just take a little getting used to, sometimes."

Ridley laughed, a hollow, humourless sound. "Yeah, I get that. What's she doing now? Do you think we can trust her?"

Kayla sighed. "I do. I think you're right, though. We need to keep her in restraints, at least for now. This has all been a lot to take in, and we can't afford to leave her to her own devices just yet."

"I agree," Ridley said, nodding. "So, we're still on for tonight? Still sticking with our plan?"

"Yeah, of course. Nothing's changed. Full speed ahead."

Ridley looked at Kayla, her young friend, so full of life, love and beauty. Yet still, soft, naive and innocent. As she looked into her friend's captivating blue eyes, however, she saw what she needed to see. Determination. She rocked herself forward and onto her feet. "Okay then," she said as she stood up. "Let's get this place buttoned up for the night. I need to find a bike."

As the women turned back to the door of the container, Kayla's phone began to buzz in her pocket. She pulled it out and checked the screen, then looked at Ridley. "It's Taara."

Chapter Thirty-Nine

The stench of piss and shit had kept Do-Hyun Kim awake most of the night. He was sitting up on the small sleeping pallet in his cell when the guards came for him. He had spent the entire previous day and two nights in their custody.

"Hands!" the smaller guard barked, while the larger one stood behind, a submachine gun levelled at Kim. Kim stood up from the pallet, stepped over towards the cell door and stuck his hands through the food slot. The guard slapped handcuffs on him and yelled, "Step back!"

Kim did so. The guard unlocked the door. He was ordered to step out, and then marched back through the narrow corridors and into the holding room where he had first been interrogated. The large guard stood back as the small one unlocked a cuff from one of Kim's hands and latched it to a metal rail that was bolted to the table.

"Wait here!" the guard said curtly, then turned on his heel and left the room with the large guard in tow. Kim heard steel bars sliding into place just outside the door.

They had treated him more or less humanely, all things considered. His meals had been on time, if not very palatable. He had eaten them and hadn't gotten sick. He had been provided toilet paper for when he needed to shit, using the stainless-steel toilet bolted to the wall in the back corner of the cell. He had not been beaten, or starved, nor had he been deprived of sleep.

He had, however, been deprived of information. The guards who came to bring his meals said nothing, except to ask whether he was ready to tell Deputy Inspector General Malek his real name yet. Each time he had insisted that his name was Jang Jin-Seung, a legal immigrant from South Korea. At hearing this, the guard would shrug, turn around and leave without saying a word.

Was that what this was about now? Were they ready to start beating the information out of him? *They will find me tough to crack*, Kim thought, almost relishing the prospect.

Or, had the people from up north in Amristar shown up, to take him away to mete their own kind of justice for stealing a government minister's car, as Malek had implied?

Kim was weighing the possibilities when he heard the locks clinking open, and the steel bars being slid from their slots in the door jamb. The door swung open, and Sahm Malek stepped through. Without saying a word, he stepped to the corner of the room, reached up and pulled the power cable from the camera mounted there. Then he moved to the table, pulled out the chair and sat down in it with a huff.

Malek said nothing for two full minutes. He simply sat there, staring at Kim, looking him up and down with undisguised disdain and something akin to boredom in his eyes. Drumming his fingers on the tabletop. Patient.

"I will have your name, now," Malek finally said, his voice calm. "Your real name."

Kim said nothing for a moment, and then began, "My name is Jang Jin—"

"I already know that is a lie!" Malek roared as he sprang from his chair. "We are through playing games! I will have your real name now, or we will start taking limbs. You are not protected by Indian law here. You are a ghost. No one knows you are here. I can do whatever I want with you. Including making you disappear, if it comes to that."

Kim maintained his silence, but he was starting to consider whether it was now time to begin talking. He could live without a finger or two, or a hand or even an entire arm. What use would holding out be, if he were going to eventually tell them what they wanted to know anyhow? Telling Malek his true identity now would bypass all of that. What could they possibly do with that information? Kim's true identity was even more invisible than the Jin-Seung alias, at least here in India. For that matter, would Malek even believe him if Kim revealed his true identity?

Yet, if that identity were researched beyond India's borders—for example, in certain countries of Europe and southeast Asia, not to mention his homeland of Korea—it would likely turn up some interesting information. Information he was sure would be better off for him if it stayed unknown to this Deputy Inspector General Malek.

Kim was turning all of this over in his head while Malek watched him intently. He was finally ready to say something. He was preparing to open his mouth to speak, when Malek blinked first.

"I guess it is your lucky day, then," Malek said, shaking his head in disgust. "There is someone here to see you," he added as he stood up from the chair and turned towards the door.

"To see me?" Kim said, dumfounded. "Who?"

Malek paused at the door, then turned and looked at Kim with a grin. "Your lawyer," he said, and stepped out of the room.

This time Kim didn't have to wait long. Only a few minutes after Malek had left the room, he heard the locks disengaging again. He looked up expectantly as the door swung open. The first man through the door was a very large Indian man, taller than Kim, and stocky, with pectoral muscles that stretched the fabric of his shirt. *Pecs?* Kim thought. *What the fuck?*

A smaller Arab man followed Pecs into the room, smartly dressed and carrying a suitcase. The recognition was complete, as Kim now knew they were the muscle from Chota's electronics shop. Pecs took up a position in the corner of the room, clasping his hands in front of him, while the Arab stepped forward and sat down in the chair that Sahm Malek had vacated shortly before. He placed the briefcase on the floor and looked at Kim.

"So, Mr. Kim. It appears you cannot keep your nose clean here in Mumbai, yes?" the Arab said, in his heavily accented English.

"What are you doing here?" was all Kim could think to say.

"Were you expecting Perry Mason?"

"Actually, no, I wasn't expecting anyone. How did you even know I was in here?"

The Arab laughed lightly. "Mr. Kim, you should know by now. Chota knows things. What he doesn't know, he finds out. And, when he finds out that a client of his has fallen into some... difficulties, yes? At times like these, Chota sees it as a... crossroad, of sorts. A decision must be made."

"What kind of decision?"

"A business decision, Mr. Kim."

"This has nothing to do with my business with Chota," Kim said.

"On the contrary, Mr. Kim, it has everything to do with Chota. You, sir, are what they call a loose end, yes? A loose end must be dealt with, in one of two ways. The easiest way is simply to snip it, so that no pesky fingers may peck at it, tug on it, and pull until the whole thing comes unraveled."

"I am not a loose end!" Kim retorted with poorly concealed anger. "I know nothing about Chota, about you, or what you guys do!"

The Arab shook his head. "You know enough," he said calmly. "Enough to be... troublesome, yes? Believe me, Malek has the means to extract whatever information he wants from you, which Chota will not allow to happen. As I mentioned, this can also be handled as simply a business decision. Which brings us to the second way to deal with a loose end."

Kim glared at him. "Which is?"

"To weave it back into the fabric, to tuck it in so that it cannot be picked loose."

"Weave me back in, then," Kim said.

"It is not quite that simple, Mr. Kim. As I said, this is a business decision. The first option, Malek would do for free, to cover favours he already owes to Chota."

"And the second option? The weaving thing?"

"Well, weavers of such skill do not come cheap. Of course, there is Malek himself to be concerned about, and those of his team who took you in, each of whom deserve just compensation for their inconvenience, as well as their silence."

Kim sighed silently with relief. Naturally, anyone can be bought. It was the way of the world. "How much?" he asked after a long pause, as if he was actually considering not accepting the offer.

The Arab laughed again. "I am not through, yet. Understandably, Chota requires his cut for brokering this transaction. By necessity, there are the fees for your humble advocate, and his stalwart assistant." The Arab nodded his head towards Pecs, who stood silently in the corner. "The fee will be one hundred thousand."

"Rupees?" Kim asked, more hopeful than expectant.

The Arab smiled at that. "Dollars. US."

Kim thought for a moment. How much money did he still have available, in liquid funds? A hundred grand might wipe him out, at least until he could free up more cash.

"Again," the Arab said, "there is always the first option. Malek can simply snip the loose end for us. Yet, the choice is yours, Mr. Kim. Which is... ironic, yes? That the loose end itself is afforded the opportunity to choose its own fate?"

It didn't take Kim long to make up his mind. "I will need my phone," he said, sighing as he slumped back into his chair. "That bastard Malek must have it somewhere."

The Arab smiled and reached down to grab the briefcase. He hauled it up onto the table, popped the latch and reached inside. "We thought you might choose that option," he said, as he placed Kim's mobile phone down on the tabletop and pushed it across to him.

Chapter Forty

The sun had sunk behind Malabar Hill and into the Arabian Sea hours ago, but its heat still radiated up from the baked streets and sidewalks in shimmering waves. Alex Ridley sat at a table inside the Bombay Roasters coffee shop, with her head tilted down to her phone, though her eyes were probing the cityscape beyond the cafe's plate-glass windows.

Her vantage point was well chosen, being on the uphill side of Babulnath Road, looking out over the buildings and businesses that lined the famous Chowpatty Beach. In the distance, throngs of Mumbaikars still walked up and down the beach, enjoying the evening's cooler air and food from the street vendors who dotted the paths.

In the foreground, directly across the street, Ridley had a direct view onto the rooftop bar of Bastion, one of Mumbai's hottest new night clubs. The constant "Oontz! Oontz! Oontz!" of electronic music could be heard even from across the street and through the coffee shop's windows. Fake palm trees and flamingos adorned the edges of the space, all lit up glaringly in neon blues and pinks, and which pulsed to the beat of the music.

Nearest to her, along Bastion's glass-lined wall which fronted Babulnath Road, a line of cocktail tables and stools accommodated those who were taking a break from the writhing humanity of the club's dance floor. At the far end of the space—mostly hidden from view under the club's partial roof and further obscured by the dancers—was the main bar, the landing from the staircase below, and doors to the restrooms and service areas. Ridley knew the layout from scouting the location earlier. One of the doors, marked "Employees Only", led to a storage room behind the bar with a walk-in cooler and shelves filled with cases of whiskey, rum and vodka. Also in that room was the doorway to a second staircase that descended to the bar's service entrance.

"The back door," Ridley mumbled, remembering how it opened into the narrow alley behind the club. It was a dirty, garbage-strewn lane that stood in sharp contrast to the building's freshly scrubbed façade that patrons and the public saw. All of the businesses up and down the beach used the alley for deliveries, garbage pick-up and their employees' smoke breaks.

She couldn't see the back door from her vantage point, but did have a narrow view of a sliver of the alley. It had very little activity at this hour and was only dimly lit by the occasional bare-bulb lamp sitting above each tenant's service door. Ridley had watched several vehicles come and go in the alley over the course of the evening, most of them delivery or service vehicles.

Returning her eyes to the activity in the rooftop club, Ridley felt her anxiety begin to rise when Kayla was no longer in the location where she had last seen her. However, she relaxed when she caught that unmistakable flash of blonde hair and tanned white skin, so generously revealed by her electric-blue party dress. Kayla was now back on the dance floor, seductively moving to the rhythm of the music. She was still with the handsome man in the white suit jacket. Kayla had been doing an admirable job of sticking to the plan by staying in areas of the bar that would be visible from Ridley's vantage point.

Yet, Ridley knew that if the plan was going to work, she would eventually lose sight of her friend.

One more time, she flicked her eyes down to the street below to confirm that her bike was still there. It wasn't actually hers, of course, she had just "borrowed" it for the night. A quick canvass of one of the tonier neighbourhoods of Malabar Hill had yielded a smorgasbord of possibilities, so she had chosen an old Kawasaki ZXR 750. The bike was over twenty years old and lacked a steering lock or much of the newer technology that would have made it harder to hot-wire. So, she had silently pushed it out to the street, away from the condominium where its owner was presumably fast asleep inside, and to the sidewalk at the darkest point between the overhead street lamps. She had started it in under thirty seconds and ridden away. The hotwire was still in place—anyone could simply hop on it and hit the start button to fire it up—thus, she had been a bit nervous about leaving it on the street. She needed it positioned and ready to go without delay, so she had taken the risk.

Once again, she was relieved to see it had not been touched. She focused back on Kayla.

Chapter Forty-One

Kayla Stone was beginning to wobble.

She had done her best to stay sober, but after several hours "under cover" in a night club, even her best efforts at alcohol avoidance had been only a half measure. She had to drink some kind of adult beverage, in order for the plan to work. But she was good at faking drunkenness, so it wasn't necessary for her to actually be intoxicated. Still, it wasn't always easy to discreetly discard the drinks that kept coming her way.

She would pour out small quantities of the sickly sweet concoctions, into the planters or other empty glasses, when she was sure it wouldn't be noticed. To stay in cover, she would inevitably have to drink some of it. And there had been a lot. She had politely declined drink offers from several men who, she was reasonably sure, were innocently looking for a hookup. A few of them seemed to match the type of the "feeders," about whom Ridley had passed on what she'd learned from the drug dealers back in Dharavi.

Also, the dealers' descriptions had matched her own

experience from her first trip into that nightmare underworld. Though it turned her stomach to do so, she had been
more receptive to the advances of those who fit the 'feeder'
type. Kavin had been just that type.

"You are so fucking beautiful," he said, for about the
hundredth time, while staring into her eyes.

Is he trying to determine how drunk I am? Kayla mused,
hoping her pupils were sufficiently dilated. She was indeed
feeling the effects of the alcohol, though she thought she
had her bases covered.

"Oh stop it," she said, lazily punching him in the shoulder. "I'll bet you say that to all the girls."

Kavin held her gaze a moment longer, and then leaned
back in his chair and smiled broadly. "Of course I do. The
difference is, this time I did not have to lie."

She had to admit, he wasn't too shabby himself. Tall,
dark-skinned with high, cherubic cheeks and a mouth full of
bright white, perfectly straight teeth displayed by his
perpetual smile. He was clean-shaven, and apparently
continued his grooming below the neck. His maroon silk
shirt was open to the fourth button, revealing a smooth,
copper-skinned chest with the hint of pectoral swells in all
the right places. He was wearing a white linen suit-coat and
matching slacks. *A bit too Miami Vice*, Kayla thought, but the
look worked for him.

She kept her eyes on him as she sipped the last of the
ridiculous pink cocktail he had brought her, swirling the
straw seductively as she held his gaze. She giggled at the
slurping sound when there was nothing left but ice. It had
tasted hideous but had been quite strong. As her head began
to spin a bit faster, Kayla thought she'd need to figure out a
way to dump most of the next drink.

"I'll get us another," Kavin said, then he rose swiftly and

made his way towards the bar. Kayla watched him go until he disappeared through the sea of people on the dance floor, pulsing to the beat of the music.

She stole a glance in the direction of the coffee shop across the street, which stood at a slightly higher elevation due to the slope of the terrain. The reflection of city lights on the plate-glass windows denied her a view into the interior, but she knew that Ridley was there. Watching. Waiting. Protecting. Knowing she was there gave Kayla the strength to continue on with the plan.

What if she weren't there, though? What if something had happened, something unforeseen, that had knocked Ridley out of the action? What if whoever had tracked them to the guesthouse in Dharavi had caught up to Ridley?

Kayla tried to push such thoughts out of her mind. She had to put her faith in her tough friend. Somehow, she knew, if anything had gotten in Ridley's way, she would have dealt with it quickly and efficiently; then she'd have kept going. The woman was unstoppable. Even frightening, in a way. Kayla took comfort in knowing that she was on her side and would move mountains to protect her, if need be.

Kayla turned back to the maelstrom of activity towards the middle of the club, trying to put Ridley out of her thoughts enough to concentrate on the task at hand: Kavin.

Could he be the one? The "feeder" in The Vulture's network that worked this side of town? Was she even in the right place for it?

Kayla and Ridley had spent hours poring over everything they had learned about The Vulture's network and Azim Alli; from the Dharavi drug dealers, from Taara, from what each of them knew from her own experiences. They knew that for their plan to work without backfiring right at the start, they needed to avoid nightclubs in any section of town covered by Azim's wing of the network. Certainly, Azim himself, and quite possibly any of the spotters and feeders who worked under him, would recognise Kayla immediately.

They had briefly considered disguising or altering Kayla's appearance somehow. Maybe a hair colour change, or cutting it short, or coloured contact lenses, or strategic makeup application to subtly alter the appearance of her facial structure. In the end, they had agreed that none of these would fool any of the men who already knew her from her previous abduction. It was her natural appearance—thick, long blonde hair, sparkling blue eyes, perfect skin and face—that made her a prime target for the traffickers in the first place.

They had decided to target locations that were likely outside of Azim's hunting grounds, which they believed from their intel covered everything to the west and north of Kamathipura, as far as Bandra East, which was too close to Azim's prostitution territory. That had left most of the east side of Mumbai proper, and south into Colaba, at the southern end of the city. They reasoned that Azim probably adhered to a "don't shit where you eat" policy. Therefore, since he lived somewhere in Colaba, that narrowed their search area even more.

Next they had researched online for "Mumbai's Hottest Night Clubs" and "Mumbai Night Life," and several similar search terms. These had turned up a few dozen likely spots in their narrowed target area. They further pinpointed their targets by reading Yelp reviews and looking at photos of the interiors of each club and its patrons. This helped them to determine which joints were most-frequented by young, active, attractive tourists looking for a fun night out.

Bastion had come in at the top of their target list. Still, there was no way to be sure it was part of the spider's web that fed into The Vulture's network. The girls had resigned themselves to that possibility and were prepared to try a different club from their list each night, until they hit pay dirt.

So, she had arrived, by herself, in a cab, in another stunning outfit. The shimmering blue clubbing dress wasn't quite as revealing as the tiny red thing she had worn to impersonate a prostitute at The Neptune Bar a couple of nights before, but it hugged her body seductively, showing off every curve. It also matched her sparkling blue eyes. It had worked, even though most of the women in the place were dressed similarly, all of them having brought their 'A game' for a night on the town.

Kayla had slipped into her role of a young, single woman wanting to see the world and experience life to the fullest before settling into a mundane career back in Australia. She had come to party and was acting the part. She had danced with several men, and more than a few girls, all of whom could not seem to take their eyes off her. However, she took care not to get attached to any one person, keeping herself in play.

Kavin had been one of several men in the club that seemed like a possibility as one of The Vulture's feeders, so she had allowed him to get closer to her throughout the evening. They had danced until her feet ached, and consumed drink after drink (with her pouring out as much as she discreetly could of each one). So far, he had been a perfect gentleman.

Perhaps he wasn't the one.

She saw Kavin working his way back through the crowd, holding a simple-looking, dark-coloured drink in each hand. *Thank god those aren't some shade of neon,* Kayla thought with relief.

"I thought we'd switch to something more... adult," Kavin said as he set the drinks down, and pulled his chair closer to hers. "Rum and coke?"

"I thought you'd never ask," Kayla replied, and took a sip. It tasted good, if a bit, what was that... salty? *Must be some sort of Indian spiced rum,* she thought. *Not everything tastes just like Bundaberg.*

Chapter Forty-Two

Ridley watched as the man in the white suit returned with the drinks. Kayla had been entertaining him for quite a while, and he hadn't tried anything suspicious yet.

"Come on, girl, kick him to the kerb," she mumbled. He was obviously just another local playboy looking for a foreign piece of arse for the night. They needed to move on. Either shoo him away to give any real "feeder" that might be in the room access to the bait, or bail out of Bastion altogether and move on to the next club on their list.

They were wasting time.

"May I refill that for you, ma'am, and put it in a to-go cup?"

Ridley jerked slightly, startled out of her concentration by the barista standing next to her chair. She looked up. "Excuse me?"

The barista smiled, sweetly but tiredly. "We are getting ready to close. I just wanted to know if you would like me to top that up and transfer it to a disposable cup so you may take it with you. Yes?"

Closing? Ridley glanced at her watch. It was a quarter to two in the morning. She had been there almost three hours. She silently reprimanded herself for not being stealthier with her surveillance.

"Oh, thank you. I'll just finish this one up, then I'll be on my way."

The barista nodded. "Take your time, please."

It's just as well, she thought. Maybe she would head on over to Bastion herself and rescue Kayla from that random guy so they could move on. She picked her phone up off the table and was scooting her chair back so she could stand up, when she looked over to the rooftop bar for one last time before heading across the street herself.

She froze, halfway risen from her chair, when she saw what was happening.

Kayla stumbled, trying to rise from her seat. She almost lost her footing, knocking her chair backward until it tumbled over. She reached for the tabletop to try to steady herself, only to flail ineffectually. Her hand knocked the drinks over, spilling ice and cocktails across its surface.

The man in the white suit bolted from his own seat and caught Kayla around the waist just as her knees unbuckled; he'd managed to keep her from falling to the floor. He gripped her tighter as one of the drink glasses rolled to the edge of the table and fell off. Ridley barely heard the shattering of glass amid the cacophony of electronic music emanating from the rooftop bar.

Kayla placed her arms around the man's neck. Ridley could see her smiling, her head lolling side to side, laughing. Then she leaned in and appeared to drunkenly try to kiss him.

It had only taken seconds. Ridley knew things were in motion. She tore her eyes away long enough to glance towards the alley behind the bar, where she saw headlights moving quickly up the narrow lane and lurching to a stop. It was a compact urban delivery van with the words "Old Port Seafood" written across the side, above a stylised fish icon.

Back on the rooftop, she watched as the man pulled his face away from Kayla's and looked around. He was waving his free hand in an "It's alright" gesture to the patrons around them who had turned to see the commotion. Then he had gripped her tighter and started guiding her towards the exit. Kayla seemed compliant, laughing and smiling, though she stumbled as they moved.

Ridley sprang into action. She bolted towards the door and barely heard the barista call out "Thank you!" as she hurried outside into the night. The Kawasaki was still parked where she had left it, the cheap black helmet she had bought still hanging from the handlebar grip.

With practiced efficiency she donned the helmet, swung her leg over the bike and hoped the hotwire she had left in place for expediency hadn't drained the battery. She pushed the start button; the big four-cylinder, 750 cubic centimetre engine came to life on the first turn.

Ridley pulled away from the kerb and accelerated as she leaned into a left-hand turn onto one of the cross lanes that ran behind the block of buildings where Bastion club was located. Luckily the bike was relatively quiet for having over one-hundred horsepower. She raced through the mostly empty street to the far end of the block, where she brought the bike to a stop. She turned off the headlight and let the engine idle as she waited. Her heart was pounding as she fought to remain calm.

To her right, around the corner, the alley that passed behind the Bastion club opened onto the street. During her scouting earlier in the evening she had determined that there was no other entry or exit from the service area behind the buildings on this block.

Ridley fought her own doubts while she continued to wait. There had been only two exits from the club, the front door and the back door. There was no way they would have hauled an abductee down to the street through the public entrance to the club and then stuff her into a car to be whisked away. Too many eyes.

Maybe doing it in plain site was the safer strategy? It might look merely like a good Samaritan giving an inebriated person a ride home.

Ridley had the sense that Kayla's compliant, almost amorous nature was not intentional. She had obviously been drugged with something that had elicited that behaviour. The whole affair didn't match Kayla's description of her more violent, first-time abduction. Though this was a different crew. Maybe they used different methods. Maybe they did make it look like simply an altruistic ride home?

She was just about to swing the bike back around to take another pass along the front of the block when she saw the beam of headlights shining out from the end of the alley. The light was bouncing around as if the vehicle that cast them was moving hurriedly, swerving between garbage bins and stacks of crates as it made its way towards the end of the alley.

Ridley exhaled, relieved.

It's them.

Chapter Forty-Three

Ridley watched as the seafood delivery van emerged from the alley and turned onto the street heading away from her. It was moving swiftly but carefully. She watched as it slowed at the intersection with its turn signal on, waiting for the traffic light to change. When it did, it accelerated through the intersection and turned up Chowpatty Seaface Road and disappeared from sight.

Ridley's thumb moved to the headlight switch and was about to turn them on, but she stopped, thinking she should wait. She fought her impulse to pursue, as she knew the van was getting farther away.

Ten seconds.

Twenty.

Thirty.

A set of headlights came on, from a car that was parked further down the block.

"I knew it," she said into the helmet. She watched the dark, four-door sedan pull away from the kerb and swiftly make the turn through the intersection, ignoring traffic rules as it sped off after the delivery truck. Her instincts had saved her from blowing her cover to the traffickers' chase team.

Ridley revved the engine, pulled away from the kerb and took off in pursuit.

Traffic was moderate in Chowpatty, despite the hour. It worked in her favour, as she was able to duck behind other vehicles while tailing the traffickers. The delivery van was ten car-lengths ahead, with the chase car tailing it at about half that distance.

Ridley maintained a discreet distance as she followed the two vehicles across town. The little convoy made several circuitous turns along the way, which she recognised early on as counter-surveillance measures. When traffic thinned out as they transitioned away from the more nocturnal sections of the city, she was careful to lengthen her follow distance, even hanging back from turn to turn. Then, when traffic had disappeared altogether, she switched off the bike's headlight and running lights in order to follow more stealthily.

They wound up in the port area, not far from the shuttered construction site where they had stashed Yasmine Alli. In fact they were only two streets over from that very location, heading up P D'Mello Road, when Ridley saw brake lights flash and both vehicles slowed down. She slowed as well, bringing the bike to a stop between two parked semi-trucks. She watched as first the delivery van, and then the chase car, made a left-hand turn onto a narrow street lined on either side by high concrete walls with the rusty, corrugated metal roofs of old warehouses peeking up behind them.

She killed the engine and leaned the bike onto its kickstand. Keeping her helmet on, Ridley sprinted across the road to the cover of a row of leafy shrubs that were growing along the side of the concrete wall. She moved up to the end of the wall, where the van and chase car had disappeared onto the side street, and peered around the corner.

The side street was narrow, with only a concrete walkway between the kerb and the walls that lined either side of the street. There were a few stacks of broken wooden pallets and blue plastic barrels here and there, along with a handful of trucks parked along the street, further narrowing the right-of-way. The taillights of the seafood delivery van were just disappearing through a gate in the wall along the opposite side of the street, about halfway down the block. The chase car sat in the middle of the street behind it, idling.

Ridley pulled the zipper of her black leather jacket halfway down, reached inside and pulled the Chinese Type 54 9mm out of the shoulder holster she had liberated from the Dharavi drug dealers. The rig had fit her too loosely when she had first tried it on. Punching a couple of new holes and cutting off excess leather had resulted in a nice, snug fit. With gun in hand, she eased around the corner and low-walked to a closer position behind a stack of pallets, which afforded her a wider view of the gated entrance.

The metal gate slid shut as Ridley watched, cutting off her view of the delivery van. And Kayla Stone.

The chase car had not followed the truck into the warehouse complex. It sat there on the street for several minutes. Ridley could just make out the silhouettes of two occupants inside. The shadows were cast by a dim, flickering streetlamp that clung to life at the far end of the block. The two heads were moving slightly, as if their owners were talking. Conversationally, not excited. Business as usual. *Bastards!*

She considered moving up on them and taking the two

at gunpoint. She would disarm them and slide into the back seat, holding the gun on them while guiding them to some dark corner to interrogate them. It might bring this whole episode to a swift conclusion.

It was too risky, though. There were too many variables. Kayla was too vulnerable for Ridley to show her hand just yet.

Then the driver made up her mind for her, when he put the car in gear and pulled away. She watched as the car disappeared around the corner at the end of the long block.

The street was now completely deserted, barely illuminated by the single, dying streetlamp at the far end of the block and by the ambient glow of city lights. There was no movement, except for the blinking lights of aeroplanes moving across the sky, and no sound other than the general din of the city around her.

Ridley crept closer to the gated entrance, stealthily moving from cover to cover behind stacks of pallets and parked trucks, to get a closer look.

She spotted a small metal plaque bolted to the concrete wall to one side of the gate. It read "Ivory Tiger Trading Co." along the top, followed by a phone number, and "Deliveries by Appointment Only". Below this was another sign which read: "KEEP OUT—Trespassers Will Be Prosecuted".

The gate itself was constructed of rusty but sturdy looking wrought iron, with closely spaced vertical bars. There was some sort of solid sheeting affixed to the inner side of the gate, maybe plywood or thin sheet metal, to block the view. The visual barrier was in poor shape, with pieces missing here and there; corners of it sat crumpled and bent, as if having been hit by a forklift or truck. The result was that Ridley could still see through it, in places, to the inside of the complex. If she shifted her position, she could view wider swathes of the interior.

Her eyes settled on a bright orange pinprick of light through one of the holes. It was moving slightly, bouncing, and trailing horizontally. She tracked it as it disappeared from view through one hole and reappeared a few seconds later through another. A cigarette. Being smoked by a guard, stationed at the gate.

There wasn't much else to see. Only the side of an old warehouse, which matched the roofs she had already seen protruding above the top of the concrete walls. The warehouse walls were made of more of that rusty, dented corrugated siding, and the warehouse floors were elevated a couple of yards above ground level to function as a loading dock. There were a series of roll-up doors arranged along the warehouse walls, all of them closed.

Ridley looked back at the building's roof, her eyes tracing along its top edge. The roofline was broken in several places down the length of the block, indicating that there were many separate buildings in there. She imagined there must be row after row of them, a few dozen buildings filling up the entire complex, with a labyrinth of alleys running between and around them.

Kayla could be anywhere inside there.

Besides, who knew how many of those guards there might be, or how well they were armed. And how well trained.

Ridley backed away from her vantage point and began to work her way back down the street to where she had parked the bike. Halfway there she felt a vibration in her pocket.

Only two people knew the number to her burner phone, and one of them was currently drugged and imprisoned somewhere inside the complex in front of her. She made her way to a dark corner, pulled the phone out, tapped the button to accept the call and brought the phone up to her ear.

"Yes?"

"This is Taara. What have you done?"

Chapter Forty-Four

"What the hell have you done with her?" Taara demanded, as soon as she stepped out of the cab. She still wore her skimpy working girl costume, though it was loosely covered with a light coat. "I trusted you two!"

"Sshhh!!" Ridley hissed, looking around. "Keep your voice down." There were only a few cars moving up and down the street near the docks, as it was still quite early in the morning. It would be a couple of hours before most of the work crews began showing up for the day. Even so, she couldn't have this woman getting hysterical. "Come with me," she ordered, then grasped Taara firmly by the arm and dragged her towards a secluded spot behind a power transformer box.

"I only told you about Yasmine as a way to find Azim!" Taara spat, her voice still angry, even though she was trying to keep the volume down.

"What have you heard?"

"Just that she's missing! Azim himself came into The Neptune tonight. We hardly ever see him... he usually just sends his goons," she said, the words tumbling out. "They were with him, but he came in like a typhoon and dragged both Stella and me into the bathroom by our hair! His men slapped both of us around while he asked us if either of us had been speaking to anyone about his family, about Yasmine."

A chill ran up Ridley's spine as she looked over Taara's face and spotted the fresh bruises. "What did you tell him?" she asked, cautiously.

Taara looked down and shook her head back and forth. "Nothing. I told him I had no idea what he was talking about. Stella said the same thing. They beat her up a little more, even though she was telling the truth. I lied, but I got off easy. They finally left when they were convinced we did not know what they were talking about. I am assuming they went off to interrogate and beat up whoever was next on their list."

Taara was now crying, wiping tears from her smudged face. Ridley tried to put an arm around her shoulders, but she shrank away.

"Don't you touch me!" she hissed. "I know you have done something to her. I could see it in your eyes when we first met. You are a killer. I recognise it. Just like Azim and his men, but with a pretty face. Oh God help me for what I have done!"

Ridley took a step back, giving the woman her space. "Taara, we haven't harmed her at all. She might be a little bit scared, but she's okay. I promise. In fact, let's go see her."

Taara blinked back more tears. "Right now?"

Ridley had been thinking it might have to come to this. She needed help. She had too many plates spinning, and some of them were beginning to wobble. She needed an extra hand if she was going to actually go inside the compound. There was nobody else. A city of eighteen million, and not a single one she could trust. At least she knew Taara, sort of. She at least knew the woman had a kind heart and supported her cause. She decided she would have to trust her.

"Yes, right now. She's just a short walk away from here. Let's go."

Taara nodded her agreement and followed Ridley down the street, along the boarded construction site fence. They made a turn at a small cross street. Taara clearly grew nervous as Ridley led her into the shadows of the narrow lane and to a gate in the construction site's fence.

"It's just through here," Ridley whispered as she stepped through the gate. She looked back and saw that Taara hadn't followed. Her wide eyes and pursed lips were evidence of the fear she felt, and which was written all over her face.

Ridley returned to her. "Taara, I know you're scared. I don't know how to assure you of this, but I'm not what or who you think I am." She reached into her jacket and drew out her pistol.

Taara's eyes grew even wider at the sight of it, and she took a step back, her feet beginning to pivot so she could run away.

Ridley grabbed Taara's arm with her free hand; with her other hand, she flipped the handgun over and caught it by the slide, holding it out to Taara, grip first.

"Go on, take it," she said, keeping her grip on the woman's arm. Taara tried to pull away but couldn't. She finally gave up, and looked down at the gun.

"Go on," Ridley repeated. "It's loaded. You can keep it pointed at me if you want."

Taara stared at the gun a moment longer, then said, "I have never touched one before. I don't know how to use it."

"It's not that hard, sweetie. Take it in hand, by the grip there. Keep your finger out of that trigger loop unless you're ready to fire it. If you need to, just point it and squeeze the trigger. You won't even need to take aim, at this range. You can keep it pressed into my back, if it makes you feel better."

Taara shook her head. "No. I-I can't. It… scares me."

Ridley released her arm. "Okay then, let's do this." She ejected the magazine and handed it to Taara, who took it timidly. "Those are the bullets," Ridley said. Then she pulled back the slide and ejected the live round from the chamber and handed it to Taara as well. "There. Put those in your purse. Without them, this thing is just a paperweight." She tucked the unloaded gun back into its holster.

Taara nodded. "You did not have to do that. Thank you. It does make me feel better."

"Okay, then. Let's go. Yasmine is right over there, in one of those shipping containers."

A few minutes later Ridley removed the lock from the container door and swung it open. Yasmine was standing just inside. She looked tired but otherwise in good health.

"Oh child!" Taara cried at the sight of her. "Thank heavens you are okay."

Yasmine had a puzzled look on her face as she looked back and forth from Ridley to Taara, and back to Ridley. "Yeah, as good as can be expected," she said, "for having been kidnapped by a couple of crazy bitches." She turned to Ridley and said, "So who is this? She's dressed like a whore."

Ridley rolled her eyes.

Taara smiled, and then laughed. "Sweet child, that's exactly right. Though I prefer the word 'escort'.""

"Okay, well now I am thoroughly confused. And you, Princess Kate, what are you doing back already? I agreed to play along with you clowns for twenty-four hours. It has only been twelve."

"Things are moving faster than we thought," Ridley stated. "This is Taara. She, um... works for your father. She's bravely agreed to help us. Right, Taara?"

Taara looked at Ridley for a minute, then turned to Yasmine. "Worked. Past tense. I worked for your father, but I recently... quit." She touched the fresh bruises on her face. "I will *not* be working for him any longer."

Yasmine's mouth hung open. "You're a prostitute? You worked for my *father?*"

"It's true," Ridley said. "Kidnapping and selling them into slavery isn't the only way your father abuses women. It appears he's quite diversified, in that regard."

Yasmine fell silent as she stared at Taara. Ridley saw a tear run down her cheek as she stepped towards Taara and embraced her. "I... I'm so sorry," she said, crying into Taara's ample bosom. "I had no idea. This is all so new to me."

"I know," Taara said as she stroked the young girl's hair. "It is a lot to take in. There is nothing for you to be sorry about. None of this is your fault. As for me, I was a willing participant, at least to a point. I was not stolen, or kidnapped, or locked up and sold against my will." She arced her neck to look at Ridley. "Like these women."

Yasmine pulled away from her embrace. "These women," she echoed, and looked at Ridley. "Where is your friend? The kinder one? Kayla?"

Taara also looked at Ridley. "Yes, where is she?"

Ridley shook her head. "She's gone back in. She used herself as bait and has been re-abducted."

"Oh my Shiva," Taara said.

Yasmine looked down and started crying again.

"She insisted on it," Ridley said. "To save any women they might have now and to bring the enterprise down for good. She's a very brave woman. So far, the plan has worked. I've learned where they're keeping her, and most likely the rest of the women are there too. I need help. With Kayla on the inside, I have no one else to turn to out here." She met their eyes in turn. "Except you two. Will you help me?"

"You can count on me," Taara said. "Though I have no skills, at least, not in these matters. I am not sure what I can do to help. But I will try."

"Do you have a driver's license?"

"Yes, I do. I would be a little rusty. I have not driven in years."

"I'm sure you'll be fine. I just need you to drive a small truck, that's all. I won't put you in harm's way. Can you do that?"

"I… I think so. I will try."

"You'll do fine."

"What about me?" Yasmine said. "I also want to help."

Ridley shook her head. "No, you'll stay clear, where you're safe. Obviously, at some point we'll need to return you to your father. That's how I intend to get Kayla back, and free the other women."

Yasmine nodded. Ridley and Kayla had already explained that much to her. It was what had convinced her to cooperate without resistance.

After a pause, she spoke again. "What about my father?" she asked quietly. "What will happen to him?"

Ridley didn't speak for a minute. With everything that had been going through her mind, she had not yet given that aspect of the situation much thought. It was indeed a fly in the ointment. Finally she said, "The truth is, I can't say, for sure. I don't expect he will let us simply make the exchange and be done with it. He's going to put up a fight. I'm sorry, sweetie, but I really don't know how it will play out. He could get hurt. Or, he could get killed. I could be killed. Kayla, too. This is a very dangerous game."

Yasmine hung her head again. "I understand," she said, and sobbed quietly for a minute. Then she looked up at Ridley and said, "Promise me though, you will not kill him if you do not have to? If he surrenders or something?"

Ridley watched another tear roll down the young girl's cheek. She thought of her own father, who had died tragically when she was only very young herself, and the daughter's love she still had for him in his absence. Then she looked into Yasmine's eyes, and for the second time in less than twenty-four hours, on the exact same spot, she lied again.

"I promise."

Chapter Forty-Five

Kayla Stone could hear voices as she slowly came awake.

Their voices were rising and falling in rhythm with her heartbeat. Each beat sent a new spike of pain through her head that momentarily overpowered all audible input. The painful spikes were in addition to a constant, dull ache that seemed to permeate her body from end to end.

After the headache, her stomach was her next worse source of pain. It felt both full and empty at the same time. Involuntarily clenching and releasing, in constant spasms. She felt as if she needed to vomit, but knew she couldn't. Though she couldn't remember where she was, or what she had done, somehow Kayla knew that she had long since puked every last morsel from her stomach.

The floor was cool and hard against her cheek. Concrete. Then she realised the rest of her body was slightly elevated. She was on a filthy old mattress, lying with her head off of one side. The stench of sweat and urine from the mattress was strong, and it began to jog her memory. Kayla had been in this place before.

The crusty old mattress. The filthy concrete floor. The smell of shit and piss from the plastic bucket she now realised was sitting only feet away. She knew that if she stretched out a leg or an arm very far in any direction, it would come into contact with the stiff, wiry lattice of steel chain-link fencing.

I am back.

With both dread and satisfaction, she began to realise it. She was back inside. Back in prison. Back in the bowels of the Mumbai human slave operation.

Though she had not yet moved, and her face was still planted on the floor, a faint, grim smile formed on Kayla's lips, almost as though she were kissing the filthy concrete.

It worked.

Now what?

She ached all over and was still trying to break through the cobwebs in her mind. She had been "roofied," that much was clear. She was now inside The Vulture's compound, though she had no idea how long it had been since she had lost consciousness.

Kayla had not yet opened her eyes, yet instinct told her it would be best not to. At least not yet. Who knew what might happen once someone realised she was awake?

She tried to push the pulsing pain out of her mind and concentrate on the noises she could hear. They, too, were familiar. Closest to her, she could hear whimpering. A little farther away, snoring. And sobbing. This time there was no screaming. She remembered that from her first trip through this place. The ones who screamed and cried the loudest were kept drugged or beaten.

From another direction she heard different voices. Male voices, speaking English, the common language of India, though thick with different ethnic accents. Arabic. Hindi. It was him. Azim Alli, the son of a bitch whose crew had abducted Kayla the first time. The same guy who had transported her and the rest of the girls to the slave market under Mount Kailash in Tibet.

She deduced that the other man was his boss, The Vulture. Kayla tried to concentrate on their conversation, picking out the words from among the din of the whimpering and snoring women closer by. The men were walking across the room, towards the small office cube that was near her end of the warehouse. As they got closer, she was able to pick up the conversation. She continued to feign sleep, with her head turned away from them, in case Azim Alli should glance in her direction and possibly recognise her.

"I do not care," she heard The Vulture say, in his calm but menacing voice. "You have had plenty of time to deal with your personal matters—"

"She is my *daughter!*" Azim broke in.

"That is the last time you will speak over me. Is that clear?"

Kayla did not hear a response. Yet, when The Vulture said, "Good," she pictured the big Muslim having grudgingly nodded his assent.

"Now," The Vulture continued, "while you have been on family leave, Nandu and the other teams have picked up your slack. We are now ready to fulfil the order. They brought the final three in last night."

Kayla heard Azim sigh. "Okay, that is good. I will evaluate them. Is that them over there, in the last three pens?"

"Do not worry about them. Nandu and I will handle the quality assurance checks. You have other work to do. Finding these three last night proved fortuitous, as I have learned the ship must leave ahead of schedule. It seems there is a typhoon forming out in the sea, and the captain wants to get out ahead of it. It leaves tomorrow."

"Tomorrow?" Azim said, sounding surprised. "That brings the shipment into port weeks too early! They will not be ready yet, on the other end."

Tomorrow? Kayla repeated in her mind. *So soon?* She began to feel a pit forming in the middle of her aching stomach. Would that be enough time for Alex to work? She felt panic beginning to set in.

"The timing will work out," The Vulture stated. "It turns out we can not send the cargo through Suez into Europe anyhow. There will be too much scrutiny from customs. Which is why we have re-booked it to a ship that will be going around the cape, making several stops along the west coast of Africa along the way before entering the Meditterranean the conventional way towards Genoa and Milan."

Genoa? Milan? Kayla thought. *They plan to send us to Italy?* She wasn't sure she had heard correctly.

"In future," The Vulture continued, "we will make port in Agadir."

"Agadir? Is not Tangier a better choice?"

"When the time comes, you will advise them of the change. They will understand our concerns. Besides, Agadir is closer to their base in Marrakesh. The port in Casablanca is too big. Too many eyes."

"And what about Marrakesh? Is that going to work out?"

"Do not worry about Marrakesh yet. I am still working out the details. I should have everything worked out by the time you have harvested your next crop. For now, focus on getting things ready for this shipment. You will need to stock extra supplies inside the container. It is a much longer voyage, and we can not afford too much spoilage. I am guaranteeing no more than fifteen percent loss of the inventory in transit. Any more than that will come out of our own pockets."

"Understood. I will make the arrangements."

"Good. One more thing. I need you to go and visit Chota."

"Chota? What for?"

"He informed me he has some information we will want. You know how he is. You had better take some money from the safe."

"That godless fuck works for us. Why are we always paying him?"

"Me," The Vulture corrected. "That godless fuck works for me. Not us. And I pay you, too, do I not? Not unlike you, Chota has certain skills that are best kept honed by the liberal application of money. Besides, I have always found his services to be a bargain. Go and see what he has for us this time. Pay the man if it is useful."

Kayla heard the sound of footsteps fading away, followed by the click of a door shutting with a loud echo. Then all she could hear were the cries and moans of her fellow captives reverberating around her.

She decided to stay in place for a little while longer to think about what she had heard. They planned to ship out the "inventory," including herself, the very next day. They would be trapped inside an ocean container for weeks; it was acceptable if up to 15% of them did not make it. Their destination was unclear. Was it Italy, or the deserts of North Africa? She wasn't sure. However, she was sure of one thing.

We don't have much time, Alex! Where are you?

Chapter Forty-Six

What the fuck am I doing back here again? Kim asked himself as he pulled up outside White Tiger Electronics on Lamington Road.

It had been less than a day since Chota's creepy Arab had sprung him from Force One headquarters up in Aarey Colony. Of course, he had been grateful, but that was yesterday. Today was a new day. For how long would this Chota bastard expect that he would come running at the drop of a hat?

Maybe Chota had some information for him. Kim couldn't deny that the bastard was useful for that, at least, even though everything that came out of his mouth came at a hefty price. Ever since he had gotten out of jail, Kim had hit nothing but dead ends in his search for that fucker Alex Ridley and her new sidekick.

He had gone right back to his last known location for her, right back to the King's Rest Guest House in the Dharavi high rise. The cute Asian woman with the nose ring was at the reception desk again, but this time her hair was pink.

"Mister Man! You come back!" she had exclaimed. She offered to show him any room he wanted to see this time, personally. She winked and licked her lips as she said it. Kim briefly considered it. He had just gotten out of prison, after all, and could use a bit of cleaning of the pipes. He was too busy, too focused on finding and killing Alex Ridley. So he had declined, thinking he might just have to come back and pay her a visit later, after this fucking Ridley business was over with. Perhaps give it to her a little rougher than she wanted.

He had asked the receptionist about the two women from the other night. Naturally, they were long gone, she had confirmed. Kim had expected as much. Maybe they even knew he had been there, though he had been as careful as possible to leave no evidence of his visit.

After leaving King's Rest, Kim considered doubling back even further, to the Orchid Hotel where he had first picked up their trail, with Chota's help. He had left a dead maid in one of the rooms there, who had most likely been found by now. He couldn't afford to go back there just to have a look. He also reasoned, reluctantly, that Ridley was too smart to return there anyhow.

He had been out of leads and was sitting in a street vendor's stall in the Marathi section of Dadar, wolfing down a heaping plate of *bhaji*, when his phone rang. Once again it was the unmistakable voice of Chota's pet Arab.

"You will come to the shop in one hour," the Arab said in lieu of a greeting.

Kim was dumbfounded. "Oh, and fuck you, too," he retorted.

"This is no joke. You will be here. You will ask for the Governor."

"Oh yeah? What does he want now? I'm out of money, as you know, because he already has it all." That wasn't true, but there was no use letting a carrion-eater like Chota pick his bones clean.

"You will be here," the Arab repeated.

Kim was about to lay into him about not ordering him the fuck around, when he realised the line was dead. *The motherfucker hung up on me? Fuck that guy, and fuck Chota.*

Kim had to concede that he had nothing else to do until something broke in his search for Alex fucking Ridley. Maybe Chota had some tidbit for him? Something about her? Her location, even? The bastard knew he was looking for her, and that he would pay for information.

As it turned out, the Arab had been right after all. Here Kim was, where the bastard had ordered him to be. At the prescribed time.

The door chimed as he stepped into White Tiger Electronics. Two men stood behind a counter at the back of the shop. The small one said, "Welcome to White Tiger! Can I interest you in the new iPhone?" Pecs was standing next to him, the logo on his shirt stretched and distorted.

"Cut the shit, I'm here to see The Governor," Kim said, rolling his eyes.

Pecs turned to the door behind him and knocked. The door opened, and he spun back to Kim. "Follow me."

Kim followed Pecs into the back room, where the Arab was waiting, his gun drawn. "Weapons, phone, wallet," the Arab said.

Kim sighed audibly. "You know this isn't necessary," he said, but complied anyway, dropping his things on the table.

The Arab nodded to Pecs, who opened the back door of the room and stood aside.

"Chota will see you now," the Arab said.

Kim shook his head and stepped through the door into Chota's electronic domain. He had forgotten how hot and stuffy it was in that small room, with the whirring of cooling fans and hard drives making conversation difficult to hear.

"I am Chota," the man sitting at the workstation said.

There was a rickety old office chair on the visitor's side of Chota's desk. Kim pulled it out and sat down. "Yeah, no shit. What brings me here?"

"Such insolence," Chota said, "from a man newly liberated, towards his emancipator."

"Cut the shit," Kim said. "You got paid."

Chota leaned back, the faintest hint of a smile on his lips. "Handsomely," he said.

"Why am I here? You have something for me on Ridley?"

"Alex Ridley? That file has been closed. The contract fulfilled. Did you wish to open another?"

"Possibly."

Chota stared at him for a moment, his eyes hidden behind the glare of status lights reflecting off his glasses. "Perhaps we will set that aside, for the moment. Another matter has come up."

"A matter that concerns me? How?"

Chota spread his hands. "I do not know the nature of the concern. It seems you are a, how shall I put this... a person of interest? Yes, that seems right."

"Of interest to whom? The police? I already paid you for that."

"No no no, Mr. Kim. Someone much more important than that. You are not native to my country, so perhaps you are not familiar with one of our proverbs. 'If you live in the river, you should make friends with the crocodile.' I have found that to be sage advice, especially in a river such as Mumbai, and for a humble little enterprise such as mine. We all have our crocodiles, Mr. Kim. Those we must keep happy."

ip not make with our first. From the table. If you know much buye you should make contact with the upcoming things found them. He saw and he has had chance to start an after-all, and their thought little chirping with so many. We all have a personally, Mr. Kim. Then we must keep hapy.

Chapter Forty-Seven

"So which crocodile are you keeping happy by selling me out?" Kim asked nonchalantly.

Chota shook his head. "It is unfortunate that you see it as such, Mr. Kim. We are both businessmen, are we not? Information is the currency I deal in. I have not sold you out. I have only sold the information you might have. At a discount, of course, because they still have to extract more information from you."

Extract the information? Chota's words reached Kim's brain as bright red danger signals. He sprang from his chair and bolted for the door. He wasn't sure where this was going yet, but he didn't like the prospect of information being *extracted* from him. He needed to get to his gun. He bounced off the door with a thud. It was locked and bolted from the other side.

"You should calm yourself down, Mr. Kim. These men can be reasonable. Perhaps they will only want a conversation? Maybe even pay for whatever it is they think you can tell them? Who knows, perhaps they may be of help to you as well, in the matter you are pursuing."

Kim looked back at him and watched as Chota pressed a button on his keyboard and spoke into a boom mic. "Is Mr. Kim's appointment here yet?"

"Yes," came the Arab's curt reply through the computer speaker.

"Alright. Mr. Kim is anxious to meet him. Please come and collect him."

The door opened and Pecs stepped in. Kim considered punching him in the throat and then bursting through to take the Arab out with a flying kick. However, the odds of success were low, as the Arab most likely had his pistol out. Additionally, he wasn't sure yet whether this situation was going to be cordial or hostile. After mulling it over for two seconds, Kim nodded at Pecs and stepped through the door.

He had guessed right. The Arab had his gun out and levelled at him. That had been standard procedure so far in his experience, whenever coming or going from Chota's lair.

"Can I have my shit back?" Kim growled.

"After your meeting, perhaps," the Arab replied, then he looked past Kim to where Pecs was standing. "Show Azim in."

Kim turned as Pecs opened the other door and a tall, stout and dark-complected man walked in.

"Is this him?" the newcomer asked.

The Arab nodded.

The newcomer turned to Kim and said, "My name is Azim Alli. You are Kim Do-Hyun."

"It seems I need to do a better job of covering my tracks," Kim replied.

Azim stared at him, then nodded. "Yes, it would seem

so. Do not be disappointed in yourself. Mr. Chota is the best there is at uncovering tracks."

Kim raised an eyebrow. "Sounds like it. It also sounds like I haven't paid him enough to buy his loyalty."

Azim let out a sound that was half grunt, half laugh. "You cannot afford his loyalty, Mr. Kim. That is, you cannot beat the current bid for it."

"Who, might I ask, is that high bidder? You?"

"No, it is not me, but it is the man I work for. His name is not important."

"Okay, then, what can I do for you? Or him?"

Azim gestured to one of the two chairs that sat at the small table in the room. Kim reluctantly took a seat. Azim lowered himself into the other chair.

"You were recently in Tibet. Mount Kailash."

Kim couldn't believe what he had just heard. How could this man know about Kailash? He had said it as a statement, not a question.

"Please, save me the unpleasantness of extracting a confirmation from you involuntarily, Mr. Kim. It has already been confirmed. Mr. Chota has many resources at his disposal, you see. And he investigates every thread. Every person he finds of interest. I believe he does it for sport, mostly to keep his skills honed. Sometimes he stumbles upon a useful morsel, as it seems he has done again this time. When his information was combined with things that I already knew, and people I know... well, everything just sort of fell into place."

"I'm not following."

Azim sighed. "I really do not have time for this. I am a busy man, Mr. Kim. I have problems at work, I have problems at home. I do not have time for games. It would be easier to simply kill you and have you fed to the vultures in the Tower of Silence. I will give you the benefit of the doubt, and gamble that you might have some useful information. So, to convince you I am not fucking around, I will tell you that Captain Chang Zhu is a friend of mine."

Chang? Kim thought. *The captain of the Chinese guards at the Tibetan border? Fuck!*

"I will take your silence as confirmation. It seems we both have an interest in what happened under Mount Kailash that night a couple of weeks ago. Chang told me you had come through his checkpoint, not long after a bus load of women passed through. However, he did not have a name. It took a man of Chota's ingenuity to make that connection."

Finally Kim spoke. "You are the slaver?"

Azim seemed to wince slightly at the term. "I prefer… trader. I am merely selling and transporting a sought after commodity."

Kim nodded. He had no moral dilemma over the issue. He had delivered the Ridley bitch into that same industry. "Okay, then. Yes, I was there. So what?"

Azim leaned back, satisfied. He looked up at the Arab and Pecs, who still stood in the room, and turned back to Kim. "Not here. Come with me, to see my boss. There is much to talk about." Then he looked up at the Arab and said, "Give him his things."

Chapter Forty-Eight

Kayla Stone was beginning to lose faith. Not her faith in Alex Ridley—she knew that Ridley would move mountains to rescue her and take down the trafficking ring—but she was starting to think that there simply wouldn't be enough time for her powerful friend to make her move. They had both understood that it would take time for Ridley to set up and execute her plan. Neither of them knew, at that time, that Kayla and the rest of the abducted women would be loaded up and sent out to sea in only a matter of hours.

Ridley, she kept reminding herself, had no clue that time was running out. In turn, Kayla had no way to warn her. Kayla was haunted by visions of Ridley, prepped and ready for war, showing up to an empty warehouse long after she and the rest of the women had been shipped out.

She started to believe she would have to take action on her own. Yet, what could she do? She was athletic, strong and confident. She was a skilled martial artist. She was not afraid. Yet she didn't have Ridley's skill at arms, or her taste and natural penchant for violence. She was no match for the armed men around her.

She looked through the chain link fencing at the girl in the cage next to her. Kayla didn't know how long she, or any of the others, had been here. As far as she could see, the cages were all full, as they had been since she had awakened in hers.

The girl in the next cage had long, dark hair. Kayla couldn't see her face. She had been sitting there on the small patch of floor in her caged space since Kayla had awakened a few hours before, her knees drawn up and her head hanging between them, rocking back and forth and crying softly. Kayla had tried to call out to her, but she hadn't responded. It had only earned her a visit from one of the guards, who had stepped up and kicked the chain link of her cage.

"No talking!" he had hissed. "Unless you prefer to be bound and gagged."

Kayla noticed that several of the girls in other cages were indeed tied up, their hands behind their backs, with a filthy towel tied around their head, holding another rag into their mouths. Kayla complied by staying quiet thereafter. She would be of no use to herself or the other girls if she were incapacitated, or worse.

She needed to make a move, she was sure of that now. Kayla needed to do something, and soon. She was starting to come to grips with the likelihood that she and the others would be shipped out before Ridley could strike. Kayla knew that, once she was locked up inside an ocean container and put on a ship, nobody would know where she was or where she was being sent. Not her family. Not Ridley. She might even die during the voyage, as part of the acceptable 15% *spoilage*.

Kayla decided that she would rather die here, in this warehouse, while taking out as many of the traffickers as possible before they managed to bring her down. At least she could count that as a victory, of sorts. If Ridley showed up later and found Kayla's lifeless body here? At least she would know what had happened to her. She would leave signs that she had not gone out without a fight, and hopefully with a body count of her own. She hoped that Ridley would be proud of her.

Kayla looked up when she heard the door opening at the far end of the warehouse. Two men stepped in, one carrying an assault rifle and the other one pushing a cart laden with a large plastic drum. They stopped at the first cage along the opposite wall. The guard with the gun levelled it at the girl in the cage and ordered her to lie down on her mattress, on her stomach, and with her hands clasped behind her back. The girl wordlessly complied. The other man stepped up to the gate, unlocked it and stepped into the cell. He picked up the shit bucket with gloved hands, carried it out to the cart and emptied it into the large drum. Then he returned the empty bucket to the cage, stepped out, then re-locked the gate before he and the guard with the rifle moved on to the next cell.

This might be my only chance, Kayla thought as the stench of shit and piss intensified from the bucket-emptying process. After the first few cages, Kayla calculated how long it would take them to work their way across that side of the room and to start working up her side, until they finally reached her cage at the end of the line.

As she was thinking of how best to exploit the situation, the doors at the end of the warehouse opened once again and two more men walked in. They were followed by another guard, who took up position just inside the door after it closed. Kayla kept her head down and watched out of the corner of her eye as the two men approached the centre of the room.

She recognised one of them as Azim Alli, who she had heard speaking a few hours earlier, but had not seen because she had been feigning sleep. She did not recognise the other man, who appeared to be Asian.

"As you can see, Mr. Kim, our inventory is now at full capacity," Azim said. As they walked, he gestured outward with his hand to indicate the cages that lined either side of the space. "We have been working hard to successfully fill an order for a new client."

Kim nodded. "With the Mount Kailash operation destroyed, you have wasted no time finding an alternate market."

"My employer has been cultivating that relationship for some time already. We were ready to transition right into it, as if Kailash had not even happened."

"I understand you had something to do with the destruction at Kailash," a third voice said. At the other end of her field of vision, Kayla saw The Vulture step out of the office door and stride towards the other two. They met in the centre of the room.

"Kim, this is the principal of this enterprise," Azim said. "You may address him as 'sir'."

"Sir? That's it?"

The Vulture smiled. "My name is not important, Mr. Kim. I value discretion above all else. I am sure you can appreciate that."

"If you care whether or not I know your name, that must mean I will walk out of here at some point."

"Of course. We have no quarrel with you. We are not barbarians, Mr. Kim. On the contrary, there may be certain circumstances in which we might work together."

"Work together? On what?" Kim nodded towards the cages. "I'm not usually a flesh trafficker."

"You know how to move things," Azim said. "Things that require just as much skill and connections."

"What do you know about me?"

"Much," The Vulture said. "Our mutual friend, Chota, is quite thorough. But I will not bore you with those details. I am much more interested in learning more about what happened in Tibet. As you might imagine, that was an organisation which was important to our commerce, and it behooves me to know what happened, to understand whether it might pose a threat to us here in Mumbai."

Kim was silent for a minute. Then he spoke. "Yes, I was there. I knew the people there too, though more so for weapons trading."

Kayla monitored the progress of the crew emptying the shit buckets. They had completed their work along the opposite side of the room; they were now on her side, working their way towards her.

"I see," The Vulture continued, nodding. "And on that specific occasion? You were there to complete a weapons transaction?"

Kim hesitated before answering. "No. Well, not entirely. I brought them something else. An asset more like that which you deal in."

"Oh?"

"Just one woman. I was in the area anyway, and a chance opportunity presented itself."

"I see. I admire an opportunist like myself," The Vulture

said, nodding again. "What caused the decimation of the facility there? The deaths of the staff, the apparent escape of the inventory? Did you have anything to do with that, Mr. Kim?"

Kayla could only see part of Kim's face, as he was mostly blocked from her view by Azim, who stood with his back to her. She could, however, see beads of sweat forming on Kim's face.

Kim shook his head. "I did not have a hand in that. I was assaulted, along with the others. I nearly died along with them."

"Then what happened?"

"A team came in to rescue one of the captives. It was the woman I brought. Her friends engineered a rescue. It turned into mayhem."

"In other words, you led this team right to Mount Kailash?"

"I... I did not intend that. They had known nothing about the Kailash facility. They must have learned about it elsewhere and guessed that their friend had been taken there."

The Vulture was silent for a minute. He stared at the floor, in thought. Kayla checked the progress of the sanitation crew. They were two cages away from her own.

"And this woman you took there," the Vulture finally said. "She must be the one you have been looking for? Alex Ridley?"

"How did you know her—" Kim started.

"Chota," Azim cut in. "It seems she was among the escapees. Is that why you are seeking her?"

"Yes, it is. I have a score to settle with that bitch."

The Vulture nodded, a faint smile appearing on his face.

"Revenge, then. I can respect that. You have tracked her here, to this city? What do you think she wants in Mumbai?"

Now it was Kim's turn to smile. "She wants you, of course. She wants to kill all of you."

Chapter Forty-Nine

The sanitation crew was just finishing up in the cage next to Kayla's. She knew that she would need to act when they reached her. She tried to concentrate on what to do, while also listening to the conversation happening at the centre of the room. *They know about Alex,* she thought, *and they know she's here!*

She was even more certain, now, that she had no choice but to make a move. It might be her only chance, and it would likely cost her life. Yet, it didn't matter. She was determined to take as many of theirs with her as possible.

"Coming after us will be no easy task," The Vulture stated to Kim. "Especially for one weak woman acting alone. We are not a soft target, even assuming she can find us."

Kim laughed. "She is not weak, I can assure you of that." Kayla heard that clearly, and hoped the words tasted bitter as he said them. "She's not alone, either."

"Lie down on your stomach!" ordered the guard outside

Kayla's cage. "Face down and place your hands behind your back. Now lace your fingers together."

Kayla complied.

"How many are with her?" The Vulture asked.

"Do not move, or I will put a bullet in your skull. Do you understand?"

Kayla nodded, as she heard the lock on her gate pop open. The chain rattled as the links slipped free.

"Only one, that I know of," Kim said.

The squeak of un-oiled hinges as the gate was pushed open.

"Let me guess," Azim said. "She is working with another woman… "

Boots on concrete as the sanitation worker stepped into the cage and headed towards the bucket at the back wall.

"… and her name is Kayla Stone?"

The footsteps stopped.

"Yes! How did you know that?"

Kayla jerked her head to the side as she swept her legs off the mattress.

A shot rang out as a hole appeared in the mattress where Kayla's head had been.

She reached out and grabbed the wire lattice of the chain link fencing to give her legs more leverage as they continued in their arc. Her bare feet struck the sanitation worker's boots just as the man was starting to lean forward, squatting to pick up the waste bucket. Being off-balance already, his feet were swept out from under him and he lost his control, falling over sideways.

Kayla let go of the fence and hopped to her feet as another shot rang out and left a hole in the room's corrugated metal wall. The sanitation worker landed on his side as Kayla reached down and grabbed the bucket by its handle and lifted it into the air.

The worker was starting to regain his composure. Kayla saw that he had a sidearm in a holster, and that he was reaching for it.

Kayla began to swing the bucket in the direction of the guard.

The three men in the centre of the room had been slow to react but were now aware that something was going on. They began to turn towards the commotion while reaching for their weapons.

The guard fired a third shot, which passed through the bucket and whizzed past Kayla's chest, missing by mere inches.

The open mouth of the bucket was pointed towards the guard when it reached the end of Kayla's reach. She hung onto the bucket as forward momentum launched its contents in the direction of his head.

Kayla didn't wait to see the result; she looked down just as the sanitation guy pulled his handgun free of its holster.

"Shit!!" she heard the guard scream, followed by a wet splash.

Kayla flipped the bucket over in her hands and fell down on the sanitation worker, bringing the bucket, still dripping piss and excrement residue, down over his head. She let go of it and grabbed the man's forearm with one hand, pulling it towards her, while her other hand shot out and struck his gun hand in the opposite direction.

She heard the crack of bone, felt it reverberate through her grip on the arm as the wrist of the man's gun hand bent unnaturally backward from the blow. There was a muffled scream from inside the bucket as his grip on the gun loosened.

Kayla caught the gun as it fell from his hand, fired once into the man's stomach, and then rolled onto her back as she brought the gun around and trained it on the guard with the rifle.

She could now see that her aim with the shit bucket had been dead-on, as the guard's face and shirt had been soaked with it, and he was gagging and spitting. Kayla lined the pistol's front sight with his chest and pulled the trigger. The man fell.

By now, the guard—who had been posted at the door at the other end of the warehouse—was sprinting in her direction. Azim and Kim had their weapons drawn and were flanking to either side to achieve tactical separation and triangulation. The Vulture backed away, towards the cages along the other side of the room. The women in the other cages were also now aware of what was going on; several of them were getting to their feet and looking in her direction.

Kayla aimed the gun first at Azim, then at Kim, and then back at Azim. "Put your fucking guns down!" she screamed.

"You are outnumbered!" Kim yelled back. "Drop your gun, and you might still get to go on that ocean cruise."

"Ah, yes, Kayla Stone," Azim said. "So nice of you to save me the hassle of looking for you. Now drop that gun."

"Not before I take at least one more of you mother-fuckers out! Which one of you will it be?"

"Neither of them," The Vulture called, from somewhere across the room. Kayla looked towards him and saw that he had opened the gate of the cage nearest to him. He had dragged the girl who had occupied it out onto the floor by her hair. He held his gun to the girl's head. "This one will die next," he said, "if you do not drop that gun in three seconds. One…"

Kayla held the gun on Azim, pointing it directly at his chest. She didn't know much about guns, but Ridley had been giving her some pointers. She had also practiced wielding and dry-firing the one Ridley had confiscated from the drug dealers. She had advised to always aim for centre-mass. It wasn't guaranteed to be a kill shot as much as a bullet to the head was, but heads were smaller, faster-moving targets. She began to apply pressure to the trigger. Azim was right there, in her sights. The man who had abducted her and sold her into sex slavery. This was her reason for coming to Mumbai.

"Two…"

Yet, so was the girl at the end of The Vulture's gun barrel. She was here to protect her and the rest of the girls here. She could not sacrifice that poor girl to her own need for revenge.

She tossed the gun onto her mattress and fell to her knees.

Kim and Azim both rushed forward. Azim reached Kayla first and punched her in the side of the face with his massive fist. Kayla fell sideways and almost passed out.

"That is for Yasmine. You will tell me where she is before I kill you."

Kayla sat back up straight, her head swimming. "Fuck you," she said, trying hard to force a grin. "She's probably already dead."

Azim drew back to deliver another punch when The Vulture yelled, "Enough!"

Kim, Azim and Kayla turned towards The Vulture, who still had his gun barrel against the crying girl's temple. He pulled the trigger. The girl's head snapped sideways, and her body fell to the ground.

Kayla screamed.

Chapter Fifty

Kayla's arms were nearly numb. Her hands had been tied behind the back of the chair she was seated upon. Her ankles had also been bound to the chair legs. She could not move at all. She kept flexing her arms and wrists as much as she could, to promote circulation and to keep testing the restraints.

I'm sorry Alex, she thought. *I have failed you.* She looked over at the crumpled corpse of the murdered girl and then to the other girls in the rest of the cages. *I've failed all of you, as well.*

They had subdued her—crying and hysterical from The Vulture's murder of the innocent girl—and dragged her out into the middle of the room. One of the guards had run and fetched a chair and rope from the office; they had tied her up, there, in the centre of the space. Kayla was beginning to think they conducted most of their business there, in view of all of the girls, as both an act of arrogance and a show of force.

"Where is Yasmine?!" Azim roared for the tenth time.

"Your daughter can wait," The Vulture said, also for the tenth time. "Alex Ridley is more important. Tell us where she is, Ms. Stone, or we will start killing more of the captives until you do."

Kayla could see the hate on Azim's face as The Vulture spoke. She began to wonder whether it was directed at her, or at him.

"I don't know where Yasmine is," Kayla said, looking at Azim. "Alex put her somewhere and did not tell me the location, for this very reason. I was coming inside; we both agreed it would be best if I didn't bring that information in here with me. As for Alex Ridley"—she turned towards The Vulture—"well, you won't know where she is until you feel the point of her blade being shoved through the base of your skull."

Kim moved swiftly in front of her and delivered a punch to her gut, knocking the wind out of her. She gulped and gasped for air, flailing in her seat. That's when she first noticed how rickety the old wooden chair was.

"Alex Ridley," Kim said. "What are her plans? When will she strike? It matters little. I will be waiting for her!"

When Kayla regained her breath, she looked at him and said, "I'm sure she will be just as happy to see you. She's going to love the opportunity to kill you for a second time."

The Vulture sighed dramatically. "All of this posturing is getting us nowhere. Azim, fetch the bolt cutters. Shall we start removing fingers?"

Azim turned towards the office just as the phone in his pocket began to ring. He pulled it out and glanced at the screen. He looked at The Vulture, then brought the phone up to his ear.

"Listen carefully. If you want to see your daughter again, alive and in one piece, I will exchange her for all of the girls you are holding."

Azim cleared his throat. "Excuse me, miss…?"

"You know who I am. You're fucking dumb, but not that dumb, Azim Alli."

"Ridley, then. My daughter better be unharmed and—"

"She's unhurt, for now… but only if you do as I say. Is your boss there? That pathetic sack of shit who everyone calls The Vulture? Put me on speaker so I can talk to both of you."

"You do not speak to me that way—"

"Put me on fucking speaker, arsehole!"

Azim pulled the phone away from his ear, tapped the screen with a finger and held it out from him so the others could hear. "Go ahead," he muttered.

"Is The Vulture there?"

"I am here," The Vulture said. "Though I have to advise you, only a very select few associates may call me by that moniker. Anyone else who does so, dies."

"Save it, tough guy. Did you hear my terms? Your right-hand man's sweet young daughter currently has a knife to her throat. However, I will exchange her for all of the girls you are holding in your prison."

The Vulture laughed. "Do you think one child means anything to me? Go ahead, kill her. She is nothing compared to the market value of my inventory."

"Suit yourself. You will find her body floating in Mahim Bay near Worli Fort, somewhere beneath the Sea Link by morning. Goodbye."

"Wait!" Azim yelled. "Ridley!"

The phone fell silent. Azim tapped the screen desperately. "Are you still there?"

"I am. I am also getting impatient."

Kim stepped forward and spoke into the phone. "Hello, you vile bitch. I will give you every one of these slaves if you show up in person to collect them."

"Who is that? Kim? Do-Hyun Kim?"

"It is me. Of course, I am sure you thought you had left me for dead. But I am very hard to kill, Ridley. Now I will kill you."

Ridley was silent for a moment. *"Well congratulations, then. I am impressed. Release the girls, first. And then I will meet you anywhere you'd like."*

"They are not his to release," The Vulture chimed in, remaining calm. "As I said, my inventory is not available to barter. Except, perhaps, for one of them. It seems that, among my collection here, is someone quite dear to you."

"You're holding Kayla Stone."

"Of course you knew that. She is here as part of whatever scheme you are planning. It will not work. My inventory is not available for negotiations. It is a shame the daughter must die, too. But, Kayla Stone will die first. Right this moment, as a matter of fact."

"Don't you touch her! The girl will die! Ask Kim. I am not joking."

"Oh, I do not doubt that at all. Yet, as I said, Azim Alli's daughter means nothing to me. My assets, however, mean everything. And your friend, Ms. Stone, has already proven to be too troublesome. I am afraid keeping her around is a poor investment. Say goodbye if you must." The Vulture pulled out his gun and pointed it at Kayla's face.

"Alex I'm sorry!" Kayla screamed.

"Don't do it!" Ridley yelled through the speaker.

A shot rang out.

"Kaylaaaaa!"

The Vulture fell to the floor, a crimson bloom spreading on the chest of his Armani suit.

Kayla Stone sat paralysed. Her frozen stare locked on to Azim Alli as he lowered his gun.

"This is Azim," the big Muslim said into the phone.

"The Vulture is dead. We will take your deal. These girls for my daughter. All of them, for Yasmine."

"All except for one," Kim added. "The girls for this man's daughter. As for Kayla Stone, we will only exchange her for you." Kim looked at Azim.

Azim nodded.

They waited for a response. *"Okay,"* Ridley finally said. *"Yasmine for the captives. Then I will take Kayla's place."*

"Agreed," Azim and Kim said, in unison.

"Okay then," Ridley continued. *"This is how it will work. I will send a van into the compound. The driver is innocent in this, and you will not harm her. Your guards will admit her through the gate and guarantee her safe passage. You will load the girls into the van, and she will take them away. Once they have safely reached a destination I've designated, I will drive the van back to you myself, with Yasmine. Azim Alli can have his daughter back, and you will release Kayla Stone."* The phone was silent for a moment, before Ridley continued. *"I will stay in her stead."*

"That sounds too complicated."

"Maybe so," Ridley said. *"But that's too bad. My primary concern is getting those girls to safety. There's no other way to guarantee that."*

Azim and Kim looked at each other. Both nodded.

"Okay, then. Send the van."

"It's already in the neighbourhood. It will be there in five minutes."

Chapter Fifty-One

The gate slid open. A compact man wielding an AK-47 waved her through.

Taara steered the delivery van through the opening and watched the armed man as she passed. His weapon was pointed directly at her, tracking her as she moved along. Taara shuddered and returned her focus to the road ahead of her. Her mouth had never felt so dry. A second guard waved her towards the right, and she obeyed.

Ridley and Taara had left Yasmine in the room at the guest house in Pathak Wadi, deeming the ocean container by the docks no longer necessary to contain her. Now that Yasmine understood the stakes, like Taara, she was fully cooperative and eager to help Ridley and Kayla in any way she could. Yet, Taara remained uneasy about how the women had treated her. Nevertheless, she understood that helping Ridley carry out her plan was the best hope for the women her former employer was holding captive.

She thought of Alex Ridley. A woman of uncommon strength and valour, according to Kayla Stone. However,

Taara knew the men she was up against. The monsters. She shivered at the thought, and then said a silent prayer for both of them:

> *O Mother Durga!*
> *Enter our bodies in Thy Yogic strength.*
> *We shall become Thy instruments,*
> *Thy sword slaying all evil,*
> *Thy lamp dispelling all ignorance.*

Taara arrived at the centre of the complex three turns later. There, another guard signalled for her to stop next to a loading dock with a series of roll-up doors, all of them currently shut. An enormous ocean container, like the one Ridley and Kayla had used as a safe house for Yasmine, was mounted on a semi-trailer and backed up to the loading dock at one of the bay doors. Next to where the container was parked, a short flight of rusty metal steps descended from the floor of the dock to the cracked concrete surface of the truck yard.

The guard stepped around to the driver's side of the van and motioned for Taara to roll the window down. "Step out of the vehicle until the cargo has been loaded," he ordered.

As Taara climbed out of the driver door of the van, Alex Ridley slipped from her perch between the van's frame rails and dropped to the ground beneath the vehicle.

Lying on her stomach amid the shadows, Ridley could see the boots of the guard, herding Taara's smaller feet a short distance away from the van. She moved to the opposite side of the van and low-crawled out from under it, rising to a low crouch in the shadows between the van and the container trailer. She stealthily crossed to the trailer and disappeared into the shadows of its undercarriage.

Ridley found a suitable vantage point between the double rear axles of the semi-trailer and peered out between the tyres. The guard was holding Taara at gunpoint, across the yard from the front of the van. Ridley couldn't help but notice the frightened look on her face.

Stay brave, Ridley said in her mind. *This should be over soon.*

Ridley heard a door opening and turned to see a pedestrian door, situated between two of the roll-ups, swing open. Another man stepped outside. He was large, dark-skinned, and held a coal-black handgun in one large hand.

That must be Azim Alli, she mused. She watched as the man stepped to the side of the door and waved his gun in a "hurry up" gesture.

Ridley breathed a sigh of relief as she watched first one young woman, and then another, emerge through the door, soon followed by a constant stream of women. They all looked tired, some of them seemed drugged, and most of them bruised, but otherwise they seemed in relative health. Ridley counted twenty-two women in all. Her heart began to soar as she realised it was actually happening. These women would all be free soon.

A third man followed the last girl out through the door. This one she recognised immediately. *Do-Hyun Kim.* The hint of a smile curled her lips, though she felt a surge of adrenaline at the same time. *I will deal with you soon.*

Azim and Kim herded the women down the short set of stairs and across the cracked concrete to where the van waited.

"This is all of them," Azim called out as he approached Taara and turned his attention towards her, away from the captives. "You can tell Ridley I—wait... Taara? You are working with these *Gori?* Oh, you stupid fucking whore."

Taara shrank away from him. "I am only helping because they have your daughter," she pleaded. "You should be careful, that woman is dangerous! She will not hesitate to kill your daughter; I am quite sure of it."

Azim sneered as he stared down at the small woman. Then he called out to Kim. "Load them into the van!"

"I will decide what to do with you later," he promised, and stepped past Taara towards the roll-up door at the back of the van.

Ridley watched as the women shuffled towards the van and, one by one, climb up into it. It was a tight fit, with the last of them taking a seat right at the back of the van's interior. She watched as Kim lowered the door and latched it shut.

Once the women were loaded, the guard motioned for Taara to climb back up into the driver's seat. After she had done so, Azim stepped up to the window and said something to her that Ridley could not hear. Then he and Kim stepped away and headed back towards the door of the warehouse.

Taara turned the truck around and returned along the route by which they had come in. Ridley watched until the van disappeared around a corner, after which the truck yard fell eerily silent. Azim, Kim and one of the guards had stepped back inside the warehouse.

The guard positioned outside had retreated to the shadows under the eaves of the loading dock to have a smoke, as Ridley could see the small orange glow of his cigarette. She considered moving up and taking him out first but decided against it. He might have to be dealt with later, along with the various guards positioned throughout the complex and the front gate, but she had more important business to attend to first. First she had to find Kayla Stone.

She knew that Kayla was here, most likely inside the warehouse that Kim and Azim had disappeared into. Those two would be inside, waiting. Preparing. Anticipating. Licking their lips in anticipation of her arrival.

That was fine. She would be making her appearance much sooner than they expected.

Ridley backed away from her vantage point underneath the container trailer, away from the guard, and away from the entry door Kim and Azim had stepped through. She would find another, stealthier way inside.

Then she would deal with whoever or whatever got in her way.

Chapter Fifty-Two

Do-Hyun Kim strummed his fingers on one of the cardboard crates stacked at the edge of the room, next to one of the warehouse's large bay doors. The guards had been bringing the crates in from one of the other store-rooms, but had stopped once the deal had been struck to send the women out. The crates contained cases of bottled water and canned food, apparently in anticipation of the shipment of women that was to be leaving soon.

That shipment wasn't going to happen now. The women were gone, sent away in a deal to bring Alex Ridley and Azim's daughter to them. Kim couldn't give two squirts of piss for Azim's daughter. Perhaps he would kill her, too, along with her Neanderthal of a father, before this was over. Alex Ridley was his primary goal. His prey. Finally, he had caught up to her after chasing her down from the Tibetan mountains, across India and through the filthy streets of Mumbai. She would be here soon, and finally, they would dance.

He hoped there might be a way to keep hold of Kayla

Stone as well. He glanced at her, bound to her chair in the middle of the room, still struggling weakly against her restraints. The Vulture's lifeless body remained crumpled on the floor next to her, his pooled blood beginning to dry and harden.

She caught him looking at her, and said, "You're dead, you know that, right?" She forced a grin. "You are both dead. Alex will see to that."

Kim grinned back but ignored her taunts. He let his gaze linger on her. She was a fine specimen, he thought, even beaten and battered as she was at the hands of these goons. He thought it might be good to have a turn at her, once he had dealt with Ridley. Perhaps he would save her the second dance.

Azim Alli paced back and forth across the room with a two-way radio in his hand, which he was using to keep in contact with the outside guards. As he watched him, Kim thought about how he had always worked mostly alone. Partners, employees, right-hand men? They would end up stabbing you in the back. Or shooting you in the head. The Vulture had learned that lesson the hard way.

This time, it had worked out in Kim's favour, in the end. Azim killing his own boss would return his daughter to him, and deliver Alex Ridley to Kim. It was an elegant solution.

The radio in Azim's hand squawked to life, with some static-laden message Kim could not quite make out from across the room. Azim brought the radio to his face and said, "Report. Are they here?"

More static from the radio as Azim listened. "Bring them inside but frisk them for weapons first," he said, then added, "Make it thorough." Kim nodded in agreement at that notion and walked towards the centre of the room.

Azim joined him there. "They are here," he stated, and looked over at Kayla Stone. "Should we unbind that bitch?"

"What the fuck for?" Kim answered. "She is not going anywhere. The Ridley whore will be here, too. I see no reason to let either of them leave this place alive."

Azim smiled. "I am glad we see eye to eye."

They heard the van moving into the truck yard outside, followed by doors slamming. Kim and Azim took up position to either side of Kayla Stone, facing the small entry door. Kim glanced down at Kayla, who for once had stopped her struggling and moaning through the gag; now she was also watching the door intently.

The door opened, and one of their guards stepped through, followed by a teenage girl and a woman.

"Yasmine!" Azim yelled. Kim heard real emotion in the man's voice for the first time. The girl ran to him and stopped short, her eyes wide with what looked like fear and confusion.

"Father? What have you done?" the girl asked, looking around the room at the cages, the bodies and the chaos. Kayla Stone sat there, beaten and bruised, tied to a chair. There was a dead man in an expensive suit, and nearby, the lifeless body of a young girl dressed in soiled rags. A few paces away, two more dead men lay on the floor in, and one near, a stretch of what appeared to be cages. The stench of blood, shit and urine permeated the air.

"I will explain later," Alli said. "Yasmine, please step behind me, I need to speak to—"

It was then that both Kim and Azim realised the woman who had followed Yasmine into the room was not Alex Ridley, as she had stepped into the light cast by the overhead fixtures.

"Taara? What the fuck are you doing back here?" Azim demanded. "Where is the Ridley woman?"

Taara answered, and her voice remained steady. "She is already here."

Chapter Fifty-Three

Kim saw the hint of a smile on the whore's face as something like fear began to grip him.

"Guard!" he yelled, and waved the armed henchman over to the centre of the room. "Kill this woman!" he ordered, gesturing towards Kayla Stone, while he dove for cover behind one of the stacks of canned goods.

The guard stepped up behind Kayla Stone, then drew his pistol and brought it up to the back of her skull.

"No!" Azim screamed as he shoved Yasmine to the ground behind another stack of crates and moved to take cover himself. Taara dove for the safety of the shadows at the edge of the room.

A single crack of gunfire rang out, loud and violent inside the metal building. A small red hole appeared on the guard's forehead as the back half of his head exploded behind him. His body crumpled to the floor; the pistol he had been holding landed on the concrete behind Kayla with a dull, metallic thud.

Kim glanced over at Azim's position. The shot had not come from his direction.

Ridley! he thought. Kim peered around the crates in the direction from which he thought the blast had emanated. The opposite end of the room was mostly dark, with the now-empty lines of chain-link cages marching into the blackness along either side of the warehouse.

"Ridley!" he called out. He was answered by another blast of gunfire as several cans in the stack exploded, raining chickpea soup and baked beans down on him. *You fucking bitch,* he thought, as he pointed his gun around the corner and fired two shots in her general direction.

Another shot came from Ridley's direction, striking the concrete floor only inches from Kim's feet. Just when he thought she had him pinned down, Kim heard another shot from only a few feet away, aimed downrange. Azim had joined the fight.

"Alex, there are two of them!" Kayla yelled out. "Both armed. Probably more outside!"

Kim glanced towards Kayla. He saw that she was struggling harder against her restraints and rocking back and forth on the wobbly wooden chair. It would be a shame, but he thought he just might have to put a bullet into her to shut her up and to keep her from causing any more problems.

"Ridley!" Azim called out. "You are outnumbered! We had a deal!"

Kim shook his head. *He doesn't know her like I do,* he thought. *She was not going to honour that deal any more than we were going to. We are in this to the death. Hers, or ours. The fool might serve as a distraction. If only he could draw her out, just enough to reveal her position...*

Ridley didn't answer. However, Kim could just make out the faintest of shuffling from her end of the warehouse. She was on the move. He decided it was time for him to start moving as well. He crept to the opposite corner of the stack of crates and started plotting a course from stack to stack, to work his way in Ridley's direction.

Kim began to move towards the next stack of crates when he caught faint movement in the shadows beyond. Ridley had already outflanked them. He instinctively dropped to the floor as another shot rang out. She was close enough that he saw the muzzle flash. Kim rolled onto his back and returned fire, sending two rounds towards the source of Ridley's last shot.

He heard a shriek of pain. It wasn't coming from Ridley's direction. *So, not Ridley. Who then?* It was behind him. It wasn't a woman's cry. It was Azim. Kim pushed himself back behind the stack of crates he had started from and moved to the side he judged to be in the lee of Ridley's gunfire. He glanced over his shoulder towards Azim's position.

"Told you so," Kayla mocked. "She's going to take you both apart. Piece by rotten piece."

"Shut your mouth, bitch!" Azim roared. Kim saw that he was holding his leg, keeping pressure on a wound. Blood was spreading outward from his hand, soaking the fabric of his trousers. Azim had managed to drag himself back to relative safety behind his own stack of boxes, but Kim saw that his pistol was left on the floor where it had fallen, in the open and out of reach. Azim was out of the fight, for now.

It was time to stop playing games. Kim raised his pistol towards Kayla and pointed it directly at her face.

"Ridley!" he called out. "This is over! I will kill Kayla Stone in ten seconds if you do not show yourself. Place your weapon on the floor and step forward! One!"

"Don't you do it Alex!" Kayla called out. "Please! He's a coward. He won't shoot!"

Kim looked at Kayla and laughed. "She knows me better than that," he told her. "Five seconds!"

"Don't fucking do it!" Kayla screamed as she strained maniacally against the ropes that bound her.

Four... Three... Two... Kim ticked them down in his head and began to apply pressure on the trigger.

"Okay," he heard from across the room. "I'm coming out."

"Alex no! They'll just kill us both!"

Kim edged his face around the corner of the crates and saw Ridley emerging from the shadows at the far end of the room. *Finally!*

"I had no choice, Kayla," Ridley said, her voice softened somewhat. She advanced to the centre of the room and stopped about fifteen feet from Kim's position behind the stack of crates.

Kayla was hysterical, struggling against her restraints and crying out. "They'll just kill us both!" she yelled, over and over.

She's not wrong, Kim thought, as he continued to hold Kayla in his gunsight. "Place your weapon on the floor," he called out to Ridley. "Then kick it in my direction!"

"I'm sorry, sweetheart," Ridley said as she began to kneel.

Kim peered around the corner to see that Ridley was complying. "On the floor!" he barked.

"Alex! *No!*" Kayla screamed, and shifted her weight backward as far as she could, bearing down on her restraints with every muscle in her body. There was an audible crack as the old chair splintered.

"Be fucking quiet, bitch!" a now rattled Kim yelled as

Kayla's chair collapsed, dropping her to the floor. Kim had had enough of the Stone woman, and fired in her general direction, a bullet whizzing through the air where her face had just been.

"No, Kim!" he heard Ridley yell, and Kim turned to face her, a grin spreading across his face.

Ridley winced as Kim fired at Kayla, and an enormous wave of relief shuddered through her as she saw the bullet miss her friend by mere inches. She knew she should finish this now, knew she should shoot the bastard in the head and end him. Yet, as the chance arose to shoot him, distracted as he had been by Kayla, something held her back, despite the pep talk she'd given herself sitting outside the dockyard container. A bullet to his head was simply too good for Do-Hyun Kim, and Ridley felt herself warming to the idea of a second fight with the dispicable human, in which she could dish out justice, Ridley style.

The Korean gangster turned to face her, and she wasn't surprised to see him grinning. Though, as she appraised the man, she also sensed a wariness about him, and that didn't surprise her either. They had fought like tigers beneath Mount Kailash, and although Ridley had come out on top in that battle, it had been very close. Too close. But she couldn't help it. She just had to fight him again, and more than just fight him. She had to beat him. Destroy his mind as well as his body.

Only then would she end him.

She dropped the gun at her feet, and kicked it away. Ridley half expected Kim to sieze the moment and shoot her. But she knew this man. Knew his weaknesses, and knew she had humiliated him up in Tibet. Men liked Kim couldn't handle that. Couldn't handle being bettered by a mere woman.

Instead, and to Ridley's great satisfaction, Kim also dropped his gun, though he didn't kick his as far away as Ridley had hers.

Ha, fucking coward, she thought, then said, "How nice to see you again, Do-Hyun. I'm going to enjoy watching you die."

Chapter Fifty-Four

Kim came at her fast, the knife leading in a vicious vertical thrust towards her chest. Ridley arched right, feeling the blade slice through the air inches from her ribs. She countered immediately—a snapping side kick that slammed into his thigh, surely rupturing blood vessels on impact.

He growled but kept coming, moving the knife into a reverse grip and slashing down hard. Ridley skipped back, the tip of the blade catching her shirt and opening a thin gash beneath her shoulder blade. Blood welled instantly, warm and stinging.

"I enjoyed that," Kim snarled, scarred knuckles white around the handle.

Ridley blocked out the pain and settled into her fighting stance. Kim was taller and stronger, and had a knife, but he wasn't skilled, and he fought like a caged animal—all wild aggression and zero control. Ridley knew she could use that to her advantage.

Kim lunged again, this time reaching for her exposed throat with his left hand while the knife came up hard in a belly-ripping motion. Ridley snagged his wrist and spun, using Kim's momentum to pull him off balance. Her sudden elbow strike crashed into his ribs, though his taut muscle absorbed most of the impact.

Kim twisted with the throw instead of fighting against it, straightening again with a backfist that bashed Ridley across the cheek. Her head snapped sideways, her vision blurring for a moment. Kim pushed his advantage, thrusting the knife towards Ridley's neck with a direct lunge.

Somehow she managed to squirm low under the blade and drove her knee up into his solar plexus. The man doubled over, but he managed to snatch at her leg before she could retreat. Kim yanked hard, sending Ridley off balance and crashing to the concrete floor.

She rolled as the knife came down fast, the point sparking off the floor where her head had been a fraction of a second before. Ridley scissored his legs, dropping him to one knee with the strength of her own, then scrambled to her feet.

"Stay fucking down, bitch!" Kim roared, spittle flying, and swishing the blade left and right in wide arcs to keep her at bay.

Yet, Ridley *was* skilled, experienced and, worse for Kim, she was patient. She awaited the right opening, dancing just outside his reach. This went on for several seconds, but Kim did not share Ridley's patience, and his naivety caused him to overextend on a particularly vicious slash, so she stepped in fast and drove her heel into his knee. She heard the joint buckle with a satisfying pop.

Kim screamed and stumbled, but Ridley expected the pain would only make him more wild, thus more dangerous. He switched the knife to his off-hand and began swinging wildly, abandoning any semblence of technique, and going full berserker.

One wild swing sliced Ridley across the forearm, yielding a gash from wrist to elbow. She hissed through her teeth but kept on the move, blood dripping steadily to the floor.

Kim was limping now, slowing slightly, favouring his damaged knee, but he was not yet finished. Far from it, Ridley guessed. She didn't know his full background, but she doubted he had become a human trafficking gangster because of a penchant for flower arranging. Besides, they had fought before and she knew he was tough. She remained cautious.

He feinted low then went high, the blade slicing towards her throat. Ridley strode back, but her heel caught on a steel O-ring set into the concrete floor. Her arms wind-milled, trying to keep balance. Kim was on her in a flash.

With an animalistic growl, his shoulder caught her in the sternum, driving her back into a concrete pillar. The hefty impact forced the breath from her lungs. Kim pressed his sudden advantage, pinning her against the pillar with his body weight, bringing the knife back up towards her neck.

Ridley thrashed, then grabbed his knife wrist with both hands, fighting to keep the blade away from her neck. Kim was stronger, and with slow, incremental gains, the point crept closer to her jugular.

"Should have... stayed in Tibet," Kim grunted, spittle flying from his lips. "Dead beneath that mountain."

The blade was an inch from her throat now. Kim's eyes were wild with bloodlust and the promise of revenge. Ridley could smell his sweat, and felt his hot breath on her face. Her arms shook from the effort of repelling his strength.

Then she remembered her training, and that sometimes you had to give ground to gain it.

"But I wasn't dead," Ridley growled, then suddenly released his wrist and ducked. The knife scraped against the concrete beam, sparks flying as Kim's momentum carried him forward. She squirmed under his arm and came up behind him, her hands quickly locating the pressure points Master Jae-won had taught her.

Her left thumb dug into the nerve cluster at the base of his neck. Her right hand struck the radial nerve in his forearm. Kim's grip spasmed and the knife clattered to the floor as her forehead slammed into his nose with an audible crunch.

But somehow, Kim still wasn't done. He spun about, his good arm swinging in a wide hook that smashed Ridley in the temple. Light flashed across her vision in an explosion of stars, and she staggered, almost falling.

Kim lunged for the knife, his fist closing around the handle just as Ridley's boot stomped hard on his wrist. Bones crunched under her heel, and he bellowed in agonised rage.

Ridley kicked the knife away and began to back off, but Kim grabbed her ankle with his uninjured hand. He yanked hard and, caught off guard, Ridley crashed down beside him. They tumbled across the concrete, Ridley grappling as if a life depended on it. But it wasn't her own life she was fighting for.

Kim scrambled on top of her, his hands closing around her neck. His damaged right wrist was useless, but his left hand was strong enough to potentially crush her windpipe. Black spots began flickering at the permieter of Ridley's vision.

With everything Ridley had left, she drove her knee up

into Kim's groin. His grip weakened as he rolled over in agony and she scooted out from beneath him.

Ridley struggled to her feet, exhausted, and with a collection of gashes and bruises. Kim cradled his destroyed wrist, his face a mask of fury, his pain evident. Ridley's throat felt on fire. Yet, as she raised her hands in a fighting stance, they remained steady as she remained poised.

She glared at Kim, remembering what he'd done to her in Tibet. How he'd tried to sell her to the monsters at the human market. How he'd tried to kill her. She also remembered how she'd told herself she had to finish this quickly, removing her emotion and thirst for revenge, and to simply kill him. But proper justice wouldn't really be served that way, she understood. She needed him to suffer. Needed to watch him die.

Kim charged one more time, leading with his shoulder in a desperate tackle. Ridley sidestepped at the last second and caught him with a perfect spinning heel kick to the temple. The impact sounded like a cricket bat hitting a melon.

Kim's legs collapsed from under him. His head hit the concrete hard. The Korean gangster did not get up. He didn't even move.

Ridley inhaled, and moved to stand over him, blood dripping from her various cuts. Kim was unconscious, but was still breathing as his body twitched slightly. She allowed the blood to fall onto the exposed skin of his arms. Ridley nudged him with her foot—no response.

The fight was over. She had beaten Kim, but barely. Her entire body ached, and the blood on her tongue from where she'd bitten it tasted like an old penny.

She was alive. She had won. Do-Hyun Kim was finished.

She spotted the fallen knife and kicked it towards Kayla, whose expression was one of shock and relief. "Are you okay?" Ridley called over to her friend.

Kayla was struggling to her feet. The legs of the broken chair were still lashed to her feet; her arms were still bound behind her, along with what remained of the shattered back of the chair.

Kayla nodded. "I'll be okay," she called out as she shuffled towards where Azim Alli lay, half-conscious from blood loss. Kayla reached Azim's gun and kicked it further away from him.

Ridley glanced at Kim, and saw that he was still alive. She inhaled again, slowly, and exhaled even slower. Then she raised her gun and pointed it at his face.

"Alex, don't!" Kayla cried. "He's already down! You beat him. It's over. You can't kill in cold blood!"

Ridley shook her head. Images of their brutal fight under Mount Kailash swirled like a kaleidoscope in her mind. How he taunted her. How he'd threatened to rape her and then kill her. "No," Ridley said calmly, towering over Kim's inert form. "You're wrong, sweetie. He's already dead. He has been dead since the moment he met me in India. He was dead the moment he decided to kidnap me. He was dead the moment he failed to kill me in Tibet."

"No, Alex!" Kayla screamed, at the same moment Kim suddenly twitched and sat up, which was exactly the same moment Ridley grinned down at Kim and squeezed the trigger.

Chapter Fifty-Five

Azim Alli sat in The Vulture's office chair, which Taara had fetched from the office cubicle. After untying Kayla from the remnants of her restraints, she and Ridley had lifted him up into the chair. Ridley used a length of Kayla's rope to cinch around Azim's thigh as a tourniquet, to try to staunch the flow of blood.

Taara stood a respectful distance away, watching.

Yasmine had emerged from the shadows and stood in front of her father, crying.

At the sound of her cries, Azim lifted his head slightly, and opened his eyes. "My little flower," he said weakly.

"Father! What have you done?" Yasmine cried. "How could you? All those women? Girls? Like me?"

Azim slowly blinked, his eyes moist. "I..." he started, "I... I did everything for you. And your mother..."

Yasmine's cries turned to anger. "Do not say that!" she yelled. "Don't you dare say you kidnapped and killed... for me! Don't you say that!"

Azim was silent for a long moment, fidgeting on the

spot, eyelids flickering as if fighting back tears. He faltered too, as if weakening from blood loss. Finally, he spoke. "I am... I am so sorry." The big man closed his eyes.

"Yasmine," Ridley said softly from behind her. "You have to go now. Taara will take you outside."

Yasmine turned and looked at Ridley, then over at Kayla. Tears streamed down over her now puffy cheeks. "I am not going anywhere," she stated.

"Sweetie, this is not over yet," Ridley said. "Far from over. You know what we have to do next. You shouldn't be here for this."

"I am not just a girl anymore," Yasmine said, a determined expression hardening her features. "My eyes are opening now, finally. I see the world as it truly is, not just as it has been presented to me. I know, now, that evil exists, and sometimes it is closer to us than we realise. But... I also understand what must be done about it." Yasmine stepped back two paces.

Ridley nodded, and stepped forward.

Kayla moved closer. "You don't have to do this, Alex," Kayla pleaded, "please listen. This isn't you."

"Someone has to end this," Ridley said coldly as she raised the gun. The barrel was barely two feet from Azim's head. She began to apply pressure to the trigger.

Azim opened his eyes again. "There are other Vultures," he said, his voice now barely audible.

Ridley froze, her finger applying half-pressure to the trigger.

Kayla stepped closer still. "What did you say? Other Vultures?"

Azim nodded, almost imperceptibly, and exhaled, unsteady on his feet. "Yes, others, like him." He nodded vaguely in the direction of his boss's fallen body.

"Other exchanges. Like the one in Kailash. In other countries."

Ridley rushed forward now, placing the gun directly against the side of Azim's head. "Where?" she demanded.

Azim looked at Ridley, his eyes swivelling tiredly in their sockets. Then he swung his gaze towards Kayla. "You and the others were to be sent to Milan... There are more, I believe, to be delivered to Morocco... and elsewhere. I will tell you what I know. I will tell you everything... but on one condition."

"You are in no position to cut deals," Ridley spat impatiently.

Azim nodded. "I know you must kill me. It is also what I would do. I see it in your eyes. You are a killer, too. One knows another. My request is only that you do not do it in front of my daughter. I do not want my little flower to see this."

Ridley looked at Kayla. Kayla nodded. Ridley pulled the gun away and stepped back.

"Start talking," she said.

Chapter Fifty-Six

In the end, Ridley did not have to shoot Azim again, thoguh she was prepared to do it. He succumbed to his earlier wound, due to loss of blood. In the meantime, he had divulged what little he knew about a slave market in Milan, Italy. He died before he could relay any actionable information about that particular facility.

It wasn't a huge amount, but the women managed to get what they believed was nevertheless valuable intelligence from him before he expired. The merchants in Italy were based in Milan. Azim didn't have proper names or a specific address, but he directed Kayla to retrieve a certain black notepad from The Vulture's jacket pocket, which contained phone numbers and nicknames. They learned that the shipment was to be delivered to the Italian port of Genoa, along with the ship's identification and arrival date.

"There's more," Azim had said. "A safe, inside the office, over there." Azim recited the combination, which Kayla scribbled on to one of the pages of The Vulture's notebook.

"There is some cash. Give it to my little flower, as I... I will no longer be around to provide for her."

It turned out there was over half a million dollars in U.S. currency stacked inside the safe, along with various other papers and financial instruments. Kayla dumped the contents of the office wastebasket onto the floor, then removed the plastic bag that lined the wastebasket and filled it with cash.

"It's yours," Ridley told Yasmine. "Take it."

"I do not want it," Yasmine declared as she tossed a banded pack of one-hundred-dollar bills back on to the pile of money. "Any of it. It is dirty money."

The cash sat in a pile at the edge of the loading dock. Ridley, Kayla, Taara and Yasmine stood on the ground in a half-circle around it. After Azim had taken his last breath, Ridley and Kayla had emerged from the warehouse to where Taara and Yasmine were waiting, to deliver the news.

Yasmine had cried briefly when Ridley told her that her father was dead. Yet she had found her composure, stood up straight, and looked at each of the women in turn. "What is next?"

The money had been the next order of business, after Kayla had dumped it from the plastic bag into a pile at the edge of the dock.

"He wanted to make sure you were taken care of," Ridley said. "It was his final act, as a father, and as a man. It doesn't make up for his crimes, but he left this world thinking of his daughter and trying to provide for you."

"I still do not want it," Yasmine repeated. "My mother's family has means. I will be starting college soon. I will be fine." She looked once more at each of the women in the group, and then her gaze settled on Taara.

"You take it," she told the former prostitute.

"Me?" Taara said, looking up in surprise. "Sweet child, I have no more desire for tainted money than you do."

"You were a victim of these people, too, Taara," Kayla said. "Take it. Look after your family. Take it all and leave this life behind. Share it with the others."

Tears welled up in Taara's wide eyes.

"Yes," Ridley agreed. "That makes the most sense. Take the money, Taara, and use it to right some of the wrongs these people have committed. I have only one request, though. See to the girls and young women we liberated today. Make sure they are taken care of, until they are repatriated and returned to their families."

Taara was crying profusely now, the tears streaming down her cheeks as she nodded in agreement. After a few deep breaths, she said, "I will, I promise. I will make a large anonymous donation to the authorities tomorrow morning, with instructions to use the funds to help those girls."

Ridley, Kayla and Yasmine stepped forward and embraced Taara in a group hug, holding each other for several moments. "We have to go now," Ridley said. "Kayla and I have work to do, and we need to clear out of here before the police show up."

The women broke their huddle. Ridley and Kayla started backing away. "You'll call the police, as we agreed?"

Taara nodded. "Of course. After you two, and Yasmine, have left. Yasmine can take the money away; I will retrieve it from her afterwards. I will wait here for the police and explain to them what has happened here."

Ridley nodded. "They will find several more bodies scattered throughout this complex. Let them find them on their own. It's important that you know nothing of the others. Only what you have seen yourself."

Taara nodded. "Of course. I will direct them to the location where I left the freed captives."

Ridley looked at Yasmine. "You were never here. You know nothing about any of this."

Yasmine nodded in understanding.

"And you?" Taara asked. "They will want to know who did all of this."

Ridley thought for a moment. She looked from Taara to Kayla, and then up at the warehouse that now entombed Azim Alli, Do-Hyun Kim, The Vulture, one of the female captives and a handful of the guards. She thought of the chain link cages that had held the abducted women. The shit buckets, and the stacks of canned food. She looked at the ocean container that was still backed up to the loading dock, which would never receive its human cargo to be delivered to the port. Finally, she looked back at Taara.

"Tell them it was… just some Vigilante."

Epilogue

Alexandria Ridley felt at peace. Relatively.

She had mentally blocked out all the noise and bustle of the frazzled passengers as they angrily tried shoving over-sized hand luggage into any tiny space they could find in the overhead compartments. She ignored the whining of a child in the seat behind, repeatedly asking her mother how long the flight would take. Ridley inhaled as she turned away from the ignorant bastard who hadn't noticed he'd rested his considerable arse on her shoulder. She took a long, deep breath, then exhaled slowly.

It was okay. Something had grasped her soul.

Long, silken notes of Italian opera picked their way through the chaos, bringing with them four hundred years of history and the passion of an entire country. The music was being pumped into the Alitalia 747 to give passengers a taste of the place into which they would arrive some dozen hours later. Ridley glanced about. Most of them didn't even seem to notice it was playing.

But for Ridley, the rising and falling notes in the female

singer's voice, delivering anguish and delicate beauty all in one bar, had transported her to another world, transcended her above the humming maelstrom of the cabin. Just for a moment. Before the real world pulled her back.

"Alex!" Kayla Stone said for the third time. It was the first Ridley had heard. "He needs to get to his seat!"

Ridley looked up and saw a man towering over her. Black curls of hair were matted to his huge, round head. His shirt—which may have been light brown through either dirt or design—was so drenched in sweat it was being sucked into the crevices of his ample belly. As she stood to let him pass to the window seat, the guy fixed her with a look that said, *Don't you ever make me wait again.*

Refusing to look away, Ridley held his stare. She was not surprised when, barely five seconds later, the look in his eyes morphed, shifting from threatening, to confused, and finally, to afraid. She knew that most people who delivered threats crumbled at the slightest resistance. He lowered his gaze to the floor and shuffled with some effort into his seat. Ridley hadn't practiced the look she had given him. It just came naturally. It had worked again.

"You okay?" Kayla asked her friend.

"Yeah. Why?"

"You seemed miles away."

"Huh! I guess I was."

Five minutes later, as the final pieces of luggage were being packed away—forced would've been a better adjective—the last of the passengers finally took their seats. A member of the crew then announced "Boarding complete." It was obvious the flight was only half full. Ridley abstractedly mused that there was way too much luggage for so few passengers. *Ah, consumerism.* There were rows of empty seats, and people who wanted to get some shuteye were already eyeing the vacant spots.

The big man was staring longingly at a row across the aisle. He plucked up the courage to look Ridley in the eye, and smiled at her the way a child smiles at his kindergarten teacher. He was now at her mercy. The two women stood to let him out. Ridley forced herself to smile back.

His smile said, *I'm no threat to you, so please don't hurt me.*

A few minutes after takeoff, the aircraft had levelled out and the seatbelt signs had pinged off. The serenity of the opera was long gone. Ridley suddenly felt anxiety gripping her chest. This was almost always how it took hold of her. She believed she was comfortable, her mind at rest. Then the distress would come from out of nowhere, unbidden, like a black dog leaping from the shadows in the night. The trauma she had experienced in her mid to recent past had not been the cause of this affliction. She had suffered from it for most of her life. It was fair to say that dealing with those demons had not been made easier by recent experiences.

She tried to ignore the feeling and eyed the drinks cart being trundled far too slowly in her direction, taunting her with its snail-like progress. When her hand was finally around a cold plastic cup containing her double gin and tonic, she turned to her companion. She looked into Kayla's sparkling green eyes and felt a wave of affection.

"How're you doing, sweetie?" Ridley asked.

Kayla smiled and touched her cup to Ridley's. "I'm good. For now," she said. Ridley assumed the warmth of the alcohol, the drone of the engine and being 30,000 feet from any of the horrors they had recently faced had afforded a calming effect on both of them. "How about you?" Kayla muttered, motioning with her head to the big man now across the aisle. "I thought you were going to kill that guy!"

"He's okay. As long as he doesn't have the audacity to make me... stand up again."

The two of them enjoyed a moment of feeling normal. Drinking, talking and resting. It wasn't much to ask.

"Seriously, though," Kayla said, "we've both been through a lot. If you ever need to talk to me, please do. About anything."

"I will."

Ridley looked into her drink, then back into Kayla's eyes.

"What is it?" Kayla asked.

Ridley paused for a beat, then nodded, as if to herself. "We'll never be the same, you know. What we've seen. The things we've done. There's no going back."

"I know," Kayla replied quietly. "That doesn't make us freaks. Most people know about the appalling shit we've seen, even if they haven't witnessed it with their own eyes. Yet they go about their business, having fun, killing time. Wilfully ignorant. It's depressing."

"You're right. While there are still women suffering like those we helped in Mumbai, how the hell can we stop? How could we focus on anything else? I couldn't deal with wasting my life like that. I won't do it."

"Exactly right." Kayla turned away and rested her head on the seat.

Ridley knew and understood well the emotions her friend was experiencing. Sad resignation. She'd felt it herself, in the past. Recently, those feelings had been replaced by only one thing; unwavering determination. She thought about the women she had seen in chains in the caves in Tibet, where she too had been held. She remembered the brutality of her captors. She saw the faces of those in the cages in Mumbai. Unlike, she suspected, most who had lived through what she had, Ridley did not want to forget. She did not want to recover or heal, and believed she never could. It was better not to let the faces of those people who had tormented her and others fade from her memory. Remembering the coldness in their eyes, the evil, would spur her on as she sought out others just like them. Other disgusting predatory criminals.

She was now a hunter, and it was her job to understand her prey. Her duty!

The bleak, broken world that existed beneath the surface of Mumbai life also entered her mind. The children who had no idea that their privileged education was being paid for by the ill-gotten gains of human trafficking. The kids on the other side of the equation, who would have no education at all after their mothers were cruelly taken from them, all to satisfy fleeting lust and to funnel wealth to people who did not deserve it. The horrific effects of such crimes would be experienced for generations, and Ridley forced herself to acknowledge that as motivation for the challenges and dangers to come.

Ridley badly wanted another drink. But tiredness overcame her. She glanced at her friend, who had closed her eyes and appeared to be peaceful, and for the first time in too long, with not a care in the world. She wondered how many other people on the plane were suffering beneath their serene exterior. Then, she tried to get a few hours rest.

After fitful sleep, in which Ridley had dreams about things she'd never mention, she was awoken by an announcement from the pilot. She leaned over and gave Kayla a gentle shove. Passengers began to shuffle around them, their spirits lifted by thoughts of Milan's magnificent sights and enchanting culture. Probably the shopping.

For Ridley, and surely Kayla too, she thought, it will be different. Ridley's thoughts were filled with altogether more sombre things.

Horrors that beckoned. Dangers that lurked around corners and in holes they would deliberately seek out.

Another world waiting for them, down on the ground.

I, Guardian: Prologue

MILAN, ITALY

The late afternoon sun embraced Parco Sempioni, its rays falling on couples strolling arm-in-arm and families enjoying picnics on the vivid green grass. A lazy, languid feel graced the area, which provided a welcome change from the noise, traffic and loosely organised chaos of central Milan. Beneath a range of towering trees, a small but relatively appreciative crowd had gathered to watch a local busker. He was tall and, he supposed, reasonably handsome—his mother told him he was—with long, black hair pulled into a tight knot that stretched his olive-coloured skin over high cheekbones.

The performer smiled as he wrapped his mouth around the words of an enchanting love song. He knew tourists were often smitten by the way he delivered the Italian language to their ears. Equally, Milanese natives enjoyed hearing songs they remembered fondly from their child-hoods, family gatherings and youthful romantic encounters.

Once upon a time, many years ago, he used to get a buzz from the adoration he received. Maybe it had been vanity, or maybe he had genuinely enjoyed making people happy. It was difficult to remember. Most of his memories were blurred for one reason or another. Yet, *happy* was no longer a word that entered his mind, at least not often. He was delivering joy coldly. Joy was a means to an end. Happiness had become a commodity. The end in question was a long, long way from joyful.

At the southeastern end of the sprawling park, shadows began to fall across the medieval ramparts of the giant Sforzesco Castle as the busker worked his way through a set of carefully chosen songs. The jagged 15th-century architecture of the looming fortress became increasingly imposing as dusk slowly took hold and the final visitors departed through the massive castle gates or dispersed throughout the park.

A level of darkness had arrived that ushered out the slow, carefree afternoon and gave people the sense they should perhaps head home, or head on out to dinner. He suspected many others were beginning to anticipate the hi-octane vibrancy of a night on the wild Milanese tiles.

Francesco finished up his song and the crowd dispersed, offering weak smiles of appreciation or simply turning their backs on him. Only a few threw coins in the receptacle at his feet. He would love to have told them where they could stick their paltry coins, of which he had no need.

One person was still watching. Francesco was well aware of her presence, though he was able to avoid looking her way too often. Just one glance, and one smile, that was sufficient. For now, it was enough for her to know that he had noticed her. It was also enough for him to have clocked the contours of her perfect figure through the thin fabric of her colourful floral dress.

As people moved out of the park, away to bars, restaurants or the comforts of home, Francesco changed his song. He chose a sorrowful ballad about the loneliness of a lover scorned. His notes drifted through the air, long and soft.

The woman eyed him intently, observing his mouth as it formed the words and watching his long, dexterous fingers caress the frets on his acoustic guitar.

He could almost be described as *beautiful*, she thought. An unusual word to be used to describe a man, but in this case it was the word that came naturally to her mind. Conversely, he also appeared rugged, and she imagined rough hands and scuffed boots, though she was too far away to know for sure. She had come to Italy for adventure. This guy looked as if he could bring it right to her.

She was lying on the grass, and could smell the soil, still warm from the heat of the day. She realised that she was digging her fingers into the ground, massaging the earth. Her manicured nails would be dirty, but she didn't care. Picking up her small plastic cup filled with cheap red wine, she looked up to the sky that was bruising purple over Milan.

She took a sip and ignored the sharp edge of the flavour, instead managing to pick out the sweet and fruity notes beneath. One facet of her trip had been to become more aware of herself. She had recently been practicing meditation and mindfulness. Part of this mindfulness focused on paying attention to all of her senses, that culminated now, drinking warm red wine in a darkening park, in a joyous moment in which she was thrilled to be on this Italian odyssey. An odyssey that was only just beginning.

The busker's final note lingered before fading out and floating away on the gentle breeze. The girl clapped, which is when she first truly realised she was now forming an audience of one. He nodded at her and offered a shy smile, seemingly careful to acknowledge her only casually, making her wonder for a moment if he was really interested in her presence at all. He took a moment to slowly and carefully place his guitar into its case. Then, almost coyly, he beckoned her over, waving a bottle of wine in his hand and raising his eyebrows, as if to say, *You can join me—if you wish?*

The girl waited for just a few seconds so as not to appear too keen, then pushed herself up off the floor. She glided gracefully towards him, her dress swaying lightly in the warm breeze.

"You are very talented," she said when she reached him. "Oh, and, hello."

"Grazie," he replied, then added, "Thank you. But if I was really talented, I wouldn't be playing in a park to only one person."

They had both defaulted to English. She assumed the guy was Italian, but he couldn't know where she was from.

"Well, your very small audience really enjoyed your playing," the girl said.

She caught him admiring her blonde hair, that fell down onto her feminine shoulders in voluminous curls.

"A happy audience of one is better than a bored audience of one thousand," he replied.

She nodded, smiling shyly. "That is true."

"Um, how about some wine?"

"Why not?"

The handsome busker pulled another small bottle from his bag and twisted off the cap. He unleashed the whole lot into her plastic cup, and she smiled as she watched the large measure being poured.

"Do not worry," he said. "Wine in Italy is cheap!"

"I know. I've been buying plenty of it since I arrived."

"What's your name?"

"Eliise."

"I am Francesco."

They touched cups.

"Nice to meet you, Francesco."

"Piacere di conoscerti," he said, the words rolling off his tongue like they did in the movies. "Nice to meet you too… um, Eliise?"

She nodded.

"Where are you from, Eliise?" he asked.

"Guess!"

"You are not Italian, I think. You have a… a different kind of beauty."

Eliise felt a sudden warmth in her chest when he described her that way. She was impressed by how he had managed to deliver the compliment subtly, instead of telling her she was beautiful too directly. However, she combined a smile with a frown, as if the statement had been strange, not pleasing. As if she were surprised that anyone would take note of her beauty, despite the reality that people did it often.

"Your appearance is quite Nordic," Francesco continued, his eyes slowly taking in every detail of her face. "However… I think you are from… no, I am sure of it. You are from Estonia… si?"

Ellise had to stop her mouth from falling open, she was so shocked. She then noticed what seemed to be the nervous glance Francesco gave to a passerby over her shoulder. She turned, but only saw another guy passing by without paying them any attention.

Ignoring the slightest hint of confusion, she said, "That's amazing," then turned back to him, realising the soft pronunciation of the 'z' in her accent probably hinted at where she was from.

Francesco had studied a lot of accents and a lot of faces. People always loved it when he 'guessed' where they were from. It had proven to be a very useful skill to have.

"Am I right?" he asked, turning his attention back to her. It wasn't a question.

"Yes! How did you know?"

"Just a lucky guess! How long have you been in Italy?"

"Only a few days. This is my first time in Milan."

"Really? Well, if it doesn't seem too forward, would you let me show you some places? I love to teach people about my city."

"Yes, please. That would be wonderful. So, you're from Milan?"

Francesco nodded. "Yes, I am. Bring your wine," he said as he pointed towards the edge of the park. They made their way over to the treeline. The purple sky had morphed quickly to black, and this corner of the park was barely lit, but for the uplights illuminating a series of modern sculptures.

As they walked across the grass, Francesco caught a glimpse of the girl admiring the Arco della Pace, the grand triumphal arch that stood at the far end of the park. She gazed in awe at the stunning monument. Francesco took the opportunity to have a quick look around.

"Here," he announced when they'd reached a striking, angular sculpture. "This piece is by Antonio Verdi. There are several sculptures in and around this park, but this one is my favourite."

He watched as Eliise tried to speak, likely to say something about the sculpture. But she couldn't say anything at all. He knew her head was fuzzy and that her legs were suddenly feeling weak. He counted down from five in his mind, and just as he got to three, she reached out, then collapsed into Francesco's arms.

A sudden wooziness had come over Eliise, and she reached for Francesco, feeling nauseous and assuming it was down to dodgy wine. She felt him grab her around the shoulders, preventing her from falling, and though she fought it, her eyes closed.

Then, and with the last of her consciousness, Eliise felt branches slapping at her legs and ripping at her dress. Things were suddenly moving fast, and her heels were dragging across the ground.

Then, the world went as black as the sky.

I, Guardian: Chapter One

Here we go again, she mused, with no pleasure at all. There would be no fun Alexandria Ridley in Milan. Not this time.

Luckily, fun was the last thing on Ridley's mind. There would be some satisfaction if she were succesful on her mission, and she would allow that satisfaction in whatever form it took, and whatever level. But that was all. It would be business as usual, and she would get in, get the job done, and get the fuck out of there... on to the next one.

And that would be enough. Would it always be enough? Probably not. But for now the mission was simple: bring the bastards down.

She took her place in the immigration line after a surprisingly short time getting from the aeroplane into the terminal, via a bus and a long walk. In front of her in the line was a family of 6... just her luck... and behind her a young, glamorous couple, Italian, she thought, who couldn't keep their hands off each other, despite the very public nature of the surroundings. Ridley almost grinned. Not quite.

She had been young once, and if she were really honest with herself, she'd even been in love. Yet, she quashed all thoughts of whimsy and turned back to the queue. Her mind focused itself on getting through this latest small challenge... immigration. She had a fake passport, and her tickets were under a fake name. Although confident she would get through unhindered, it was by no means guaranteed, and in her stomach a small knot began to form and tighten just a little.

A flicker of movement to her right caught her eye and she turned casually to take a look. Two men stood beyond the lines, leaning casually against a wall in quiet conversation. Neither were looking at her, but she sensed they had been. It wasn't unusual to feel eyes on her. Men would smile at Ridley often. Although she wouldn't admit it, she had been told often she was beautiful. With her long, dark hair and flawless skin that had once been described as café au lait by a cheesy, would-be suitor, people were somehow drawn to her, which both amused her as well as surprised her and made her uncomfortable all at once. She had enough experience to know when a smile preceded a come-on. In those cases, she almost never smiled back. She could handle those situations with a firm stare of her own and a raised chin, as if to say, *I know your type... don't even think about it.*

It was the subtle, sideways glances that bothered Ridley more. Not the come-ons... not the slimy bastards she'd see in bars or on street corners. It was the subtle, yet confident attention she got from strangers, usually well-dressed, often good-looking. These men weren't trying to make a move on Ridley because she was beautiful. It was because they saw her as a commodity. An object. Something to be bought, or sold, or traded. She knew those types all too well, unfortunately… and luckily her spidy senses were well tuned to those fuckers.

But there was another kind she was aware of, and right now they concerned her the most. The two men she sensed had half an eye on her were from neither of the other two categories. Right now, these were more troublesome. They looked official: authorative, unfussed and unflustered. The type who might just arrest her for the criminal that she was. And Ridley being arrested was something she could not allow right now.

Yet, once again Ridley understood she was at the whim of fate. She *was* a criminal, that much was true. Though of course, the criminal deeds she had committed in India recently were more than worthy of the acts. The people she had hurt to emancipate the poor stolen women had deserved what she had done to them, and more. A lot more. But she knew that would not be enough to convince the Italian authorities of her crusade.

She glanced over at the two men again, and caught one of them staring at her. Not in a threatening way; it was more of a *I know who you are* look, which worried Ridley more than anything.

It was possible they weren't official airport security or border patrol at all. That would have been bad enough. No, the worst case scenario was that they were part of the same criminal world she was here to destroy. If they knew who she was, then word had gotten out of India—Mumbai in particular—and had made her presence in Italy known. Which meant that she would likely get through immigration without any issues, but then her real problems would begin.

So, what could she do? There was nothing for it. Keep her head down. Speak to immigration officers only when asked a question. Smile when it was appropriate. Then get the hell through here and out into the arrivals hall, meet up with Kayla Stone, remain vgilant at all times, and be prepared for anything.

For if there was one thing Ridley knew above all else, it was that the people she had dealt with in India, and the people she would be dealing with here in Italy, were cold, calculated, clever, decisive, and willing to do whatever it took to maintain their criminal operations. Killing Ridley in cold blood... even in public... was definitely something they were capable of.

But Ridley would be ready. For anything.

Fifteen minutes later, she had passed through immigration with a nod and a smile, and no shortage of relief that her fake passport had passed the rather casual examination by the young border agent. With no luggage to collect, she made her way towards the Arrivals hall and looked out for Kayla, who had been in another immigration line due to her Australian passport.

With her head on a gentle swivel, keeping her eyes busy looking out for threats and more importantly, the two men she believed had clocked her in immigration, she soon spotted Kayla emerging from a bathroom and made her way over to her friend as casual as possible. One couldn't miss Kayla Stone. Tall, perhaps five ten, with blonde hair and a figure to die for, she could have stepped right out of Sports Illustrated, though Kayla was barely aware of her stunning natural beauty herself. Between the two of them— Ridley was a similar height and build, though her hair was the colour of a raven's feathers—Ridley understood they tended to stand out in most places... though if there was anywhere that would be diminished, Milan would be high on the list, with all the glitz and glamour on show, even in the airport.

"There you are," Kayla stated as she spotted Ridley. "You had me, you know, worried there for a moment. Glad you made it through."

"Me too," Ridley replied, allowing herself a slow exhale as the relief of getting through finally became real. She remained serious when she asked, "Erm, so... have you seen anyone who kept an eye on you a beat to long? As in, do you think anyone recognised you?"

Kayla shook her head. "No, I don't think so. The usual stares from hormonal boys, and the occasional nod from an Armani-wearing, slick-haired grandfather, but that's it. How about you?"

Ridley didn't feel the need to raise attention to the fact she thought she'd been recognised, and instead just shook her head. Kayla was good, but if she suddenly started looking around nervously if Ridley did mention the two guys from immigration, that would only serve to prove they were 'people of interest'.

So, she said nothing, and led her friend to the exits amid the throngs of tourists and locals returning home from who knew where.

Oustide, they soon reached the front of a taxi queue, and within minutes were racing through busy streets towards downtown Milan, and to dangers known, but as yet, untold.

I, Guardian: Chapter Two

The stifling heat of the day still radiated back off the ancient red brick walls of the church of Santa Maria delle Grazie.

Filippo leaned against the 15th-century edifice, his mind completely oblivious to any of the building's numerous wonders. He absentmindedly lit another cigarette as his eyes moved along a queue of people waiting to enter the famous church.

Inside the historic walls, Leonardo Da Vinci's *The Last Supper* was pride of place, displayed in all its glory adorning the entire back wall of the refectory in the convent. The world famous painting was not only housed by the church, but was entwined within its history. Da Vinci was commissioned by Ludovico Sforza, Duke of Milan, to complete the work in the late 1400s as part of the church's renovations.

It is said that Da Vinci found inspiration for the appearance of people in the painting by walking the streets of Milan and studying faces. The prior of the convent supposedly complained to Sforza about the artist's laziness in trying to find a criminal on the streets who would inspire his depiction of Judas.

Had Da Vinci walked the streets today, Filippo's surly countenance might have caught his eye. In the darkness, it was hard to tell the scars from the wrinkles among the deep lines on his weathered face. Although only in his forties, the man had chipped, tobacco-stained teeth and dull, lifeless eyes beneath greasy, thinning hair. His less than attractive facial features contrasted with the fine, expensive clothes he had carefully chosen.

Unlike his younger brother, Francesco, he never had been able to rely on his looks when it came to attracting female attention. He had given up on that long ago, and it was convenient that he could abuse his body—or use it to abuse others—however he wanted. He didn't have to worry about any good looks to ruin.

His clothes were what made him stand out, at least to those who were drawn in by that sort of superficial exterior. Beneath his heavy leather jacket was an immaculately white Dolce & Gabbana shirt, pressed to perfection by his house-keeper, an illegal Indonesian immigrant, who lived in constant fear that he would punish her for the smallest mistake. She had tried to leave his service once. In turn, he had made it clear that the consequences if she left would be unbearable. In his cold, calm manner, Filippo had promised Mai that he would let her live a new life for an undefined amount of time, before seeking her out and delivering his punishment at a moment of his choosing.

The evil he committed against other women was not usually centred around psychological attacks. Instead, it was physical in the extreme. He had decided that inflicting psychological torment was something to savour, at least as a build up to the physical suffering that would come later.

Filippo's haute couture shirt concealed tiny red punctures on the inside of his arm... an occasional pleasure he believed he could keep under control. In reality, he only had limited control over almost everything he did. His temper, for example, was something he had never been able to keep a grip on. Instead, he preferred to focus on the things he did well. Seducing women, or rather tricking them, was a skill he was proud of. He would be putting that skill to good use tonight.

For now, Filippo was keeping himself hidden in the shadows created by the lights that illuminated the church. Soon, he would make himself known. His eyes remained fixed on a group of young women chatting excitedly at the entrance to the church. Through the buzz of Milan's traffic and the chatter from customers outside nearby cafes and bars, he could just about make out their conversation.

"I envy you," one girl said to a companion, who had long, toned legs, dark skin and a figure-hugging evening dress that had clearly been picked out for a special occasion. As Filippo well knew, there was a special event tonight. It allowed entry to the gallery, and included free bubbles and canapes, and a talk from a local art historian.

"Sorry!" the long-legged girl replied. "I was lucky to get this ticket, but I wasn't lucky enough to get two. My brother knows someone who knows someone at the University of Milan."

Filippo believed her accent was Swedish. Picking out accents was something he was good at. It was a very useful skill to have, and one he shared with his brother.

"Just enjoy it," the girl's friend told her. "Tell us all about it later. See you at the bar."

The Swedish girl showed her ticket to the guy in the booth,

then made her way into the church, turning to give her friends a final wave before going inside. As the line of people slowly shuffled their way into the building, Filippo dropped his smoke to the floor and stubbed it out with the tip of his pointed leather boot. He strode over to the entrance, throwing a brief but knowing glance towards the man in the booth. He received a subtle nod in return, and the slightest hint of a smile.

Inside the church, Filippo's eyes scanned the vast space, which appeared unlike any church usually would. It was tastefully and understatedly lit for an evening of art and conversation, as much as for a place in which to be seen, as opposed to a religious service. It had the vibe and feel of an upscale Milanese bar, rather than a place of worship. People were supposedly there to admire a famous piece of medieval art, but the event itself was ultra-Milan.

Instead of a sanctified deity, the place now represented the religion of glamour and the worship of aesthetics.

Not that Filippo had the slightest concern for those aesthetics. His eyes searched for that woman. That figure. It didn't take long. He caught sight of the Swedish girl, lingering awkwardly next to the table that displayed abundant glasses of complimentary prosecco lined up in several long rows. The display suggested that the organisers of the event thought artistic masterpieces were best enjoyed with double vision, and added to the deliberate impression that this was an opulent occasion. Clearly, Filippo realised, his target wasn't used to these kinds of events. She was out of place, and it was obvious. He smiled inwardly. *That makes things easier…*

Curling one side of his mouth into a charming outward smile, Filippo deftly picked up two glasses and made his way towards the girl.

"You look thirsty," he said, smiling and offering her a glass.

The girl looked down at his diamond cufflink glistening under the lights.

"I am thirsty," she replied, smiling back.

"Then I hope this will refresh you. I find prosecco highly refreshing. Where are you from?"

"Sweden. Malmo."

"Ah yes, Malmo. It is a beautiful city. I have been many times, mostly on business."

Filippo watched as her eyebrows rose in predictable surprise. "Oh, really? What business are you in… if you don't mind me asking."

"I don't mind at all. I'm an art dealer."

"Wow. That's so cool."

Filippo shrugged. "Kind of. I love that it takes me to so many interesting places all around the world. But the people I have to associate with… "—Filippo leaned in towards the girl with a conspiratorial manner—"… not so much. To tell you the truth, they are all a little fake."

"Well, I hope the art you deal in isn't fake!"

Filippo grinned. He sensed this young woman could be very likeable. Witty, pretty and… that body. This kind of thing occurred to him from time to time. Fortunately for Filippo, he had become very skilled at dehumanising most people. In fact, all people, but especially women.

"No, no. I only deal with the very finest works. And the most authentic. In fact, I'm thinking about picking up that attractive looking piece before the end of the evening."

Filippo tilted his glass in the direction of *The Last Supper*. He gave a wry smile to let the girl know he was joking. She turned her head towards the huge, world-renowned mural painting, then laughed. She was no art expert, but even she knew that masterpieces like that are not 'dealt.' Besides, it was painted directly onto the immovable wall. It wasn't going anywhere.

"So, may I ask… what's your name?" Filippo said.

"Maja."

"I am Antonio," he lied. "Shall we survey the room, Maja? You know, most people are only here to look at each other, and be looked at in turn. They will barely appreciate the artwork at all."

Filippo led Maja around the atmospheric interior of the refectory, quietly whispering the names of artists, fashion leaders and other Milanese glitterati he saw mingling around the room. He made sure to keep Maja supplied with bubbles, and smiled inwardly as she finished the third.

Maja hiccupped, and apologised, suitably embarrassed.

I feel a little tipsy already, she thought. *And only two glasses. Or was it three?* From attending weddings and a few other family celebrations, during which she had previously consumed the drink, or similar bubbles, she knew it brought about a strange kind of drunkenness unlike any other type of booze. The kind that makes you light-headed, spacey and a little giddy. From experience, she knew that if she'd been in hot weather all day or had been in a chaotic, unfamiliar environment, being tipsy on bubbles often felt more akin to being stoned.

Maja looked around the space. The people filling it were either fairly young and ridiculously thin, or slightly lumpy and packed into ill-fitting clothes. No doubt the latter were examples of what the former would become, after what they believed were simply a few years of youthful indulgence, slowly becoming an addiction to rich food and fine wine.

She felt almost certain many of them had semi-controllable compulsions for white lines of fine powder, but that was more difficult to ascertain from appearance alone.

Either way, through slightly blurred vision Maja saw a scene of contorted bodies and faces, their mouths rattling away and their eyes rolling with self-importance. Even the chiseled jaws and pouting lips seemed grotesque. She didn't know it—would never believe it— but Maja was by far the most beautiful person in the room.

After a while, she heard Filippo say, "The free prosecco is almost gone." He motioned around the room with a flamboyant wave of his hand. "So, these… guests… will all be going to the party soon."

"What party is that?" Maja couldn't stop herself from asking.

"The kind of party that costs more to throw than most people make working for a year. It is kind of sick really. But also a lot of fun. Would you like to join me?"

I, Guardian: Chapter Three

Alex Ridley was surprised to find that, despite the shitty reason she had come to Milan, she still felt the stirrings of excitement and the buzz of travel she had always felt when she stepped onto new streets. This time these emotions were unbidden and most unwelcome. She was here on business, and streets filled with pretty buildings and scores of fancy shops and restaurants... and especially the world-class bars... were not going to distract her eye from the prize.

As she dodged the busy residents and tourists rushing by along the pavements, her mind wandered back to the journeying she had done with Hiram Kane. Kane was a good man who Ridley had met way back at university. In their first meeting, she had shocked him by defeating him on the tae-kwon-do mat. He certainly hadn't been the last man to underestimate her. She had bought him a beer to take the edge off his embarrassment, and they had warmed to each other immediately. Yet, like most other aspects of her life, things were complicated. Her undoubted love for Kane was too often interrupted by life's turbulence. By Ridley's own design, they were far apart right now. She knew that was a blessing in disguise.

Her travels with Kane had taken them into the heart of incredibly dangerous situations, and they'd had adventures together that were anything but routine sightseeing jaunts. They had also shared breathtaking moments, like the time they'd stood together in silent awe beneath the majesty of the Taj Mahal in India. Sadly, Ridley couldn't look back on that trip—a journey that should have been about relaxation and recovery—without recalling the horrors that followed in the days after.

They had headed up to McLeodganj, a peaceful hill station in the shadows of the Indian Himalayas. It's where the Dalai Lama had chosen to make his home in exile after fleeing from Tibet following Chinese occupation. Mcleodganj had come to be known as "Little Lhasa" due to its large Tibetan population, and the fact that the Tibetan government-in-exile was headquartered there. Amid the serenity of that place, they had heard whispers of a supposedly virtuous people-smuggling operation determined to help more Tibetans out of their homeland to join their compatriots in India. However, the darkness of that clandestine world soon reared its head when Ridley was brutally kidnapped by connected human traffickers.

In the caves of Mount Kailash, she'd experienced the vile world of sex-trafficking operations, and was thrown into a cell while waiting to be sold. Kayla Stone had been one of her fellow captors, and their eyes had first met through the bars of a cage when Ridley was making her escape and trying to engineer the same for the dozens of other women being held.

There was no way those caves and cages were ever going to hold Alexandria Ridley, though her bid for freedom had occurred amid chaos and flames and too much death. She had emerged with Kayla and ended up on the streets of Mumbai, India, fighting with everything they had to bring down the traffickers and save at least a few other women from the fate they had endured.

It quickly became clear to the two women that they shared an incredibly strong bond, despite not having known each other very long. Sometimes, it felt the relationship was so strong it had become difficult to handle. There was a strange kind of spark. Part matronly. Part awe. Part friendship. Whatever was happening to Ridley during these days of emotional turmoil, there was no doubt Kayla had replaced Hiram as the person by her side, and whose side she felt reluctant to leave.

Which of the two was better or worse for her sanity was hard to say. Ridley decided it was best not to dwell on it, and as she negotiated the bedlam of late afternoon in downtown Milan, she refocused her mind on the present task at hand.

Bringing down the bastards!

Grab your copy…
vinci-books.com/iguardian

About the Author

Englishman Steven Moore grew up by the seaside, thus his first true joy was the great outdoors. His innate love of travel and a degree in anthropology, archaeology, and art history, help inform his fiction writing. Steven also loves painting, photography, and both playing and watching sport.

The travel bug bit the now perpetual nomad early, and to date Steven has lived and worked on five continents, and visited almost seventy countries. Steven combines an age-old writing adage; Write what you know, with his own mantra; Write where you know, and sets most of his novels in places in which he has either lived or spent an extended period of time.

When not on the road, Steven divides his time between Norwich, UK, and San Miguel de Allende, Mexico, which he shares with his rescue cats Ernest Hemingway and F Scott Fitzgerald (Ernie and Fitz), and his rescue puppy, Charles Dickens. Oh yes, and his beautiful travel writer wife, Leslie.

A lifelong love of food, wine, and beer, have demanded a new-found love of yoga and hiking in order to fend off the imminent arrival of middle age.

www.ingramcontent.com/pod-product-compliance
Lightning Source LLC
Chambersburg PA
CBHW011757010726
47497CB00013B/3254

* 9 7 8 1 0 3 6 7 0 6 9 0 6 *